MEDIUM RARE

Also by
A. Natasha Joukovsky

*The Portrait of a Mirror*

# MEDIUM RARE

*a novel*

A. NATASHA JOUKOVSKY

MELVILLE HOUSE
BROOKLYN • LONDON

Medium Rare
Copyright © 2025 by A. Natasha Joukovsky
All rights reserved
First Melville House Printing: November 2025

Melville House Publishing
46 John Street
Brooklyn, NY 11201
and
Melville House UK
Suite 2000
16/18 Woodford Road
London E7 0HA

mhpbooks.com
@melvillehouse

ISBN: 978-1-68589-247-0
ISBN: 978-1-68589-248-7 (eBook)

Library of Congress Control Number: 2025948173

Designed by Beste M. Doğan

Printed in the United States of America
10 9 8 7 6 5 4 3 2 1

A catalog record for this book is available from the Library of Congress

The authorized representative in the EU for product safety and compliance is Easy Access System Europe, Mustamäe tee 50, 10621 Tallinn, Estonia.
gpsr.requests@easproject.com

*For Michael J. McDuffie*
*who is . . . a Duke fan*

But tragedy blossomed forth and won great acclaim, becoming a wondrous entertainment for the ears and eyes of the men of that age, and, by the mythological character of its plots, and the vicissitudes which its characters undergo, it effected a deception wherein, as Gorgias remarks, "he who deceives is more honest than he who does not deceive, and he who is deceived is wiser than he who is not deceived." For he who deceives is more honest, because he has done what he promised to do; and he who is deceived is wiser, because the mind which is not insensible to fine perceptions is easily enthralled by the delights of language.
—Plutarch, "On the Fame of the Athenians"

and the expensive delicate ship that must have seen
Something amazing, a boy falling out of the sky,
Had somewhere to get to and sailed calmly on.
—W. H. Auden, "Musée des Beaux Arts"

# MEDIUM RARE

# "FIRST FOUR"

I see Phil. And when I now see Phil? I see a man with a ball. Not just any ball: a basketball. But any man. You might even call him *every* man—though I do want to be fair to him. The everyman figure is a composite of specific ones, and fairness and truth close enough acquaintances a dispassionate observer would almost certainly call them friends. When I say *I see a man*, I mean I see a human being: singular like any other. Nothing more—but also nothing less. Something ordinary and something amazing. A world and a grain of sand.

### 000

The odds of filling out a perfect March Madness bracket are so infinitesimal statisticians disagree just how infinitesimal they are. Disregarding the "First Four" play-in games—because honestly, who doesn't—proponents of treating every game as a fair coin flip will tell you one in *nine quintillion, two hundred twenty-three quadrillion, three hundred seventy-two trillion, thirty-six billion, eight hundred fifty-four million, seven hundred seventy-five thousand, eight hundred and eight.* This was, indeed, the estimate favored by Phil Fayeton himself, not just for its magnitude but also its precision; for its neat, edgy literalness—the way it accounted for every possible eventuality, from our alma mater's landmark loss the previous season to their poetic redemption in 2019.

The best sixty-four college basketball programs in the country score invitations to "the big dance" each year; it takes sixty-three single-elimination games to crown a tournament champion. *That's two to the sixty-third power, mathematically speaking,* Phil would explain, rattling off each digit with memorial pride. After his first few public appearances, he googled a series of analogies to help contextualize a number of that size, as if to improve its marketability—almost like he was lobbying for it. *Pick a single grain of sand from anywhere in the world,* he'd say, *and you'd be twenty-three percent* more *likely to find it again at random than to fill out a perfect March Madness bracket.* He relayed such anecdotes with a specious kind of authority in his voice; Phil unironically trusted the internet in that natural, unexamined way it is easy to trust generally helpful things.

The main problem with the coin-flip method is that it's not remotely accurate, bracketologically. It assumes the probability of winning games is fifty-fifty when seeding is asymmetric by design. If you always choose the higher-seeded team, you'll correctly predict not 50 percent, but something closer to 75 percent of the games. And that's only on average.

Certain individual contests carry far more lopsided odds. Yes, in 2018, UMBC famously beat the University of Virginia in Cinderella style, but only after the top seeds had prevailed the previous 135 consecutive times. There is a lexically subtle but hard-and-fast mathematical difference between *uncertainty* and *randomness*. The winner of a basketball game is always uncertain, but random only *sometimes*. Sometimes it just has the appearance of randomness, because the factors and influences driving the outcome are too multivariate and complex—even for generational minds like Jim Nantz and Sir Charles Barkley.

More legitimate stochastic estimates on the odds of a perfect bracket are still intimidatingly, incomprehensibly huge. The most optimistic computer models quote one in two billionish, and then only in certain years, like 2019. Had Phil latched on to this ratio instead, he might still have offset it dramatically. As Georgetown University Assistant Professor of Mathematics and Statistics Lucas Hadley explained to Sunny Sanders in a courtside pregame segment early in the second round, his legs crossed at the thigh in that almost yogic manner so often exhibited by stylish men wearing slim suit pants:

—*All else being equal, when the championship buzzer sounds, you're less likely to fill out a perfect bracket than to be one of the five winning players on the court.*

Phil never connected his own penchant for waxing analogic back to Lucas Hadley. And yet, he remembered this segment well. It had aired back when Sunny's 4K hotness still had that unidirectional, abstract quality of telegenic women on television, and any national intrigue surrounding Phil took the form of a broader statistic. There were thirteen verified perfect brackets at the time—few enough, certainly, for Phil's inclusion to be a novelty within his own circle of personal acquaintance, but still too many for any of the networks to start thinking "personal interest story" on the individual bracketologists. No, the bright, hungry spotlight of fleeting sports-media attention landed instead that night on the flexing avian ankles and (frankly, in Phil's opinion, offensively tight) wool gabardine suit pants of a Georgetown statistician. Georgetown *hadn't even made the tournament*, Phil later complained. They'd given floor seats at the DaedaDome (formerly CapitalOne Arena, formerly formerly Verizon Center) to *a math professor*, while Phil himself watched from the obscurity of his townhouse living room, just across the river in Arlington, VA.

Their television at the time was a fifty-inch flatscreen, suspended below a synthetically weathered home decor sign reading "Love Is Never Having to Say You're Sorry," which Phil's wife, Raleigh, bought after spotting it on HGTV. Dear Raleigh; it was the type of object that, within a certain context (soaring ceilings, marble countertops; i.e., on HGTV) looked glibly high-end, but veered maudlin in an architecturally unremarkable suburban living room. The piece was outrageously expensive for what it was, and Raleigh had lobbied hard for it, squealing when the package arrived. As soon as

Phil hung it up, though, there was a twinge of disappointment on her face. Like she'd expected it to alter the fundamental physics of the place and was baffled when there still wasn't any crown molding or a decorative barn door.

—Do you want to return it? Phil asked hopefully.

—No, of course not!

Like Phil, Raleigh was from the South. The Deep South. She had been bred to subsume her heart's desires in amiability.

—It's okay if you want to return it, babe.

—But I don't! I *love* it!

So complete and exalting was Raleigh's devotion to the god of politeness I wonder she herself didn't find it heretical. And yet, if this devotion was one of her greater weaknesses, she possessed the rare corresponding strength to mold her own mind, shaping and polishing her thoughts until the polite mirrored the true. She'd never admit to her disappointment, but it also wouldn't eat at her—not the way it would have many women; not the way it would have me. Privately, subtly, Raleigh would manage to reframe the narrative, imbuing the synthetically weathered sign with *hope* and *appreciation* in a manner that somehow recalled neither cloying Pollyanna nor the Goopy "gratitude" of late capitalism. It was a useful temperament in a nurse: this staid, deliberate brand of positivity. And being a nurse—as Raleigh was, in emergency medicine at George Washington University Hospital—was likewise helpful in recategorizing the disappointments in other spheres of one's life, such as the discordant aesthetics of one's living room.

Phil didn't press her further, probably figuring that keeping the thing at least meant he wouldn't have to take it down, wrestle with the box, drive to the UPS Store, and patch the marred drywall. He wouldn't have argued with the message, per se. It wasn't like it said "Happy Wife, Happy Life" or something. Not apologizing was a sentiment Phil could get behind.

—*So I take it you don't see anyone banking the billion-dollar prize, then?* Sunny Sanders said to Lucas Hadley on the television.

The professor smiled wryly; flexed his dangling ankle again—*Jesus*, thought Phil, *was he* flirting *with her?*—but Sunny continued before Lucas could answer:

—*For our viewers who aren't already aware, Arun Patil, the CEO of Daedalus Industries, has pledged to give a billion dollars to anyone who fills out a perfect bracket this year.*

—*Alas, it's all but certainly a contest without a winner,* said Lucas. *Or, rather, a contest Patil himself is foretold to win. I mean, look at all the free advertising we're giving hi—*

—Phil? What do you want to do for din—

—Shhh! Phil hushed his wife.

Raleigh looked at him, incredulous, but said nothing. She was thirty-four weeks pregnant; the question of dinner was not an insignificant one.

—I mean—just hang on a second, please, Phil amended.

—*When you say "all but certainly," though,* Sunny

beamed, her tone beginning its upward modulation toward the segment's inevitable, rosy wrap—*that means it is still technically possible, right? For someone to win the money? You can't say for certain.*

—*Statistics is never having to say you're certain,* said Lucas.

Sunny laughed, giving his shoulder a chummy squeeze.

—*Well, there you have it, folks!* she said, turning to the camera. *Hope springs eternal, right? Now, back to—*

Me.

Yes, *I*—the seer. Your narrator. Surely you want to know more of me, even if the story is Phil's?

The salient facts of my life are these: I always tell the truth; I am never believed. Please remember this should it ever seem surprising for a woman of my narrative gifts to so exert them on Phil Fayeton, on basketball. Remember the polarities of magnets and how they attract; that sight is not an anecdote, but the origin of envy. If I see more than the average person—and I do—remember incredible gifts nearly always carry some hidden price, deep in the belly. That I yearn for *credibility*—not as much as "the average person," but *more.* Remember fiction is where the incredible finds credibility. Glory, even. For incredible fiction is not a falsehood: It is the visionary recourse of truth.

And so to fiction I turned, its pull not professional, but human. Perhaps a mad strategy, without any modern credentials—"so competitive, the literary world"—but *we all go a little mad sometimes*, soothsayers more often still. Remember that "sometimes" is a word of such fraught probabilities. Never is this truer than in the month of March, as it was for Phil. O Phil! My subject, my foil, my rival, my friend. *I see you.* And when I see you, with all my incredible gifts? *Sometimes* the Madness of March extends to me, too.

# PART 1: PRIME TIME

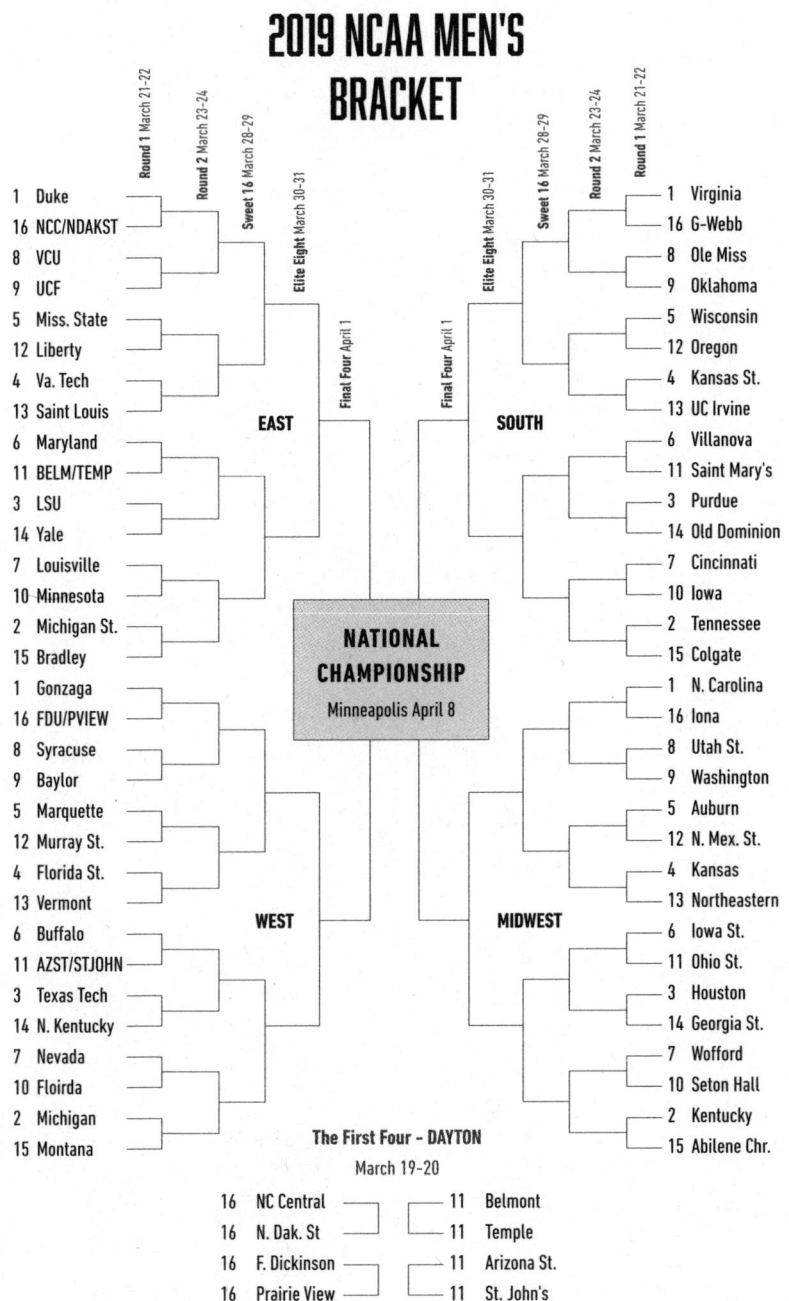

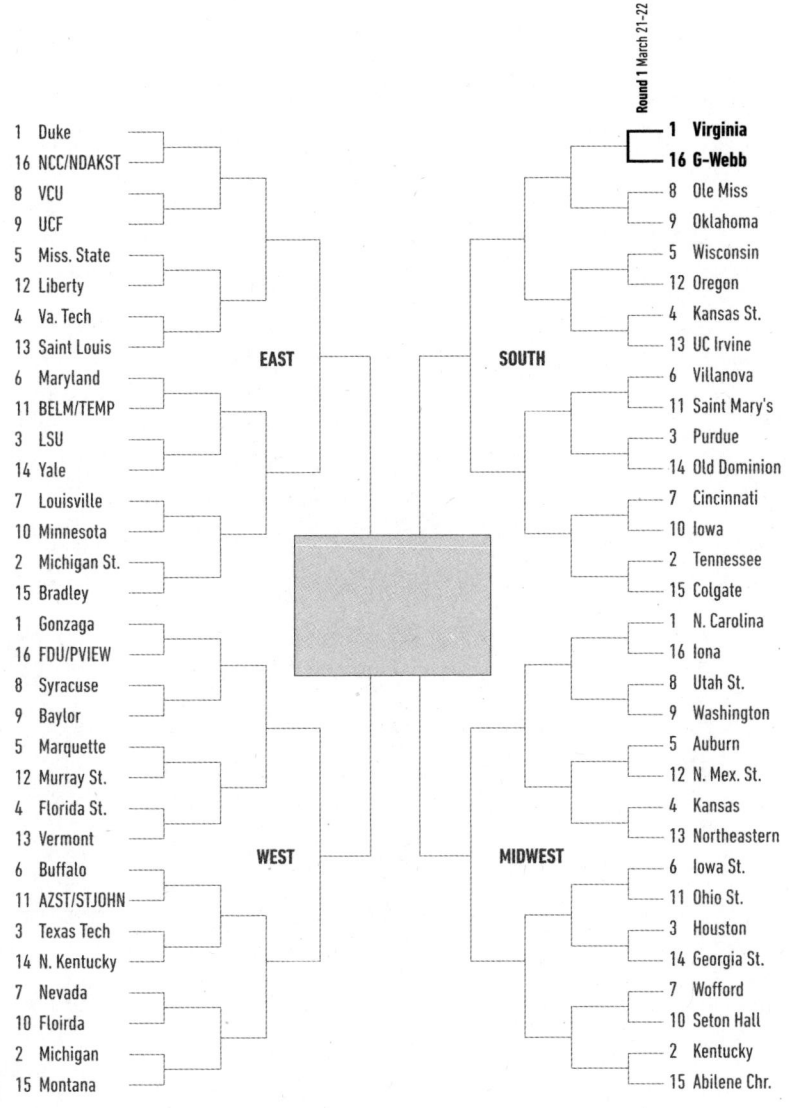

# ROUND 1

## VIRGINIA (1) VS. GARDINER-WEBB (16)

On Thursday, March 21, 2019, Phil Fayeton drove his large automobile east, his morning ardor fresh upon him. Even outside of March, the best twenty-five minutes of his day were nearly always these, alone in his Audi SUV, with his yacht rock and a stainless-steel tumbler of premium coffee. It was in the liminal space between his home and Capitol Hill, on the roads he very (very) indirectly helped to build, that Phil was able to forge some brief connection between the idea and the reality of himself. This rare, gratifying union had the superficial overlay of millennial self-actualization but fundamentally boiled down to an older archetype of American maleness, the one pioneered by Neal Cassady and Jack Kerouac, which invariably anoints *the car* as the essence of freedom, and *freedom* as the exemption from personal responsibility. It is an archetype that runs uncomfortably close to the radioactive brand of "Great" the president was always trying to Make Happen Again. Phil hadn't voted for him, of course—though he couldn't quite bring himself to vote for Hillary either, and had written in Mitt Romney instead.

When you work in politics—which Phil did, as an in-house lobbyist for the American Association of Stone, Sand, and Shale—for whom you cast your ballot is not merely a personal, but also a business decision. Phil had graduated the year before me, in 2006, into a Republican Congress under Bush the Second, and doubling down on the party he'd been raised to favor not only pleased his white, working-class father back in New Orleans, but was also professionally expedient. He fashioned himself a "moderate" one, though, a *Reagan Republican*, clear to distinguish his greater liberalism on social issues, and in particular those for which Democratic values seemed to be disproportionately favored by sexually liberated post-collegiate women.

Phil's first two years in Washington had been good to him, with the caveat that both Senators whose offices he'd worked to forge ties with as an aide to the Senate Appropriations Committee retired in 2008, one losing his seat to a Democrat. Having been on the Hill just long enough to have established the sort of clear partisan alignment it is tough to walk back, Phil experienced a sudden decline in his prospects that persisted through much of the Obama administration, with brief glimmers of hope on the campaign trails of Romney and Jeb Bush. It was when the 2016 Bush push dissolved that Phil reconciled himself to mid-level AASSS lobbying—and to marrying Raleigh, after years of on-again, off-again posturing.

This was the same year my twins were born, and following my return from parental leave, I started finding myself in the odd elevator with him.

For example: that Thursday morning, at the Democratic National Committee, when his stainless-steel tumbler forced the doors to reopen. Will van der Wende was with me.

—Hey man, Phil said to him, then to me, in pointed greeting, my name. *Cassandra.*

—Hey, Will pseudo-acknowledged Phil without looking away from me, all but refusing small talk in so momentumless a return.

A feature of the Hill, seen elsewhere but perhaps not quite so violently, is that the precise social hierarchy is not just evident to everyone in the room, it is inherent to it—to the room. The status gradations within our bicameral system are so fine as to operate practically at the individual level, an ever-evolving stack-rack of influence largely tied to one's office and reflected in its physical space. The building, the level, the layout, the view; these things are elaborately metered and codified conveyers of status and clout. If New York is ruled by the invisible hand, Washington is so by a highly visible one. Its sheer visibility acts as a narrowing mechanism in behavioral governance, the strictures of its spaces and roles enforcing social mores that stiffen and shift predictably depending on who's present—and even within the same group as it moves from building to building, from office to office, from room to room.

All of these *froms* are hardly an afterthought; it is with good reason we say the *halls* of Congress are hallowed. And if the halls are hallowed, the elevators are sacrosanct. Members—that is senators, representatives, the capital-B *Bosses* of the American legislature—often have their own, invite-only elevator cars, the privilege of riding in which might well supersede a personal office visit for one crucial reason: It is easier to be seen. Appearance, in Washington, is just reality before it's brushed its teeth, a procedural gap that's easily remedied.

We were in one of the regular elevators that day, me and Phil and Will, but that hardly mitigated the jockeying. As the chief of staff to freshman Representative Maria Muñoz (D-CA-43), Will sat a couple of rungs above Phil—but just a couple, the distance not so great as to block free-flowing conversation, in which Phil would attempt obsequence without seeming obsequious, and Will superiority without seeming to act superior.

My own relative position was harder to parse. Fundraisers—we who rule the events, who plan the literal political parties—glide along a parallel track, one that largely shields us from Washington's cruelest humiliations, if also limits our rise. Mine specifically, with my reputation for well-nigh perfect events comingling with that of overstepping my role overseeing them; for having the sort of outspoken integrity that can pose a liability to loyalty, valued over truth in Washington as a whole. Rumors of my literary pursuits did nothing to ease such concerns, painting me attentionally divided at best and a flight risk at worst. My client list was, accordingly, a bit of a revolving door. Yet there were always new Bosses clamoring to work with me. Even the most senior members of Congress rely on fundraisers, know the value of a good one. That it's we who connect them to copacetic lobby pocketbooks (like Phil's and lavisher), filling their reelection coffers while we fill their bellies. We set ourselves apart by bringing the rest of Washington together—and there is real power in our work, in guest lists and seating charts; in tuna tartare and filet mignon. Our pretty little decisions birth alliances and whip votes and above all offer or withhold opportunities for everyone else's positional reshuffling. Phil was not insensible to this; he was humbled by my power, even as he dismissed my ways and means, and this sharpened a social surface on which his shoulder was already inclined to chip.

He tested what my presence in the elevator foretold—but not on me. Phil readdressed Will instead:

—Do I . . . take it your Boss will be dropping in at the DEMO-W PAC event next week?

I cut in before Will could answer:

—Will the AASSS double-max if she does?

Even if I hadn't pronounced it *ass*, this would not have been particularly kind of me. The American Association of Stone, Sand, and Shale was hardly a plum agency. I doubted Phil had the funds to so much as consider this level of donation. Alas, I had my own incentives like everyone else.

Lobbyists pay to attend fundraising events via their political contributions, while members merely bestow the honor of their presence. I'd recently parted ways with a powerful boomer congressman due to "stylistic incompatibility," saw Maria as a potential client, and wanted Will to understand my event would be well worth her time.

I've said Maria was a freshman, and this is true, but it's important to understand Maria Muñoz was not your average freshman congresswoman. For starters: She was twenty-nine, younger than any of us, and controversial—boldly progressive, with transformational policy proposals. While I hesitate to veer to the physical, to the standards by which even the most brilliant young women are so absurdly, firstly judged, her vision and charisma inevitably benefitted from her beauty. I'm not saying she was a starlet or anything, but on the Hill? If she didn't have a million followers on Instagram already—if she hadn't been so immediately, singularly recognizable as *her*—she would likely have been mistaken for one of us. For a fundraiser, like me.

Go ahead and object. Accuse me of stereotyping, of reinforcing patriarchal norms, of—that most feminine sin—*superficiality*. The reality is that most stereotypes, like most politicians, harness their power less from abject falsehood than partial truth. In our fear that uncomfortable facts will run wildly away, it becomes taboo merely to observe them: that most fundraisers, on both sides of the aisle, *are* conventionally attractive women from affluent backgrounds; that this tendency springs not only from mimicry and exclusion from Congress itself, but from a well-groomed competitive advantage: We are uncommonly adept at throwing exquisite parties for powerful men.

I knew Phil's answer to my double-max bait would be noncommittal yet face-saving, a falsely nonchalant *maybe*, leaving the donation door ajar, even if just a crack, in Will's mind.

—Maybe, said Phil. We do like the Green New Deal's investment in infrastructure.

—Everyone likes infrastructure, I said. That's why significant bills for it almost never pass.

—I don't think that's the reason, said Will, not without humor.

—Yeah, that makes no sense, Phil agreed, with less.

How grating to be dismissed for even the most innocuous insight! But in their shared disbelief, I could see Will coming to reevaluate the AASSS anyway, even if his eyes were presently more focused on mine. I let them travel, my looks subtly reinforcing my event's appeal in the way I theoretically loathed yet practically cultivated. My suit had all the outward markers of (sartorial) conservatism, but blazers are so ruthlessly unflattering on most women, having been originally designed with men's bodies in mind, that the act of looking good in one amounts to a disproportionate achievement. That's the irony of dress codes: They're intended to be this great equalizer, but ultimately only enhance beauty's advantage.

Will would see what he could do re: the DEMO-W PAC event. Maria was wary of lobbyists, of big donations; she'd legitimately won her seat through grassroots support, against a powerful incumbent in the primary. The calling card of her campaign was "authenticity"—though what is more authentic to American politics than corporate lobbying, I do not know. But then my event, in support of electing Democratic women to Congress, was as aligned to her brand as a PAC mission could be; Sheila Campau, a fairly senior senator from Michigan and longtime client of mine, was sure to be there, and the only thing that eclipsed Maria's authenticity was her ambition. She wouldn't have hired a career staffer like Will van der Wende to run her office otherwise.

Phil soured visibly at being sidelined, the palliative effects of his drive gone before the start of his first meeting. Regressing to a personal topic after broaching business risked feeling desperate, but it was the only plausible move Phil had left.

—Fill out your bracket yet? he asked Will.

—Shit, no, thanks for the reminder. Georgetown is so bad this year, I haven't really been paying attention. Who do you have winning?

—My Cavaliers, obviously, said Phil, smiling harder to hide the sting of Will's lapse undercutting his victory.

—Oh right, I forgot you went to Virginia.

—I went there, too, I said.

The conversation halted, Will's lip half upturning.

—Yeah, right, he said. Everyone knows you went to Harvard.

—That was for my masters. Do you seriously think I don't know my own bio?

—I can vouch, said Phil. We were at UVa together.

—Oh, okay, said Will, my résumé suddenly clarified.

The elevator stopped.

—By the way, Cassandra, Phil said as he got off, a note of self-congratulation moistening his tongue. Happy Women's History Month.

He didn't ask about my bracket, though. Neither of them did, which I'm sure I would have found more offensive had I bothered to fill one out.

000

My thoughts about basketball prior to that March, insofar as I thought about basketball at all, hovered somewhere between apathy and condescension. It was not exactly the sport of choice on the Upper East Side of Manhattan, where I grew up. Nor at my boarding school, where crew reigned supreme and most rowers swam in winter. Basketball neither required expensive equipment nor issued cute uniforms. It lacked the invigorating speed of hockey and the psychological appeal of my choice, squash—certainly winter's most literary sport, with its tennis adjacency and deuce-ly theoretical infinitude.

If several of these points seem like euphemisms for snobbery, for a correlative if not causal sense that basketball could be a bit, *mm, lower class*, that's because they are. But none of them had been the foremost absenting force in my lack of interest, either. (Just add it to the list of my image problems.) What I couldn't abide about basketball was simply the immense advantage it conveyed to *being tall*. My young mind—having marinated from birth in false meritocracy, the privileged worldview that conveniently attributes material fortune to individual virtue—could not fathom the value of a system placing such great emphasis on something so obviously, so visibly, the result of sheer luck. *You can't teach height*, as they say—and what on earth, at five-foot-six, was there to gain from pursuing something one could not learn?

My indifference to play naturally extended to an indifference to watch, an indifference to both collegiate and professional ball. On television, there were too many games for any one to matter; too many games to care. The Knicks were rarely any good, overshadowed by the Giants, let alone the Yankees. Not that I had any great affinity for the Giants or the Yankees either. In the false binary that is sports versus the arts, I had naively declared almost from birth for the latter, my childhood thirst for spectacle quenched not at Madison Square Garden but at Lincoln Center, my competitive impulses already aimed at the page.

No, it was only later that I understood, appreciated, the University of Virginia men's basketball strategy in 2019, entirely in keeping with head coach Tony Bennett's signature style of play. That their vicious pack-line defense had the texture of a coloratura soprano's staccatos, that their long, drawn-out offensive possessions unspooled like paragraphs of Proust. The beauty of good passing; efficiency; patience. Teamwork. Was De'Andre Hunter a superstar, destined to be a top-five NBA draft pick? Undoubtedly. Did his sidelining wrist fracture the previous season fuel UMBC's historic upset? It couldn't have helped. But Kyle Guy still averaged slightly more points and steals in 2019, while Ty Jerome had more than twice the assists, disproportionately valued at Virginia. All three of them, I eventually learned, had offensive KenPom ratings above 119. This was a team's team, and even with Hunter on the court, they were susceptible to the fatal flaw underpinning Bennett's historical overperformance, to finding themselves on the other side of the protracted narrative grandiosity from which they so often benefit. Namely: that in dramatically slowing the pace, in minimizing the number of shots, the number of possessions, Bennett not only ensured his team could stay in the game with and upset anybody, but—as he attracted increasingly elite talent himself, those handsome Davidian eyes masking a Goliath, a 29–3 regular season, another number-one seed—well, *anybody* could also upset them.

And so it was not without reason that Phil's left knee shook violently under the Union Pub's bar the afternoon following our elevator run-in. He wouldn't have put it this way, but Virginia's greatness was also their weakness; their pace a tragic flaw. Ten minutes into their first-round matchup against sixteen-seed Gardner-Webb, and they were already down ten. *Gardner-Webb?* At least UMBC, even if he'd never heard of it, had the plausible ring of a university; *Gardner-Webb* sounded like an under-resourced public elementary school. Mamadi Diakite made a layup with his customary grace, offering the psychological assurance of a return to single digits, but three minutes later: disaster. 28–14.

Phil had already correctly predicted Murray State's win over Marquette—he'd picked three twelve-seeds over fives, actually, a famously treacherous perch for the favorites; he'd called the Minnesota upset (his cousin went there); that Maryland would hang on. He'd had LSU over Yale, of course—Phil did not trust the Ivy League in anything, let alone sports—and powerhouse wins for Michigan State, Purdue, Duke, and their ilk. Twenty final scores, twenty points, twenty little green checkmarks in the app. Maximum possible score: a perfect 192. Ranked first not just in his Republican National Committee and AASSS pools, but—in a 166-way tie—the entire Daedalus Industries NCAA March Madness men's bracket challenge. None of it would matter if Virginia lost this game. Not only would that hypothetical 192 instantly flip to 129 (his bracket, at this stage, was of secondary consideration); not only would it destroy his enjoyment of the entire tournament. As a man of middling employment and hijacked political party, of tepid performative religion and few other hobbies, whose wife had largely divergent interests, and whose first child's estimated arrival was still six weeks away—UVa basketball formed a disproportionate share of Phil's true spiritual identity. He'd already felt the unprecedented pain of losing to a sixteen-seed the year before: the alarmingly personal humiliation of it, the devout shame. He still hadn't quite recovered. To lose to a sixteen-seed *twice*? It was unthinkable. It would decimate his pride.

—Sure hope you don't shit the bed again, said Will van der Wende, sliding onto the stool next to him.

In any other circumstance, Phil would have delighted in the gesture, taken it as a harbinger of professional growth and social ascension. It would have buoyed his entire weekend. Had the Cavaliers been up, Phil might even have cherished the insult, that *you* indicative of Will's improving memory and brimming with implicit inclusion. As it stood, however, his crumbling hope in the five talented eighteen- to twenty-two-year-olds on the screen in front of them had taxed his self-control to perilous levels, and Phil wanted to hit him.

—I'm not going to start freaking out until the second half, he said instead.

—Good, because I wanted to see how serious you were about the double-A triple-S backing Maria.

—Uh—*yes*!

Ty Jerome had hit a jumper, but Gardner-Webb swiftly countered.

Phil was in the sort of rapt psychological distress that

is often more visible from across the room than within the confines of a conversation. Indeed, Will seemed to mistake Phil's genuine distraction as some coy tactic, a feigned imperviousness to his political overture that Will, while privately congratulating himself on seeing through, nonetheless had to admire. Ironically, had Phil been *more* on his game, he likely would have bumbled through another equivocal non-answer, come off as simultaneously evasive and desperate, and been written off by Will entirely—a disappointment that would not have been wholly avoidable. Maria was a high-risk, high-reward alliance even for me, even for a Democrat. While her support could lend Phil disproportionate visibility to crucial AASSS interests, her status in the court of public opinion far eclipsed her actual political power. And it was only ever in Congress, *not* in the court of public opinion, that infrastructure lacked support. Personally, Phil had even less to gain. As much as he might have liked to meet the freshman congresswoman for its novelty and clout, it made little sense for him to spend any more time and resources hobnobbing with Democrats than was strictly, AASSS-wise, necessary. The next year was an election year, and, where it was all the same to his employer (or frankly, even *close enough*), Phil would certainly have preferred to court moderate Republicans. Members and staff of whom he could later conceivably beg a better job.

Phil wasn't weighing any of this, though, and said

nothing—often the very smartest thing a person can say. It was at least the luckiest, in this case. As Kyle Guy hit a three, Will emptied out:

—I hadn't really thought about it until yesterday, but weirdly, it sort of works. There's the public works angle, for starters, obviously, but also maybe a union play. Maria's all about working-class support, and—

Ty Jerome missed a free throw but managed the second. Kyle Guy made two, and Phil started to breathe.

—look, I can't entirely promise anything because Maria takes unusual control over her calendar, but—

The game went to commercial.

—What? said Phil.

—she *is* gonna drop by the DEMO-W fundraiser next Wednesday, and if you're there and can avoid saying anything too moronic, I think I can get you a direct meet.

Phil swiveled toward Will, a tentative smile on his face. This time, he didn't miss a beat:

—That'd be great.

Virginia cut the lead to six by half and won comfortably by fifteen.

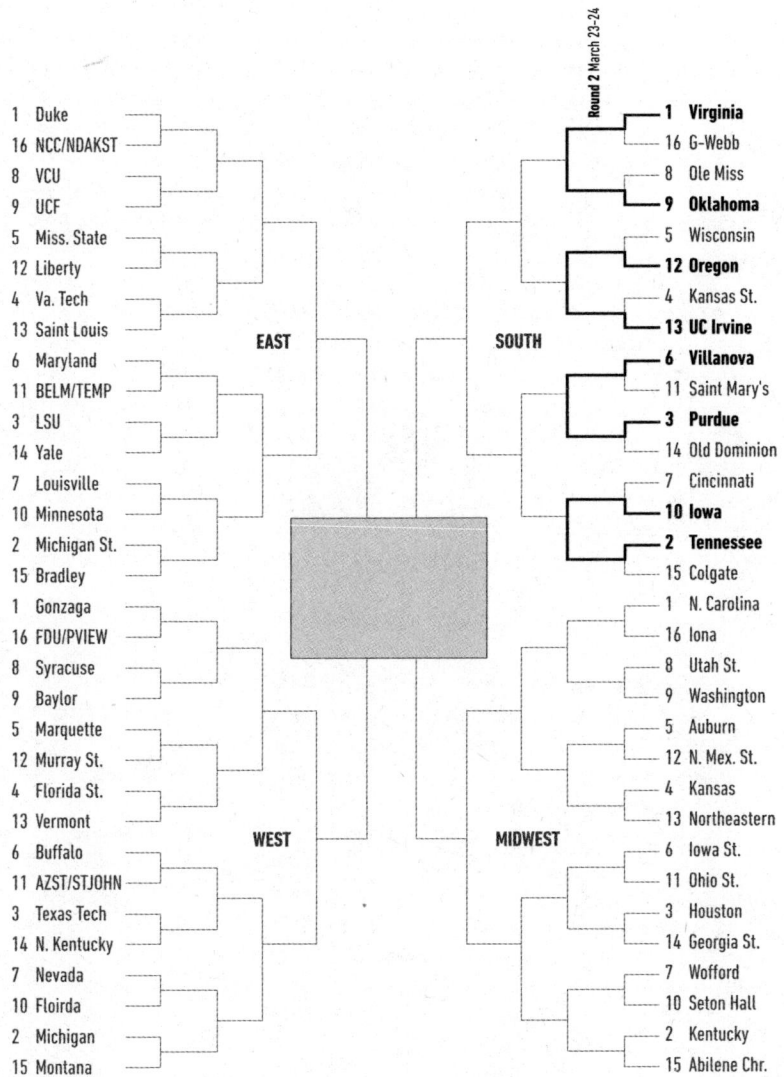

# ROUND 2

## VIRGINIA (1) VS. OKLAHOMA (9)

When I say I "knew" Phil and Raleigh Fayeton in college, I mean I was technically, and rather against my will, aware of their existence. Admittedly, my collegiate will is less a reflection of their characters than of mine. (Prophets are not infallible; it is only false prophets who claim otherwise.) Raleigh and I were in the same pledge class of the same sorority, which again suggests a closeness that did not exist. Kappa Rho Epsilon consisted of two equally powerful factions in the mid-aughts, united mostly by good orthodontia and trendy jeans. Half of the girls were much like me: temperamentally charismatic, tonally ironic, politically liberal, and disproportionately majoring in art history. The other half coalesced into a glossy-haired Christian hydra, all immaculate fingernails and unrelenting kindness. Several of them, like Raleigh, were in the nursing school, which, however unfairly, had a reputation for being the backdoor into UVa for pretty girls to earn their "MRS" degrees. Every year, two or three of them *would* get engaged at graduation—though Raleigh didn't. The practice was generally restricted to those who had made especially public promises to Jesus concerning their virginity, and with Raleigh this was only ever vaguely implied.

Everything about this second KRE contingent was highly disconcerting to me—even the kindness, which I associated at the time with a lack of intellectual rigor—and I remember recoiling, almost to the point of de-pledging, at the thought of my formal association. But then, many of the other girls in my faction felt similarly and were really very fun—and KRE was the only "top-tier" sorority at UVa I could convince myself was not a low-key white supremacist organization. So I stayed, and regularly found myself on the other side of the room at the same social functions as Raleigh and, starting in our second year, her boyfriend Phil Fayeton.

In retrospect, it was about as innocuous an outcome for which one might possibly hope in establishing social ties based on shared appreciation for the same brands of jeans. The two groups maintained a polite veneer of intimacy and benefitted more or less equally from it. The house was large and brick and ivied, simultaneously exclusive and inviting, offering glimpses of its plush, easter-egg interiors. The events at which I ignored Phil also included the sort of boys to whom I paid delicate attention; whom, on some level, I *eventually* wanted to wed and procreate with—and eventually did. All in all, it was the essence of effective mutual symbiosis. The nice Christian girls lent us an unearned air of future goodness, of—if I'm being honest (and I always am)—*marryability*, while we lent them an unearned air of fun.

And so, for all our differences, Phil, Raleigh, and I were in close enough proximity for a substantial enough period of time for me to inadvertently collect the sort of information about them that vanishes with absence but, on reacquaintance, is resurrected effortlessly. I knew, for instance, that he'd played basketball on UVa's club team; Phil had the sort of height that would have posed a formidable advantage in high school but disappeared collegiately. Six-two, maybe six-three. He had the tangential affect—and this he shared with his wife—of the hometown hero, the cursory markers of hotness failing to materialize into any subtler intrigue. And the gifts she made the most of via cleavage, cosmetics, and a frankly rapturous array of—natural, yet still enhanced—blonde hair, he had fewer socially acceptable means to elevate. Phil looked much like every other guy on the Hill, basically: like a disappointing version of the man who would play him in a movie, simultaneously insecure and overconfident in his suitability for the role.

While perfectly true, this is also a roundabout way to say that Phil looked like—almost *was*—a disappointing version of my husband. Not just because they were both lobbyists, though Miles was of the lofty, big-firm kind, or that they'd graduated from UVa the same year with majors in government. In 2007, while Raleigh was lining up a job in DC to be near Phil, I returned to New York, where Miles was suffering a stint in investment banking, and moved into his Soho apartment in lieu of my parents' place on the Upper East Side. No, I only clocked their resemblance many years later (a seer's insights do not always arrive all at once): After I left my post-collegiate job in the art world and applied not to MFA or PhD programs, but alongside Miles to the Kennedy School. After we graduated and consummated our pivots into politics as well as our more personal union, settling in his hometown of DC—eventually in the very neighborhood he grew up in, buying a Georgetown townhouse six blocks away from his parents in 2013. After our boys were born at thirty-seven weeks, full-term for twins; olive beauties with dark hair and light eyes. Even after I started seeing Phil in the odd elevator.

It wasn't until Sunday, March 24, 2019, when I again found myself, at thirty-four years of age and with my husband, on the other side of the room from Phil and Raleigh at a social function in support of some vanity charity, that it dawned on me how little separated us from them. What I'd taken in college to be opposing factions—a sharp, partisan delineation between our modern, self-aware empowerment and their stifling parochialism—all at once appeared less a difference in kind than degree. Perhaps it was because the lighting is better at adult parties, or the way the absurd ceilings of our mutual acquaintances' house dwarfed us all; perhaps it was that Raleigh was so ostentatiously pregnant I was almost getting sympathetic pains, but the few dozen feet that had seemed to form some titanic chasm in college was now, so clearly, all part of the same bourgeois room. I had made all the traditional choices of the unenlightened women I looked down on; my only distinction was having made them more elegantly.

Miles snuck a glance at the television above the fireplace, silently flashing UVa's second-round matchup vs. Oklahoma. His ego wasn't wrapped up in it the same way Phil's was, but he'd played on Virginia's D1 lacrosse team, winning national championships in his first and fourth years, and was thoroughly, if genially invested; invested enough not to notice when I excused myself from our cluster. Across the room, Phil's attention was divided. The Virginia game was in sufficient control for him to be simultaneously monitoring Houston vs. Ohio State on his phone, which was still close, and responding mechanically to the occasional social prompt from his wife.

Few people were talking to them, to Phil and Raleigh. They were among the least powerful couples there, an AASSS lobbyist and a nurse, in a room brimming with people capable of currying meaningful favors. It wasn't so obvious as to be generally embarrassing, everyone else being tied up in their own affairs, but it was obvious enough to Raleigh herself. In Phil's half-presence and of course entirely sober, she exhibited all the visible anxieties of social discomfort. And with every protective touch of her belly and stroke of her hair, I felt the uncanny effect of witnessing a scene I'd long ago predicted.

In college I'd had rather a habit of vainly warning other young women when I sensed the objects of their affections unworthy. I now remembered Raleigh had been among them. My late arrival; a single open chair; the pale tonal yellows of the chapter dining room blanching against her crimson face across the table:

—Well— Raleigh chafed against my admonition, cutting off a tiny bite of grilled chicken. I'm not about to give up on Phil *quite* yet! He's so sweet when it's just the two of us—

—But you just said he's going to "Snow Pants or No Pants" with Savannah Quincy, I balked, amazed by the speed at which her complaint had become defense.

—He promised just as friends—and they're wearing snow pants.

—I don't *snow*, Raleigh, I see you getting played. Even if you prevail, by the way. I see inconstancy and fitfulness—success portending pain. Better steer clear. It's not like there aren't other middlebrow frat boys at UVa.

I could feel the table grow quiet, the cautionary eyes of the glossy hydra resting not on Raleigh but on me, discerning the vicarious threat that I posed to the interpretive buffing of their own delicate situationships. More disconcerting: Raleigh's own eyes, hovering between hurt and something else, a look I was accustomed to giving, but not receiving. At the time I lumped her look in with the others, distinguishing Raleigh only as the direct target of my insight, naturally more affected by its personal implications. I was still learning how to share my gift, how to mitigate its side effects; that self-preservational conviction lays some of the least hospitable foundations for otherwise convincing. And yet, I was also familiar enough with collective dismissal, with awkward social balking. I knew how to rise above it. I rolled my eyes and went to see if there was any ice cream.

Now I discovered lemon cake and macarons, tiered under the absurd, adult ceilings, and wondered. That look, the *something else* from all those years ago. To fail to heed a warning is not the same as to dismiss it. Raleigh hadn't listened—but had she seen? Had *she* seen *me*? And him—Phil. Had she seen something in him that I'd missed? I passed the dessert table. I headed for the Fayetons.

Did I approach them out of some true feeling, some reconciliatory compassion for a largely private cruelty? A belated sense of "sisterhood," perhaps? Or was it more maternal, some psychic response to my flaring instincts? Was it raw curiosity? The novelty of my very uncertainty?

Or, already, did I intuit it? Did I sense the outlines of the denouement even in the rising action, something no one else could see? A crystal *basket*ball? Of my corresponding curse: There was not, would never be, any escape in status or power; no level of congressional, even executive, intimacy that could truly free me from incredibility. Did I, in looking not up, but down, happen upon *something amazing*? I should have seen it sooner, after all those seminars in art history, and enough in literature. *About suffering they were never wrong, the old Masters.* In this tableau, hiding in plain sight, was the rarest of things: a *great* story. If not an epic, then at least a piece of one, primed to unspool through the centuries into threaded derivatives, history into legend, legend into myth. I alone was the person to tell it.

I didn't even have to force it, my charm, my most precious natural resource, so great yet limited in supply; unwieldy. It blossomed of its own accord, in effortless abundance, as if having suddenly discovered the secret to its own self-regeneration.

—Raleigh, Phil, what a delight to see you both! I don't think I've had the chance yet to say congratulations.

—Cassandra! Raleigh greeted me, if not with personal affection then at least the gratitude of social relief. I—

—Thank you, said Phil, interrupting her. There are only two of us left now: me and a bracket called "roadsary." Pains me to say it, but I was worried about Duke there for a second. With Houston starting to take control, though—and look, our game's final—I might just stay perfect through the weekend!

—Well, that too, I guess, I said. But I meant the baby.

Phil blushed, though not as deeply as Raleigh. But I smiled warmly, reassuringly, and, after Phil turned back to the screen, now showing the early minutes of Oregon vs. UC Irvine, I wrapped my other hand around Raleigh's, which I was still holding. *Husbands can be such fucking imbeciles,* the gesture seemed to say—not in accusation, but conspiracy. *Believe me, I know.*

—*Thank you*, she whispered in a little exhale, and without further hesitation, let her embarrassment go. How *are* you? Am I right in thinking you're working on a novel? And your boys must be what, *three* now? Tate and Percy, yes?

—Yes, I said, uncharacteristically struck by her memory.

—Can I see pictures?

I let her scroll through my camera roll, which she did long enough to assure me her cooing was genuine. She was looking forward to becoming a mother, was going to be a good one. A better one, I thought—not bitterly or self-deprecatingly, but as a mere point of fact—than me. She returned my phone and looked down at her belly, reverently, passionately waiting. She still wasn't exactly beautiful up close, but her dense stature, the impossible breasts, lent a certain grandeur to her condition. There was something miraculous about her body, even if it was more Breughel than Caravaggio. Maybe it was just her humanness, the miraculousness, on some level, of every pregnancy, every birth—that inherent to the fresh human growing inside her was its being a specific one. Not a rarity, not even close, and yet beyond rarity. *Unique*, that most misused of words.

—Phil thinks it's a boy, but I'm certain it's a girl.

—You haven't found out yet?

—I want it to be a surprise—you know.

I didn't. It had been agony waiting even until thirteen

weeks to confirm my own suspicions. I was aware this was the new pregnancy trend, though, *being surprised*, as if not knowing your child's sex offered some feminist proof of not caring, or implicit defense of its future right to gender fluidity. In their heart of hearts? Women nearly always hope for girls, even though on some level they know life will invariably be harder for them, are grateful to have boys after all. To pretend otherwise is sort of lovely, if also lunatic. I'd been half expecting Raleigh to recount a "gender reveal party," though, so I had to give her a little credit—even if labor and delivery was, to my mind, likely to offer enough surprises without one more.

—Mm, I said simply.

—By the way, Cassandra, Phil cut in, I'll shoot you an email, too, but I'd like to contribute and attend the DEMO-W PAC thing Wednesday. . . . Cool?

—Sure, I said. *That'd be great.*

He worried I was being lightly sarcastic, or worse, temporarily humoring him to spare his wife. But you know what? I actually meant it.

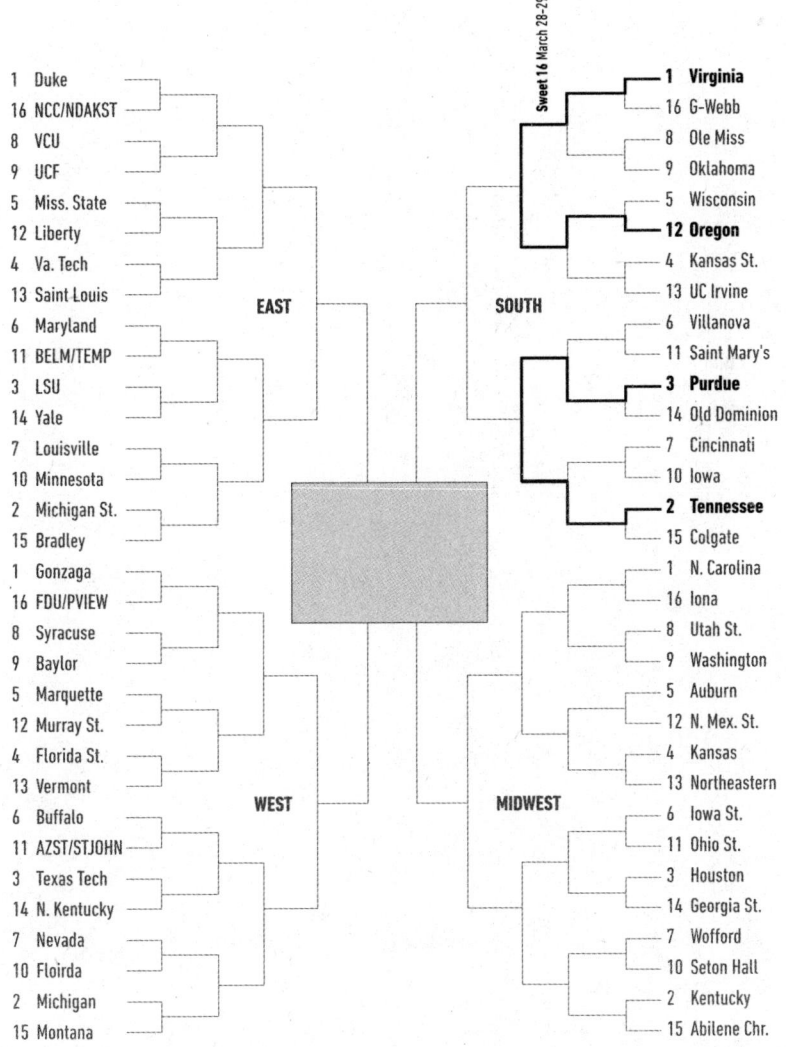

# SWEET SIXTEEN

## VIRGINIA (1) VS. OREGON (12)

The initial flurry of public attention started first thing Monday morning, with journalists and podcasters calling Phil to schedule interviews. He was featured on the UVa sports podcasts CavsCorner and Streaking the Lawn, as well as in a Skype interview with Andy Katz for NCAA.com alongside "roadsary," who turned out to be a middle-aged psychiatrist named Nigel Gregory. Nigel was a Michigan fan who'd picked Duke to win it all, and, more immediately, Tennessee where Phil had Purdue.

*—Welcome, welcome. This is an NCAA.com March Madness tournament challenge video chat,* the video began, the three of them lined up in horizontal boxes, like a low-budget version of the talking heads on CNN. *I'm Andy Katz, happy to have Nigel Gregory and Phil Fayeton on the show today. These two gentlemen have the only two perfect brackets in America right now, and I think it's safe to assume the only two globally. So, you guys have me beat at the moment—although I still have my all my Elite Eight teams*

intact. I could still overtake you. But obviously you outdid me in the earlier rounds, so let's talk about what you saw that I didn't when you were making your bracket selections. Talk to me about the first and second rounds. What were you after in your picks? I want to understand the rationale, here. Nigel, let's start with you.

—*Yeah sure*, said Nigel. *I'm just a Wolverine through and through. I watch a ton of Big Ten ball, and I know I have a Big Ten bias. Occasionally I'll throw on another game—Kentucky, Duke. Duke, with Zion Williamson, looks totally unstoppable this year. But there are a lot of teams I haven't seen play. I rely on Bracketology, obviously, on journalists like you. But a lot of it is just personal preference and a lucky bounce of the ball.*

—*For me, it's all about game analysis and metrics*, said Phil, bristling visibly at the mention of luck. *Like, yes, I went to Virginia and I want them to win, but our stats are also just* there. *Defense is systematically undervalued in college basketball—people forget that. I do keep up with, like, SportsCenter, with Bracketology, but I think it's my independent analysis that's really set my bracket apart. It's all about probability, you know?*

By the morning of Wednesday, March 27—that is, the day of my DEMO-W PAC event—the marketing department at Buick had seen the video. The aging car company, presumably as a part of some attempt to rehab its image, wanted to send Nigel and Phil to see their respective teams play in the Sweet

Sixteen. Nigel would go to Anaheim, where the Wolverines were up against Texas Tech after Gonzaga vs. Florida State, and Phil to Louisville, to see his Cavaliers take on Oregon following the Tennessee–Purdue game. Travel was booked, Buick was tweeting about its generosity by early afternoon, and within minutes Senator Sheila Campau's staffers were making the connection between one of her top corporate sponsors and the AASSS lobbyist going to Louisville on their dime—and calling me. *Yes*, I told Sheila's chief of staff, Sally Yu, *Phil bought a ticket Sunday night. No, he hasn't canceled. I still expect him to be there.* She reminded me what a big sports fan the senator was (first I'd heard of it) and said she'd like to personally congratulate Phil.

Will van der Wende called me, too. It was important, he emphasized, that Maria speak with Phil, ideally semiprivately. He wouldn't have given it a second thought before—but had I heard the Buick news? He was worried, not unjustifiably, that Phil's time would be monopolized by Sheila, who was not only more powerful, but, as more of a centrist Democrat, likely to have greater ideological common ground with Phil. *Get there early*, I advised, and texted Phil to do the same, that there were big Bosses eager to meet him. Phil texted back *ok* immediately, his cadence undercutting the blasé confirmation, the implied suggestion of *how could it be otherwise?*

Phil would have preferred to attend a Republican fundraising event in general, but especially during the heart of March

Madness. Republicans tend to be more reverent when it comes to sports. But in addition to Representative Muñoz and Senator Campau, rumor had it the Speaker of the House would be there—and Phil was riding high enough on his still-perfect bracket to endure more than the usual degree of professional hardship.

He arrived so early that I was still giving instructions to catering, but I greeted him amicably, with congratulations actually intended for his bracket this time.

—And when are you leaving for Louisville? I asked him.

—First thing, he said. I'm going to be interviewed during the Tennessee–Purdue game—like, on *national television*—so I have an hour of "media training" beforehand with people from the network.

—How thrilling! I'll be sure to watch.

—Then there's a late lunch with the Buick team.

—You'll be the perfect brand ambassador for them.

Phil frowned.

—I drive an Audi, he said.

—How pure of you to think that reflects how others see you.

—Is that so, said Phil. And what about you? How's that novel you've been working on?

—Thanks for asking, I said. I got an agent yesterday.

Phil flinched, as if unsure whether he'd heard me correctly—

—No you didn't—what do you mean, *an agent*?

—A literary agent, to help me sell the novel. Phil, are you—*jealous*?

—What? No! He said, his face contorting further, but resetting instantly as Maria Muñoz walked in the door.

On the spectrum of parties—as in social events, as opposed to factions—political fundraisers fall somewhere between a casual wedding and formal holiday office party. While people attend, on some level, for a mix of obligatory and opportunistic reasons, the purpose of these functions is rarely to accomplish anything in and of themselves, but rather to secure certain contacts for secondary meetings. And once this has been accomplished, the balance tips precipitously toward having a good time.

By all accounts, this was precisely what Phil was having far too early in the evening for his tête-à-tête with Maria not to have gone well, though he kept it together long enough to schmooze Sheila, too. *The people of Michigan, you know, are great champions of infrastructure*, I overheard her say, serving herself a canapé (in my experience, what—and who—civil servants are best at serving). He even shook the Speaker's veiny hand—a bit too vigorously, the rush of his proximity to power outweighing any ideological hesitance.

—And thank *you* for supporting the important work of electing Democratic women, the Speaker croaked mechanically.

—Oh, it's our pleasure! Phil enthused. We think women

can benefit from stone, sand, and shale, too—

—Too true, Phil! I jumped in before this inanity could register, leading him subtly away.

I put him in a cab shortly after that, before the wax could melt on any of his sociopolitical achievements, texting Raleigh he was en route—and would she like to watch the Louisville games at my house the following evening? I'd added this with some ambivalence, if not trepidation. There was the standard anxiety of potential rejection, but also of personal exposure should she accept, the asymmetric intimacy of opening one's doors. Either way I was ceding social capital to her—and while comfortable in my conscious knowledge of this (secure in my interior contents, if you will), the more primordial parts of my brain buzzed in warning about an act so brazenly unstrategic.

*That'd be great!* she texted back, with the cat heart-eyes emoji. It nearly made me regret my decision.

### ooo

Raleigh arrived in Georgetown a little after seven the following evening, bearing a mid-shelf bottle of white and little gifts for Tate and Percy, identical fire trucks they were immediately consumed by.

—Did you know Raleigh has a baby in her belly? I asked them, as she beamed and caressed it.

They weren't specially interested though, and, with a gentle push from Miles, skated off to bed. Only when the boys had left the picture did Raleigh register the living room's understated grandeur, the kind that is the product less of elegant design than authentic patina, charming not in spite but because of its little cracks.

—You have a beautiful home, Raleigh said, looking around in admiration, but also as if something was missing.

—The television's in the basement, I said.

It was more of a home theater, with a sizable sofa and worn Eames lounger, which I gestured for Raleigh to take while I ditched the wine—I wasn't about to drink alone. I needed my wits about me, to understand what I was up against in resurrecting an acquaintanceship I'd once so casually elided.

—*Who on earth is going to guard Carsen Edwards?* Brian Anderson was asking Chris Webber. *Let's find out from Sunny Sanders. Hello, Sunny.*

—*Thanks, Brian. Purdue's Carsen Edwards, the Big Ten player of the year, has been blazing hot all tournament—it will take everything Tennessee has to guard him. And yesterday? We learned Lamonte Turner injured his big toe in Tennessee's second-round game versus Iowa. He's been either out or limited in practice all week. A related story we're following here? The only two remaining perfect brackets in the Daedalus Industries NCAA bracket challenge have different picks in this game, and Turner's injury would seem to give an edge to Phil Fayeton. Thanks to Buick, he's here in person tonight—*

Raleigh's hand flew over her mouth to cover her gasp as the network cut to a voiceover shot of Phil in the stands, looking astonishingly average in his orange V-saber polo shirt and ball cap, staring at his phone. A guy in the row behind him tapped his shoulder in recognition, and Phil turned to exchange pleasantries, shake hands.

—*I'll be talking to Phil a little later about why he chose the Boilermakers and how he's feeling about his number-one seeded Virginia Cavaliers, so stay tuned, guys.*

—*You heard it first from Sunny, folks. All right! Listen to that crowd. Twenty thousand of our closest friends, Chris. And we're off—Tennessee ball at the tip! It's the Sweet Sixteen! And how sweet it is.*

Tennessee scored on this first possession, a rattling triple. Raleigh's anxiety was palpable, that specific brand of nervousness springing less from personal investment than the secondhand fear borne of managing the precarious emotions of others.

—I know it's just a game, she said apologetically. But Phil's put so much pressure on himself for some reason. He's starting to think he might actually win a billion dollars.

—I think he might, too, I said.

Raleigh laughed as if I was kidding, and I excused myself to whip up some guac.

There had been one other post-collegiate encounter with Phil and Raleigh, I remembered. A more casual, intimate one, ironically, though this is perhaps why I hadn't recalled it until she was sitting in my basement while I chopped tomatoes. It was during our first summer in DC, I think, or perhaps our second: Another KRE girl's much older boyfriend had hosted a group of us on his boat—a nice, midsize cabin cruiser—for *a leisurely Saturday on the Potomac,* as the email invitation had said. Phil and Raleigh had been late to the waterfront due to parking woes and showed up sweaty and overdressed.

Onboard, Raleigh was effusively complimentary. Her gratitude was genuine, but its outsized expression seemed, as such outsized expression often does, simultaneously sycophantic and imperious, the way a privileged person might extol a humble, tidy house. Phil, meanwhile, latched onto the older boyfriend, asking him endless boating questions, as if preparing for a licensing exam himself. Their whole performance betrayed—what? The discomfiting sense that we were all performing a bit, even if the rest of us were better at it.

—I wish *I* had a boat, Raleigh sighed toward the end of the day.

I remembered this because I'd cringed at the transparency of her desire, her lack of self-awareness. But was honesty irrespective of social consequence not something—*the* thing—I prided myself on? Again, I'd fallen in the commonest of human traps: the facile blame of difference for a repugnance born of similarity. And Raleigh hadn't finished. Her coda was exemplary:

—It's so nice being able to treat your friends, you know?

By the time I returned to the basement, Purdue seemed to have the game well in hand.

—You're just in time, Raleigh said, her eyes meeting mine.

I studied them for any sign of lingering resentment, and the utter dearth made me want to apologize.

—Raleigh—

—Phil texted me. He's being interviewed in the next—

—*and she's with Phil Fayeton now.*

—Ah! Raleigh gasped.

—*So, things are looking* pretty *good for you, Phil,* said Sunny Sanders, zhuzhing her rapturous array of—natural, yet still enhanced—blonde hair and sending it behind her shoulder before resting her hand on his. *You have one of only two perfect brackets left in the country—and if Purdue wins this one, not only will you have the last, but it will be the longest consecutive streak in NCAA March Madness bracket challenge history. Tell me how you feel right now.*

—Honestly, I'm feeling great—really thankful to Buick for sending me out here, and not at all surprised to see Purdue pulling away. Edwards is electric, and this is basically the sort of game I was expecting.

—*I love that confidence*! Sunny said, giving the camera a quick smile before returning her gaze to Phil. *And I'm sure you've seen Gonzaga's also up early—you have them advancing to the Elite Eight, too. What was your thinking there?*

—Yeah, the Zags are a perennial threat. Good fundamentals; good coaching.

Wow, *perennial*, I thought. A lot can be accomplished in an hour of media training.

—*And then we have to talk about Virginia—they're your team, you have them going all the way. What is it you love about them?*

—*Well, it's said a lot but bears repeating, Sunny—*

The way Phil said her name, looking not at the camera, but into her blue eyes, eyes like the platonic form of Raleigh's, took his wife's breath away.

—Chip? I offered, trying to diffuse the tension.

She didn't seem to hear me.

—*Defense,* said Phil. *Defense, defense, defense.*

—*Did you register that, guys? Let's go to Greg in the studio.*

—*All right, thank you Sunny,* Greg answered. *Man, how about that guy?*

—*His bracket's looking a little better than yours,* said Clark Kellogg.

—*A little better than pretty much everyone's—*

—He did well, Raleigh, I assured her.

But she frowned. He'd gotten a little too close to Sunny.

—You think I should call him?

I hesitated, remembering Savannah Quincy, afraid of what I would say. Sunny Sanders was emphatically *not* wearing snow pants. The best I could muster was a deferential gesture. Her call went straight to voicemail.

—I'm sure he's busy, she said. Or maybe it didn't go

through. There are a lot of people there.

—Mm!

Purdue extended their lead to eighteen at one point in the second half before it happened: Tennessee scored fourteen unanswered to tie the game with less than seven minutes left in regulation. Another minute later Purdue was down, then going back and forth, staying in it less thanks to Edwards than the hot hand of Ryan Cline. The network started cutting to Phil during breaks in the action, voicing over what he must be feeling, at one point showing a side-by-side with Nigel Gregory in Anaheim, hearing the news of Tennessee's comeback. Nigel smiled lightly while Phil rocked back and forth, his hands on his temples, then in front of his mouth, forming a vertical line that somehow both mirrored and formed the antithesis of *namaste*. Raleigh started doing it too, elbows resting on her swollen breasts and belly, as uncomfortable as she'd ever been in my most comfortable chair.

Cline nailed another three with thirty seconds to tie it, but with 8.8 left, Tennessee got a dunk. A missed shot went out of bounds, but replay confirmed it: still Purdue ball—

—*Holy moly, Carsen Edwards is fouled on a three-point attempt!*

Raleigh yelped before apologizing immediately, worried she'd woken the boys. No, no—I assured her; they couldn't hear anything up on the third floor. I was immensely relieved to see her having a good time.

Edwards missed the first but made the second. It was down to the final shot, which would either end Phil's perfect bracket and anoint Nigel's "roadsary," or send the game to overtime.

When Edwards made the shot we both cheered—loud enough, this time, to draw Miles, who grabbed a beer and settled in for overtime. It went back and forth at first, with both teams getting into foul trouble, before Purdue started to stretch its lead, closing out 99–94.

The first postgame shot was of the team celebrating, but the next was of Phil, practically mauling Sunny in jubilation, armpits wet, hat askew. Raleigh turned scarlet, but Miles managed to put her at ease again. Small talk. He'd always been better at that than me.

Phil had recovered his composure somewhat by the time the network cut to him again, hands on his own hips, telling Sunny how important it was in sports to have a short memory. He was thrilled, of course, by the outcome, but wasn't about to celebrate until after the Virginia game.

—*Well, all the best,* she said. *America is rooting for you!*

If the arena was any indication, this did genuinely appear to be the case. In a voiceover shot following the segment, with Brian and Chris trading platitudes like *this has been something else* and *March Madness at its best, amirite?* the crowd around Phil fêted him, slapping his back, queuing up for selfies like he was some kind of celebrity, even as Virginia and Oregon took the floor to warm up.

Oregon was the only double-digit seed left in the tournament, one of those storied twelves over fives, who'd also survived a second-half comeback in the second round. Their calling card was defense too, though, setting the matchup to be a potentially tough one of like vs. like. *A repugnance born of similarity*, I thought, my eye drifting again to Raleigh. But after some early tussles, Virginia pulled up eight by halftime—as did Texas Tech, over on the other network, who Phil had going all the way to the championship game—and following his half-time check-in with Sunny, Raleigh, understandably exhausted, made a gracious exit.

Miles and I kept watching, however.
—What do you make of them? I asked with a roving eye.
—What do I make of who?
—The Fayetons, Miles.
—Oh, he said, thinking. I'm not sure I "make" anything of them. We never really traveled in the same circles.
—We did, though—

But Miles just shrugged, taking another sip of his beer. Oregon was inching closer, without ever quite taking the lead—until, with some eight minutes left, they did. I hoped Raleigh hadn't turned it back on in Arlington. The game was tensely back-and-forth then, in that way of patient, defensive teams, until, with twenty-eight seconds to go, De'Andre Hunter had an easy layup to make it a two-possession game. Oregon never recovered.

Remember how Purdue needed ninety-nine points to beat Tennessee? Virginia won with only fifty-three.

000

By the time I emerged from the shower the following morning, I had three missed calls from Sally Yu on behalf of Sheila Campau. The Senator wanted to invite Phil to watch the games that night from her suite at the DaedaDome and was having trouble reaching him.

—He's probably on the plane back from Louisville, I said, throwing a handful of Cheerios in a bowl for Percy.

—Just make it happen, Cassandra, said Sally. He can—should—bring his wife. Oh, and she wants you and Miles to come, too.

—Me—

—You know Phil personally, right? Keeps everything feeling casual. Don't let him talk about work too much; help me keep it light—like, hobby stuff. Basketball—or, I'm guessing you don't know anything about basketball. You can talk about your novel or something.

—How magnanimous!

—Sheila just wants this to be a super casual social gathering, okay? She's planning to wear jeans.

—I understand, I said.

And I did. Whenever a congressional staffer tells you their Boss wants an event to be "casual," they invariably have elaborate plans—and Sally'd said the c-word twice. This was no longer about infrastructure and a double-max from the AASSS, at least not primarily. I checked social media to confirm. (Even oracles appreciate confirmation; it frees up the space for new insights.) Senator Campau still had more Twitter followers, but Phil had surpassed her many times over on Instagram. He'd already posted a carousel of his time in Louisville, garnering a hundred thousand likes.

That public presence and true fame often overlap, one generally used as a conduit to the other, obscures their essential distinction. The former is tied to *role*, the latter to *essence*. Sheila hailed from a prominent Grosse Pointe family, had gone to Yale Law—I don't want to undersell her exceptionalism in a certain sense, let alone her luck. But she was also a woman in late middle-age of unremarkable aura, more Michigoose than Michigander. The sort of public official repeatedly elected less for her personal magnetism than for her relative palatability; the least-offensive option in—sorry—a not particularly sexy state. People cared about Sheila because she was a US Senator, an objectively powerful person. But if she failed to secure reelection? She'd sail into relative obscurity again, save the occasional forgettable appearance on MSNBC.

The severe unrelatability of Sheila's predicament was no small part of its trickiness. Particularly in a state with few celebrities offering plausibly legitimate ties, any too-overt move to convert her power into status threatened trouble with her constituents—overwhelmingly blue-collar—posing a risk to her power itself.

But Phil. *Phil.* I saw what she saw in him—or, more precisely, I saw she saw what I'd seen. He was an established winner now. The greatest ever in his arena, really. And yet, he still had the look of an underdog about him, a dog going on with his doggy life. He was on the cusp of stratospheric fame *and* indistinguishable from one of her constituents; effortlessly relatable in the way she worked to passably cultivate—*jeans!*—but fundamentally, almost definitionally, never could be. Yes, Phil was a rare bird. But not *too* rare. *Medium.* Just the right amount; his rarity laced with the commonness needed to forgive it. Whether he soared or fell tonight didn't even matter much, not to Sheila. The important thing was to be on the screen with him, in the picture; to offset her green jersey with a little red somewhere, a bright vermillion; to be unmissable in the foreground—even if, in the final shot, she happened to have turned away from the scene.

Will van der Wende called moments after I hung up with Sally. He was frantic. Sheila's office had reached out to him too, with tickets for Representative Muñoz and her boyfriend, but, even after stooping to ask directly, Will had been denied a third seat.

—*Casual private gathering* my ass, he said. Campau met Phil—and Maria for that matter—the day before yesterday. Serious shit is getting brokered tonight, Cassandra. Surely you can wrangle an extra ticket for me?

It was possible, but I had no intention of trying. My compassion may have been on the up and up, but I still wasn't a sucker. Defying your client for a prospective one, let alone her minion? It simply wasn't smart. I told him as much, and Will rang off in a huff.

The DaedaDome felt all the more electric for our relative isolation in the suite's tranquility. In heavy offense to Will, it was under capacity: just twelve or thirteen of us in a space that could have easily fit twenty. There was also Phil's sparse demeanor, characterized less by nervousness than a cold tension with Raleigh, which I eventually learned sprung from her failure, the previous night at my house, to take a picture of him on the screen. He brightened, however, when during a commercial break, with Michigan State out to an early lead, the stadium announcer reported his presence in the building, and his face filled the jumbotron.

—You're on TV, too, Phil, called Miles, who understood the assignment and casually grabbed a chicken wing.

Raleigh looked up anxiously.

—Now it's you, Cassandra! She said, brightening with relief.

—What? Phil looked up. Why would they be showing her?

—*Phil!* Raleigh chastised him in horror.

I was chuffed enough by her defense to support it:

—You know I won "best eyes" in high school.

—Really? said Phil.

—Why on earth would she make up something like that? Raleigh said.

Phil's own eyes completed their arcing roll just before the camera panned back to him.

—*A lot of celebrities in DC tonight,* Jim Nantz was saying in closed captioning on the suite's TV. *Including our new favorite, the man with the perfect bracket: Phil Fayeton. He's picked Michigan State in this one. And that's Michigan Senator Sheila Campau next to him—she's having a good night too, obviously.*

Sheila was actually a Wolverine, and it had sort of pained her to don the green jersey, but I imagined this would be adequate compensation for the indignity.

—*Maria Muñoz there on Senator Campau's other side,* added Grant Hill, before they turned back to the game.

Neither of the early ones were close. Michigan State routed LSU, while five-seeded Auburn—who, having made it past the twelve, became one of Phil's "upset specials"—knocked off North Carolina out in Kansas City. Before Duke–Virginia Tech got underway in the DaedaDome, Tracy Wolfson came to talk to Phil, pulling Raleigh in at the end—a bit to both of their surprise—to ask what she was making of all this.

—I'm just really proud of him, Raleigh said beatifically.

It was so simple, touching. Borne less of actual pride than of knowing this was exactly what he would have wanted her to say—though as she said it, it was also clearly true. Phil's gratitude and relief, his sudden total forgiveness, passed for spousal reverence. And perhaps there was a pinch of reverence in it. Tracy looked to be on the verge of tearing.

—Well congratulations to you both, she said. On the bracket—and on the baby.

The segment would go viral, was destined to, but no one realized to what extent until after the game, because it was an absolute thriller—and everyone save Raleigh got very, very drunk. Duke ultimately triumphed, though, with Tech failing to convert on three last-ditch opportunities.

The stadium started clearing out, but the janitorial staff, recognizing Phil, allowed us to stay in the suite to watch the final few minutes of Kentucky–Houston. With a little obligatory hesitation, they even paused their work at our prompting, cheering for Kentucky, for Phil—exchanging high fives when the Wildcats won. It's the ultimate display of superiority, I thought, as we left the box and they resumed cleaning up: temporarily elevating someone to be your equal.

### 000

If you just count the rounds, the culmination of the Sweet Sixteen is the tournament's halfway point, but these first three comprise nearly 90 percent of the games, with only seven left in the remaining rounds combined. Phil had picked fifty-six consecutive—the odds of this one in some seventy-two quadrillion by Phil's coin-flip calculations, and still astonishingly unlikely factoring in asymmetric probabilities. Eight games more than Nigel Gregory had predicted, itself an achievement nine games over the previous record of thirty-nine. This is why Phil would have balked at the mere suggestion it could have been anything aside from his mathematical feat catapulting him overnight from passing sensation to household name, plastering the Fayetons' faces on every corner of Instagram and Twitter, every sports blog in the country, NCAA.com and ESPN and *Sports Illustrated*, the *Washington Post* and *San Francisco Chronicle*. The goddamn *New York Times*.

But it was Raleigh. Raleigh, with her shy poise, with her platinum hair almost halo-like; Raleigh with her full, basketballic body, brimming with life—larger than life, towering over Tracy Wolfson. What had looked almost like stage makeup to me in the DaedaDome played wonderfully on camera, in the photo. She looked dewy, even radiant. The most beautiful I'd ever seen her, her beauty enhanced by her sweetness, the naturalism of her manner offsetting the extremity of her aesthetic artifice. As if the softness of her blinks might have rendered false lashes real.

You could see the shoulder of Sheila's jacket in the corner, a little red sliver, but her face had been cropped out.

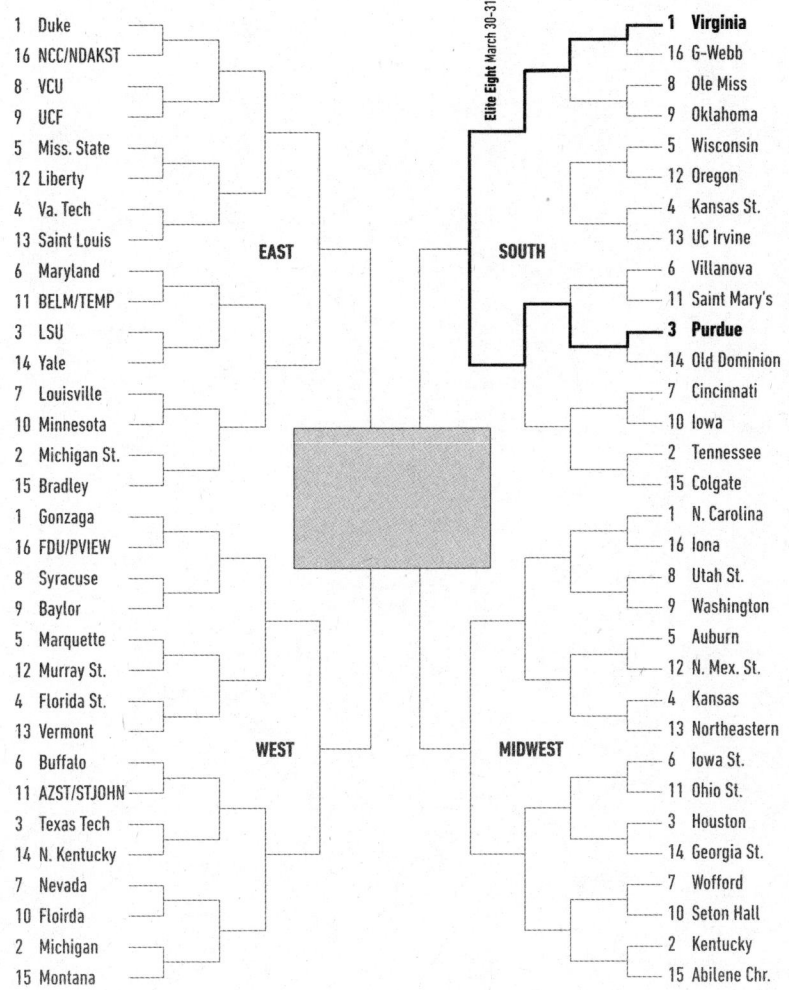

# ELITE EIGHT

## VIRGINIA (1) VS. PURDUE (3)

P hil flew back to Louisville the next morning, again thanks to Buick, going straight from the plane to the stadium for a one-on-one studio interview with Sunny. They'd invited Raleigh too this time, but she didn't want to fly so late in her pregnancy. Besides, she had a shift at the hospital. Phil didn't push her.

Raleigh did agree to be the guest of honor at the UVa club of Washington DC's watch party, however, with the caveat she would be a little late on account of her shift. They'd rebooked at the last minute to get a larger space, a colossal Mexican restaurant in Navy Yard. Still, it was already so packed before the Texas Tech–Gonzaga game, I almost regretted attending. But then, Miles was in his element, and managed to get us prime seats, and when they turned the sound on, I changed my mind. Everyone was rooting for the Red Raiders on Phil's behalf, and when his pretaped interview started airing, positively erupted. The network had slated it for halftime, while his bracket was still guaranteed to be perfect, but as the euphoric bar grew quiet, then silent, rapt, our attention infinite, I knew they needn't have hedged. I could feel the narrative envelope me, how I would tell it, the words of this very paragraph, like the story itself was alive. And yet, my sureness did nothing to lessen the prickling tension, as I watched Phil watch Sunny, the long, slow-motion shots of them strolling across the court—if anything, it heightened it. *What* alone is the province of lesser works. Truly incredible ones are propelled by *how*, to say nothing of *why*.

—*We've talked a lot about basketball,* said Sunny, *but now I want to ask you a personal question.*

—*Shoot,* Phil said gamely, in a line that had to have been scripted for him.

—*We learned yesterday that your wife, Raleigh, is having a baby in just a few short weeks. How do you feel about becoming a dad?*

The network didn't edit out the pause, more pregnant than Raleigh. I think they mistook Phil's unpreparedness for overwhelm. They saw what they wanted to see, instead of what was there. The truth was he hadn't thought about it, at least not recently.

—*Um,* he said, forgetting his media training, *it's . . . truly incredible.*

—*Aw,* said Sunny, breaking into an orthodontic smile worthy of KRE that also somehow encased a pout, her expression hovering somewhere between humanistic empathy and mooning.

The bar was with her. A few of the drunk young alumnae started to cry—softly, genuinely at first, then almost competitively. I heard one of them say Phil was "kind of hot," to nods from the others. Raleigh heard this too, having entered the bar largely unnoticed, in the shadow of her husband, of Sunny.

—*Is there anything you want to say to Raleigh?* Sunny continued.

—*Just . . . I love you, babe.*

Sunny had been explicit with the question, and it was technically the right thing to say—and yet there was a directional ambiguity to this statement, a faint sense that Phil was attempting double entendre, to say just the right thing *and*, to Sunny alone, convey a secret overture. Raleigh was mortified, but it would have been impossible for her to complain. It's the sort of complaint that never works out well for women, that invariably gets us branded sensitive and ridiculous; nervous, neurotic, and neurasthenic; irrational, crazy, hysterical. *Mad.* I should know. Her intuition was dead-on, but the facts didn't support the truth.

—Raleigh! someone said.

The cheer for her was deafening; her disquiet interpreted as sheer surprise. She was that, too, and by the time she found her way to some friends or acquaintances I knew by sight but not name, managed to forge a smile that ushered in its own sincerity. Gonzaga kept things exciting into the final twenty seconds, and Raleigh cheered along with everyone else as

Texas Tech made their free throws in the end game—until it was over, sending Sunny back to Phil. Raleigh fell ashen.

—*Congratulations on another win, Phil,* said Sunny, beaming. *The Red Raiders have been red-hot all tournament, and you have them going all the way to the championship. How did you foresee their success thus far, and why do you like them heading into their first-ever appearance in Final Four?*

—*Yeah, Sunny,* said Phil casually, hand-hipped, as if such interviews were now old hat, *I thought Texas Tech was really underrated as a three-seed. They topped the Zags big time on strength of schedule, with two of their losses coming to Duke and Kansas. I love their intangibles and—*

Raleigh made it through the interview, but excused herself to the bathroom as Sunny closed the segment, the second it wouldn't seem flagrantly unsupportive.

—His dad went to Texas Tech, Raleigh whispered in my ear a few minutes later.

It was such a banal statement of fact that I almost second-guessed my clear impression of its intimacy, that it formed if not a half-admission of my ancient warning's truth, then at least unspoken forgiveness in its good faith. I raised my eyebrows at her.

—I knew you'd understand, she said.

—Here, Raleigh, take my seat, said Miles. What can I get you ladies to drink?

—*Coverage of the NCAA men's basketball tournament is sponsored by: Daedalus Cloud: the official cloud of the NCAA, Buick: yep, that's a Buick; Oracle ERP: unbreakable, and by Taco Bell: sometimes you gotta Live Más.*

Someone had turned up the surround sound, giving the announcer's voice the aura of a higher power. A reverent hush filled the bar as Brian Anderson took over:

—*The stage is set, and the players are ready. Two storied programs, ready to write the next chapter. Tonight we're in the heart of it, folks. We'll find out who can go from Sweet to Elite, and who will go home sour. On top of it all: a still-perfect bracket rides on the outcome.*

An abstracted color-block image of Phil filled the screen, prompting nostalgic Obamaesque cheers of hope.

—*It's the South Regional final: Purdue versus Virginia. Live from Louisville, Kentucky: bring on the Madness!*

—Mad-ness! Mad-ness! someone chanted, then the whole bar. Mad-ness! Mad-ness!

—*Wow, look at the scene here, Chris. We're set for an epic clash, and just about ready to tip it off. But first: On Friday, Sunny Sanders asked Phil Fayeton, the man with the perfect bracket, what he loves about his Virginia Cavaliers. He said defense, and that's what she's talking here tonight.*

—Shh! Everyone shut up!

—*Good evening, Brian and Chris! If this Virginia team is known for one thing, it's its smothering pack-line defense, holding some of the country's top offenses to only thirty-eight percent accuracy. Now, what we mean by "pack-line" is to consolidate protection in the paint, making strong inside shots rare. The four players who aren't guarding the ball all bunch together in an unmarked area starting sixteen feet from the basket. To render the invisible visible, though, Tony Bennett tapes this area off in practice, the team growing so familiar with it that his players tell me they can see it even when it isn't there.*

The enhanced tape of Virginia sped and slowed, with mesmerizing graphic overlays.

*—So how do you beat the pack line? You have to convert on lower-probability shots. This is where you need to remember Purdue is averaging nearly ten three-pointers a game. Against Tennessee last round? They had fifteen. I checked in with Phil earlier, and he's still feeling confident in his Cavaliers, though.*

They showed him in the stands, and *confident* is not exactly the word I would have used to describe him. Mortal terror comes closer. The Elite Eight was great and all, but it's the Final Four everyone remembers, the Final Four that *the road* leads *to*, that has become utterly synonymous with the NCAA's branding, with college basketball itself. *Elite* was a solid performance, an honor—a privilege—an exclusive membership and an arena lined with envy. But *Final* was enduring fame, end game. *Final* was history.

Phil was discovering for the first time all the horrors of success. That with every basket you make, the rim shifts up a bit, and every next shot gives you something more to lose. You'll need to jump higher this time, then higher—and higher. And the higher you jump, the closer you fly to perfection, to that sunny precipice: the greater your fear of falling. It's all gravy as an underdog, a David; easy enough to lick your wounds, to scratch your innocent ass on a tree. But for Goliath? A number-one seed? A fall from such great heights is deadly.

—*All right, it's time to fly—tip's up, up, and away!*

Purdue got the ball.

—*You've been in these high-pressure situations, Chris,* said Brian, kindly eliding that Chris had spectacularly lost the biggest one on a phantom timeout in the 1993 championship. *There's so much emotion in the lead-up, that anticipatory high—what should these players do to try and settle into the game?*

Ryan Cline nailed a three.

—*That*, said Chris.

Diakite responded with a jumper in the paint, his arm extending, but Purdue countered, then banked another three. Virginia stayed in it for a while before losing ground, Purdue going on an 11–0 run that devolved Phil into a visible wreck, peeking through his fingers and pouring sweat. Half the bar mirrored him, booing loudly when, with Purdue leading 25–16 and eight minutes left in the first half, the network cut to a pretaped segment on their seven-foot-three center Matt Haarm's hair. He touched it grotesquely, and Raleigh's hands fell away from her own locks to her belly.

Virginia clawed back to within a point a few times, but Edwards seemed to hit another three against every burst of momentum. And with 2:09 to halftime: Kyle Guy, writhing on the court, grabbing his right ankle.

—*Let's go, Kyle!* a fan screamed, as he hobbled to the sideline.

Guy returned in the last two seconds before half, perhaps as a symbol of hope for the fans. There was reason enough for it—hope, that is—UVa having winnowed Purdue's lead to one.

—*A tortoise comeback,* Clark Kellogg called it. *Slow and steady wins the race.*

Sir Charles still liked Virginia, too.

—*My buddy Phil's gonna get that billion dollars,* he said.

—*He's gonna sweat for it first!* said Kenny the Jet, laughing, the guys having fun with a still of Phil peering between his fingers that would go on to become the top panel in a viral escalation meme.

It was ridiculous in one sense, the implication that any of this either required or would be influenced by some sort of physical labor on Phil's part. And yet, as Guy inbounded the ball to start the second half, apparently okay, I felt it myself for the first time: the little beads budding under my arms, my breath, my heart rate quickening. *Before the gates of excellence*, I thought, *the high gods have placed sweat.* It had been the unofficial motto of my prep school, ludicrously replete with protestant meritocracy even in situations of no personal control. It felt as if I had some then, though, a height I knew I didn't; as if my powers here extended beyond just foresight, a second heat upon the Muses' anvil: that I, Cassandra, could, from a cavernous bar in our nation's capital, will the Cavaliers to victory.

Kyle Guy hit an open three, claiming Virginia's first lead. Then, he hit another, as if the tweaked ankle had flipped a switch, not for the worse but the better. It was hard to say who was more excited, the bar, or Phil, whom the network caught in jubilation, redoubling our fervor in the bar.

Purdue stuck with it, though; Kenny was right. Sweat the gods required and sweat they would have—it was not just under my arms now, but behind my neck, my knees. I twirled my curls into a bun and felt it spread steadily across my hairline into a little wet crown as Edwards, Jerome, Edwards, traded threes. Guy hit his third, fourth, fifth—but Edwards with him; at seven minutes left, he already has thirty points, though as a team, Virginia's up one—now four, Jerome with another three. At five minutes: Edwards. At four: Purdue takes the lead. It's Virginia. Purdue. Virginia. Clark gets a steal, but Guy misses; a partial block by Haarms of the hair. An offensive board for Diakite, for Clarke—fifteen offensive rebounds total by Virginia in the game.

—*Here's Edwards for the lead—oh!* Brian Anderson is basically screaming. *And he banks it! Ex-cuse me! That's ten threes for Carsen Edwards! Purdue up two!*

—*We'll see how Virginia responds to this tempo, Brian.*

*It's not how they like to play.*

—*Kyle Guy lets one rip—short—but gets his own offensive board. Wait, did he step on the baseline, though? Oh my goodness, he stepped on the baseline! It's Purdue ball!*

—*Whooh, sometimes you have to be lucky,* says Chris—

Phil's head in his hands.

—*and sometimes your luck runs out.*

—*Could be the game right here: Edwards steps up for three—off the mark—but offensive rebound! No more shot clock! Virginia has no choice. They have to foul—*

They split the screen as Ryan Cline goes to the line, showing Phil, sodden. When Cline banks the first, I worry Phil's going to need an ambulance. It's 70–67, Purdue. The second free throw would all but seal it; a two-possession game.

But he misses.

And Purdue fouls Jerome, a one-and-one with 5.9 seconds on the clock.

—*Excellent call by Purdue,* says Chris. *You don't want to risk even a three point attempt. Better to give up two here.*

Jerome's first shot goes through. Two-point game. He lines up for the second. Phil, in agony.

—*Jerome is . . . short! Batted by Diakite! Gonna be a scramble in the backcourt! Little Kihei Clark has it, all of five-foot-ten! Virginia has a final chance here—Clark to Diakite—to win it—yes! No,* Brian corrects himself, *to tie! We're all square at seventy!*

Replay confirmed it. The shot off Diakite's fingertips

before the buzzer, the series of movements leading up to it so elegant as to be almost balletic. Clark's pass like Grant Hill's in 1992, except in full motion from the court, without the luxury of five seconds to inbound. Diakite like Christian Laettner, but lovable. As they played it over and over in ever-slower motion, the announcers going apeshit, I saw a note of something else. Perhaps you'll say it's a stretch, hyperbole; that Chris Webber would have seen it himself, having been on the wrong end enough times—but look again at the video. There was a flash in that moment, in Mamadi, of Michael. Yes, *that* Michael. Holy father of the midrange jumper. Mortal god of Air. The man who could fly.

—*Look at Phil Fayeton right now. You think he's happy? You think he's pumped up?*

—*He's incandescent, Brian.*

—*Sunny's with him. Let's go to Sunny. Sunny?*

The roar of the crowd is so intense it's clearly hard for them to hear each other, and Sunny leans close—too close. Raleigh's pain looked almost physical, and maybe was.

—Raleigh, are you all right?

—Just Braxton-Hicks, she said, bracing for another false contraction as the game cut to commercial.

—*This overtime made possible by: Mercury Incorporated, who reminds you again to* pay like a god.

—*My goodness, can you believe what we have here*, says Brian. *Overtime after a play for the ages—that mad rush—Diakite true at the buzzer. Five more minutes on the clock,* now. *Five minutes to draw the line between Elite and Final; between whose story has another chapter, and whose comes to an end.*

Purdue again controls the tip but turns it over. They score on their next possession though; Jerome answering. Seventy-two all. Trading fouls, drives. Virginia up one with twenty-seconds, and Edwards misses. They have to foul. Less than six seconds left, with two shots coming for Guy.

—*Phew, those are some epic free throws,* says Brian. *Phil Fayeton can't handle it! Look at him. He's going ballistic, and I don't blame him. The Cavs up three but Purdue still has a chance, because Edwards has been fire.*

It is almost anti-climactic, the finale, like a false contraction. Edwards doesn't miss the last shot—he never gets to take one.

—*Forty-two points in the game,* says Chris. *And he lost it on a pass.*

Or—did Virginia win it with one? With, that is, *vicious pack-line defense*? With good *passing—efficiency—patience*? With Hunter, yes, but also Guy, Jerome; Mamadi Diakite. This was still a team's team—*our* team's team. *Our* including *mine*. Remember numbers and fans are helpful in foresight; recall the wisdom of crowds. And now, our team's team, wise and sighted, replete with prophets and oracles, sibyls and bards, forecasters-cum-sportscasters—foreshadowers, diviners, and literal *palm*ists. Fanatics, bracketologists, and Washington wizards. *Mediums*. Readers, too. Yes, you, even you. All of us, turning the page and going to the holy grail, to the finality marked by that most auspicious of even numbers, the smallest composite, quadrilateral and perfectly square.

—*This is Tony Bennett's first trip to the Final Four, following in the footsteps of his father, who also beat Purdue to do so,* said Brian. *Over to Sunny Sanders, who's with him now.*

—Congratulations, Coach. Huge win. This will be Virginia's first trip to the Final Four since 1984. How does it feel?

—*Ah, pretty darn good. What a game. Purdue is a heck of a team. I can't tell you how proud I am of these guys,* Tony said, immediately turning it over to them, content to smile his winning smile, the kind that can never truly lose.

—*Kyle: He's giving all the credit to you, to your teammates. Tell me about this win.*

—*Coach is always saying you have to be able to lose together first,* said Kyle Guy, *and he's right. This win is better because we lost like that. And we have the best fans! Phil's making history this year, too! Where is that guy? Man, get him down here!*

He was on the phone when the cameras found him, as security escorted him to the floor. It wasn't with Raleigh, who sat beside me very quietly, watching. He rang off and someone gave him a matching hat, thrust him into the midst of the team as the confetti poured down.

It was Phil who made the first cut to the net, clipping it like a bird's wings. Phil who, at the top of the ladder, stared into the fiery ring, and, weightless and beaming, held up that first white piece of string, signifying everything.

### 000

—I want to know every fucking thing about him, Arun Patil shouted at a collection of executives and attorneys and assistants when Virginia won. I want to know who he's been talking to. I want to know how much money is in his bank account. I want to know every point of weakness, every skeleton in his closet. Nothing is too small, people. I want to know what Phil Fayeton ate for fucking breakfast—

Arun had paid little attention to the early rounds. Though he considered it good exercise, Arun was not, especially, a basketball fan—for five-foot-nine "meritocratic" reasons largely akin to mine. He balked at time spent watching it, or any sport for that matter, considering it a wasteful opportunity cost. His related assets—the DaedaDome, et cetera—were exactly that: assets, useful in their disproportionate emotional value to others. By the tail end of the Sweet Sixteen, though, he began to worry; by the Elite Eight, no small amount. Phil wasn't thinking about it this way yet, and wouldn't until incepted, but every win he predicted correctly was, mathematically, a form of sunk cost. With Phil having entered the Elite Eight still perfect, the probability of him guessing the remaining seven games was—at worst, even with coin-flip math—one in *one-hundred twenty-eight*. Arun Patil did not like those odds. He liked them less still after Texas Tech advanced—one in sixty-four. Just as, at the tournament's beginning, every new game shrunk the probability of perfection exponentially, with every hurdle Phil now passed, the remaining odds grew—quite vexingly for Arun—exponentially in Phil's favor.

—*now*, or else somebody's getting fired! said Arun. Maybe I should fire one out of every thirty-two employees. . . . Nah, nah, I'm just kidding.

But it wasn't particularly clear that he was. Through little fault of their own, Arun's legal team had given barely a cursory review to the whole gambit. This had not really been a bet, but a gimmick. And while Arun obviously had the funds, liquidity was another matter, as was orchestrating a cash payment of that size with tax efficiency. Then there was the principle of the thing. Arun was a competitive man. The idea of wiring a billion dollars to some bozo over basketball simply didn't sit right with him. It wouldn't have even if his team *had* been prepared for the potentiality, even if his divorce settlement hadn't likewise been looming.

Arun Patil graduated from my other, more famous alma mater in 1984, the same year the University of Virginia had last appeared in the Final Four, the same year Phil Fayeton was born. He did not, like several of his peers, drop out—his immigrant parents would have either killed him or died themselves—going instead much the way of Miles, spending just enough time on Wall Street to amass the impression of, if not the actual capital required for, risking his own rather than his parents' money. According to legend, Arun first conceived the search engine in 1989, though he didn't manage to launch his Merged Electronic Reader Option Provider Environment (MEROPE) until 1993. It was a spectacular failure. Arun excelled at bringing attention to his product; he had a publicist's Midas touch, but this is a mixed blessing when your product kind of sucks. MEROPE struggled to separate relevant results from irrelevant ones in the internet's primordial ocean, and it wasn't getting any better. Arun had spent all the money he'd made and then some. The burgeoning industry mocked him, and his first marriage increasingly floundered. Why couldn't he go back to investment banking? His wife wanted children. By 1996, she'd had enough, serving him papers the day before he flew to Palo Alto to meet a Stanford graduate student with whom he'd been emailing. Her name was Laurie Page.

True genius, whether it be in art or science, statistics, literature, basketball, or sex—is often a matter less of aptitude than of dialectic. Together, Arun and Laurie gutted MEROPE, replacing its algorithm with PageRank, a cute double entendre that estimated the importance of a website by recursively weighing the number of links to it, indexing the internet in modeling the probability of a random surfer landing on a given page. It was, in essence, an oracle based on the wisdom of crowds. They desperately needed a rebrand, but the trade name Oracle was already taken. Instead they settled on *Daedalus*. Not a literal prophet, but still a kind of one, an inventor and an artist; a figure who made things and made things happen. Daedalus could hand you the thread you needed to lead you out of the labyrinth, because Daedalus had built the labyrinth.

Arun's parents gave him another few hundred thousand dollars, to which Laurie's added significantly once they "formally incorporated"—married—in 1998. Daedalus Search grew exponentially into the early aughts under Laurie's technical leadership while Arun spun the narrative. Instead of shying away from MEROPE's former challenges, he leaned into them, crafting a story of perseverance, reinvention. It gave their IPO an even more favorable anchor—its comparison point not nothing, but even less. The comeback story is, after all, the great narrative of America. We love its extremities, the intoxicating risk of spectacular success, all the more when it's born of spectacular failure. What America hates—the one thing it will never forgive—is abiding mediocrity.

None of this is particularly conducive to sustainability or balance or a growing family. Laurie stepped back a bit with the births of their children, more when she physically lost her voice—but by that time, in 2013, Daedalus Industries had not only fully conquered search but become a leader in myriad other computing endeavors, buoyed by the kind of scale that can fill almost any gap inorganically. In his wife's relative absence, Arun acquired voraciously: apps, movie studios, sports arenas, the *Washington Post*, a gigayacht so big it had its own "support yacht," and, in 2018, the thirty-year-old mononymous Belgian supermodel, Persa.

It would have been convenient for Arun to blame the Phil debacle on the stress of his ongoing divorce, the billions he'd be paying Laurie far in excess of her own shares. Perhaps even on his more pleasant distractions—all that yachting with Persa. But the truth was Arun was far too shrewd a storyteller and statistician alike. It was Arun himself who'd thought to offer a billion dollars for a perfect bracket—not as a company, but a personal bet. It was irresistible: an astronomical prize for an event of infinitesimal rarity, a scanty promise of tantalizing value. The kind of story that linked-to stories would inevitably link to. Guaranteed virality. He'd absolutely loved it, until he didn't.

How had Phil done it? Arun wondered. *He had to have cheated somehow.* But *him? This guy? A mastermind?* He didn't seem capable of it.

The form these thoughts assumed for Arun had the tenor not of moral admiration but practical insult. Which was why he wanted to meet Phil himself. If there was foul play, he'd call it out. One of his assistants got Phil on the line, and Arun watched his shifts in expression intently on the television as they talked.

◻◻◻

Phil and Raleigh arrived early in the owner's suite at the DaedaDome the following evening to watch Auburn–Kentucky on its big screen, initially joined by several Daedalus senior executives, but not Arun himself. Sheila Campau had also extended Phil another invitation, even going so far as to dangle the offer of a position on her staff, but by this point Phil was thinking bigger. It should probably concern us that even Phil—a lobbyist, a former congressional staffer—easily prioritized a tech billionaire over a US Senator, all the more so for its failure to surprise. But Phil's social media followers were by then in the millions, and the West was calling: that lingering Manifest Destiny we can still sometimes see if we squint at the Pacific coast. He'd woken up to calls from LA talent agents, pitching their services, wooing him. *Choose soon*, they said. Win or lose, he didn't want to be without an agent at the height of his fame—someone who could help him monetize effectively, secure the best deals at the apex of his marketability. He said he'd think about it. He wanted to meet Arun Patil first—nearly as much as Arun wanted to meet him.

Arun still preferred a delayed entrance. Not just for its customary optics, the power implicit in making someone wait, but in having long since discovered the performative influence of his presence on others. He knew it would be better to give his guests time to acclimate; to set them at ease. He wanted Phil to have a few drinks first, for some of his people to form a casual rapport with him, and to watch it all unfold unobserved from another room.

Per Arun's wishes, his team had, in the past week, conducted not just background checks but what amounted to political opposition research on Phil. His affinity for Virginia was direct, obvious; for Texas Tech, familial. Michigan State–Duke, the game to be played that night in the DaedaDome, might have been a toss-up: two top programs run by legendary coaches with histories of over-performance in the tournament. Thoroughly unsurprising for a Virginia fan—routinely pummeled by and no doubt envious of Duke—to be led by desire and give the edge to MSU.

But Auburn was a mystery. A five-seed, a team who had never made the Final Four, over perennial power Kentucky as a two? When Phil predicted the other three fives losing to twelves in Round 1? Nothing in his background explained it, nor did statistics—at least none of the models Arun's team had looked at or run. Where could Phil have gotten access to greater quantitative horsepower than at Daedalus Industries? Had he adapted some political polling model? But Arun had spoken to Nate Silver, and *FiveThirtyEight* was as flummoxed as his team was. Was it possible Phil had developed some highly sophisticated novel estimation model *himself*? The more Arun saw of him, the less likely it seemed. Phil was wrapped up in the game with no evident calculation, akin to in his live TV appearances, flush with the pure emotion of an ardent fan.

And yet, there *had* been a subtle shift in Phil's affect since the previous day. His cheers for Auburn possessed all their customary enthusiasm, but when the Tigers got off to a slow start, his expression bore little sign of terror. It was closer to bemusement, as if trying to work out less whether than how they'd manage to come back. Was this hubris? Or did he know something? Arun had every indication Phil had neither the funds nor the network to throw this game or any other. Kentucky was looking so sharp Arun wondered if he'd even have to worry about it, if he could stroll in with condolences masked as congratulations, pose for a few photos, and leave early, his gimmick again a gimmick, and a wildly successful one. But by half Auburn had cut the Wildcats' lead from eleven to five, and less than three minutes into the second it was tied—then Auburn up a triple. Phil was euphoric, embracing not just his wife but Arun's associates, who seemed to have undertaken their assignment a little too believably, cheering alongside Phil as the lead bounced back and forth.

Auburn was down two with forty seconds left. Enough time for them to score, but also enough for Kentucky to win on a final shot. But the latter didn't go in, sending the game to overtime.

—Fuck! said Arun, grabbing a fresh shirt.

While he was composing himself, Auburn went up two, four, six in overtime. There were less than two minutes left.

Arun barreled into the owner's suite:

—I will give you a million dollars right now to call off the bet.

He regretted this offer the moment it escaped his lips.

Phil, rising to his full height, smiled down at him, almost with a look of pity.

—I don't think so, man, said Phil.

—*Phil*, said Raleigh, implicitly urging him to consider it.

—No, babe. Auburn's gonna win.

—There are other games left, said Arun, appealing more now to Raleigh, and feeling the need, in having made a mistake, to convince himself it hadn't been one by doubling down. Ten million.

—*No*, said Phil, more emphatically this time, almost unthinkingly, as Auburn drove in for a layup.

Arun bided his time, until Kentucky again got within three. There were thirteen seconds left.

—Offer stands, he said quietly.

—*Phil*, Raleigh whispered to him. *Ten million dol—*

But the game was over. Auburn had prevailed.

—*Anything can happen in March!* The commentator marveled.

Arun was not so sure, but, with effort, smiled nonchalantly. *One in sixteen*, he thought.

—Congratulations, he said.

—Thanks, said Phil, shaking his hand. It's great to meet you, by the way.

—You, too, said Arun, no longer meaning it.

I can hear your objections mounting. That until this point, at least I'd been in the Fayetons' direct proximity. How could

I have, even retroactively, achieved such intimate access to someone like Arun Patil? Simple divination strains credulity, and journalistic effort brands a fraud. Better chalk it up to delusions of grandeur—as if the difference between confidence and delusion hasn't generally been a little extra skin and muscle hanging between the legs. Women are always, on some level, unreliable narrators. *Victims.* But do not mistake my victimhood for weakness—this isn't like old times. There are advantages to victimhood, narratively, and I know how to take advantage of them. My *unreliability* frees me from any burden of proof. Consider that before Veblen there was George Eliot; before Girard, Flaubert. Remember every great novel is an unbelievable truth.

The first shot of the Duke–MSU game was an uncontested dunk by the Spartans, prompting the network to give us our first glimpse of Phil from home, standing with his arms in the air, which Miles clocked appreciatively. The Sunday games were early enough we'd agreed to let the boys watch, too, but their focus was on Raleigh, benefactress of their beloved fire trucks. She was wearing one of those dresses suggestive of leading an elegant life without electricity, so deeply in style then, especially in the final throes of pregnancy, and was looking very "benefactress" indeed.

—*Find coverage of the NCAA Division I women's tournament online,* said Jim Nantz in an aside. *Here in prime time: Duke's on a twenty-one to five run, with twelve unanswered points. Zion Williamson and the Blue Devils may have gotten off to a slow start, but they've been putting on an absolute clinic since then. I wonder how Phil Fayeton's handling the heat, Grant? Guess who's with him—and the man he's looking to win a billion dollars from? Let's go to Tracy Wolfson.*

Oh yes let's, Jim, I thought at home.

—*Phil, Raleigh—it's good to see you back at the DaedaDome, this time with its owner, Arun Patil. Michigan State got off to a hot start, but Duke's come back and then some. How are you feeling?*

—*Still feeling good, Tracy,* said Phil with more equanimity than I'd ever seen from him. *Michigan State's been getting in the paint. Williamson's amazing, of course—but as you know by now, I prefer great teams over superstars.*

—*Careful there,* said Tracy jovially. *You're becoming a superstar yourself. Raleigh, what are you making of Phil's newfound fame?*

—*Oh, I'm just happy for him,* Raleigh said.

—*And Arun, I bet you never imagined anyone would get this far. Have you spoken to your accountant?*

—*I'll make good on my promise if it comes to that,* he said, with a smile more forced than he'd have liked. *But there's plenty of basketball left, too. I confess, I'm a Zionist today.*

He'd been unable to resist the turn of phrase, but would, I was sure, come to see it for the grave blunder it was—and not just because there is no bigger Goliath in college basketball than Duke, even when they're not the overall number-one seed. That he'd reaffirmed his offer on tape was the least of his problems. Arun had made the fundamental error of confusing a game he'd already lost for one he was still playing—not just an error in judgment, but worse, of self-awareness. Win or lose, Phil was already America's darling, an everyman hero, one of those rare societal mirrors that manages to flatter everyone. Arun had gone into the segment everyman's patron and left it every man's adversary. Within minutes, Twitter was aflame with overzealous support for Phil—anti-Duke memes, calls to boycott Daedalus, vile personal epithets aimed at Arun. The "Zionist" line had managed to offend supporters of both Palestine *and* Israel, not to mention the vast swathes of people who found it unseemly for Americans to concern ourselves with either.

By halftime, Arun's team was starting, not without cause, to fear for his physical safety. Michigan State had gone on a run of their own to close out the half, and now up four, Phil seemed less ready to settle than ever. Arun had already bumped up his offer to sixty-two million, five—the mathematical break-even point for both, the limit his cool rationality would permit. Raleigh had gasped, but Phil, blinded by his own star shine, still declined, figuring in a ludicrous fit of optimism he could make something like that with a few sponsorships and Instagram posts if he didn't win the billion. And the billion itself was starting to feel not just increasingly likely, but inevitable. For this, I cannot fault him. I had the same feeling.

Arun excused himself early in the second half, sneaking out under oversized sunglasses and, ironically, a Michigan State hat. He didn't see the thrilling back-and-forth, the ties, the steals and rebounds, dunks and late-game fouls. He didn't see Duke miss a free throw with five seconds left—then accidentally *make* the second one. He didn't see Michigan State inbound, recovering with a straight shot to the basket; the player having the presence of mind, a point up, not to shoot, but to run out the clock.

—*Four's a pretty nice number,* Michigan State Coach Tom Izzo said, setting off more than a few tweets soliciting his thoughts on sixty-nine. *I'm thrilled, Trace.*

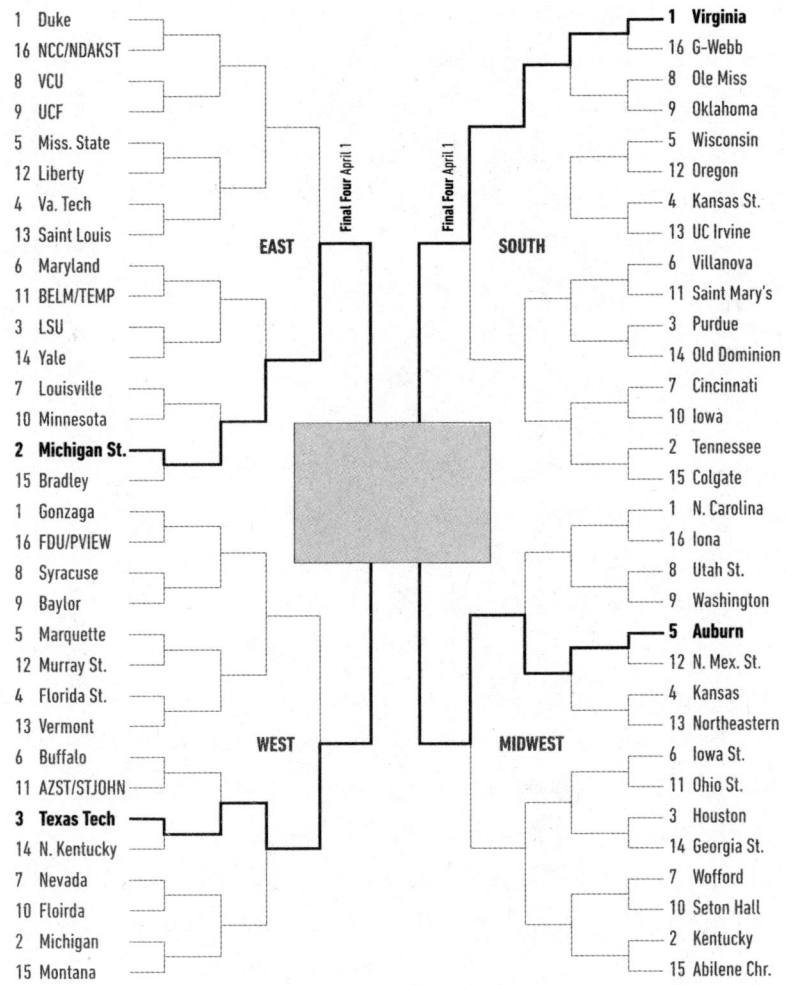

# FINAL FOUR

## VIRGINIA (1) VS. AUBURN (5)

Phil had been saving up his vacation days for after the baby's arrival, the AASSS parental leave policy not being particularly generous, but now had so many interviews and opportunities lining up he was more or less forced to take the week off. He'd toyed with the idea of quitting outright, but Raleigh, with uncharacteristic vigor, was against it unless he was going to accept Arun Patil's offer, and Phil was resolutely opposed to *that*. In his own way, Phil was as competitive a man as Arun, and the Daedalus CEO's early departure had dealt a social sting that Michigan State's ultimate victory had failed to fully mitigate. Doubtless Arun's ongoing online immolation reinforced Phil's decision. He wouldn't have thought about it this way, but Phil's first tastes of public adoration had firmly prioritized amassing status over power, and he was far more risk averse when it came to safeguarding his newfound reputation than he was in harnessing the security of funds.

Raleigh feared the harness a bit too loose—not out of greed, but sheer practicality—and was relieved, at least temporarily, when, on Monday morning, Phil called CAA back and signed with Crewe Silver, a highly touted talent agent with crossover expertise in sports and reality television. (*Now we* both *have agents*, Phil texted me—*except mine's gonna make me money*.) Crewe had a sort of sandblasted look, like cotton slub personified. He struck me as the kind of Hollywood guy who thought *Lolita* was a romance novel—but with the confidence that is often its own self-fulfilling prophecy. He set to work immediately to capitalize on the time bomb of a fiscal opportunity he believed Phil to be.

Crewe's first order of business was prioritizing and arranging Phil's calendar for the week ahead, leading up to the Final Four—or, more precisely, delegating this to one of his assistants, armed with the loosely tailored heuristic of scheduling national network sports appearances first, followed by national general interest video, print, and audio, respectively, with any remaining slots going to niche basketball outlets with large, dedicated followings. Appearances with Raleigh outranked solo ventures, as, much to the assistants' logistical consternation, Crewe sided with Raleigh in agreeing she should continue working her shifts at the hospital. Leaving the ER short-staffed to do interviews had all the makings of a PR nightmare and was wholly out of sync with the couple's team-player image. All regional and local opportunities could be deferred indefinitely—though not declined, Crewe specified, knowing there was money in the long tail there if he didn't succeed in making Phil a more durable celebrity. He'd been in the business long enough to know there was always some degree of luck in such effectuation, and bracket aside, was not yet convinced Phil had quite enough of it.

Crewe's second order of business—a credit to him that it wasn't his first, and probably the last credit I'll give him—was rounding out Phil's management team with the sort of professionals who would maximize and safeguard Crewe's cut: financial advisors and tax accountants, stylists of hair and fashion, personal trainers, makeup artists. Phil would have to get over his masculine heteronormative aversion to cosmetics, Crewe explained—even if he *was* a Republican. Raleigh would benefit, too. They had already captured the hearts of everyday Americans. The next step was to lean aspirational, but without damaging their relatability. They couldn't—shouldn't—change overnight; it had to be gradual. An evolution that would only after several years reveal itself to have been a metamorphosis. Phil nodded intently, but Raleigh frowned at this explanation.

—Are you sure they don't like us because of who we are already? She asked him.

—Oh, they do, baby, they *absolutely* do. And I don't want to mess with any of that. These are subtle little tweaks we're talking.

Crewe had a specific set of models in his mind for these

subtle tweaks—a couple he'd seen when reviewing tape of their appearances, back in the Sweet Sixteen. Friends of theirs from college, no? The man had the easy affect of a latter-day Kennedy, almost, with his swoopy hair and needlepoint belt. The woman had been darker, but with blue eyes; ambiguously Mediterranean, borderline "exotic." Turkish, maybe? Or Greek? He wasn't suggesting Raleigh go overboard—he liked her as a blonde—but he wanted her to co-opt a bit of that upmarket vibe; a more natural beauty, but with sharper tailoring.

Miles was surprised when Phil asked if he wanted to go to Minneapolis with him, but I wasn't. Phil's rise had eclipsed enough powerful people by this point that you'd be forgiven for thinking he'd also eclipsed ours. But Crewe's guidance basically aligned to Phil's natural inclination—it was Raleigh's pushback that was novel. For the first thing we tend to reach for when attaining new heights is not the top of the glass, but the rim of the basket. It is those at whom we've spent such time looking up to close-range who we most want to see us in turn succeed.

—And what do you make of Phil Fayeton now? I asked Miles glibly.

—It'd be pretty hard not to like him.

—Aw, how bromantic.

—I wouldn't go that far.

But I would. Miles was only too delighted for a free trip to the Final Four; the invitation had positively tickled him.

The NCAA itself was sponsoring this time, part of a deal Crewe brokered with them that also included a four-minute pretaped day-in-the-life in-home-plus-studio interview for the network to air in the Virginia–Auburn Final Four pregame—which I myself watched, a little surreally, sitting under the selfsame synthetically weathered home decor sign it featured ("Love Is Never Having to Say You're Sorry").

—It was overwhelming, Raleigh admitted to me in between bites of the crab dip I'd brought as an offering.

I noticed her acrylics had been removed. Her own, shorter nails were now carefully manicured with glossy orange polish.

—I don't want to complain, she said, because we're so blessed by this whole experience, but it took more than eight hours to film. And you wouldn't believe how many people were in the house!

—Try me.

But the final product started airing before she could, opening with a grandiloquent Nolanesque tableau of Phil walking into a suburban sunset with Ron Tinaldi.

—*The probability of being born with eleven fingers or toes is as low as one in five hundred,* Ron said in high-dramatic voiceover, which seemed to me an odd example, veering dangerously toward accidental satire. *Phil was born with the standard allotment. If, like Phil, you played men's basketball in high school—*

Smash cut to him squaring up at a court in a local park, shot in slow motion, black-and-white.

*—the likelihood you'll go on to be drafted by the NBA is around one in thirty-three hundred. It has been estimated that, assuming you were born in America, you have a one-in-ten-million chance of being elected President of the United States. At thirty-five years of age, Phil Fayeton, who is an associate lobbyist at the American Association of Stone, Sand, and Shale in Washington, DC, will be eligible to run in the next election—and, at the absolute minimum, two hundred times likelier to find himself there someday, swiveling behind the Resolute Desk, than he'd be to fill out a perfect March Madness bracket.*

After the ball floated slowly, gracefully through the hoop, the video pivoted to a studio interview, not with Phil or Raleigh but with Lucas Hadley, the Georgetown statistician from that early courtside segment. The initial questions rehashed much of what Sunny had previously asked him live, though Lucas himself seemed more somber this time, almost awestruck. His avian ankle, if it was dangling, was well outside the frame.

*—Setting aside a perfect bracket overall,* Ron pivoted, *just thinking about where Phil is today, perfect up to the Final Four, how rare a feat are we talking?*

*—Still infinitesimal,* said Lucas. *I heard Phil quote one in over a quintillion—though, as we've discussed, I don't think coin-flip math holds much credence. But even if we consider the absolute best-case scenario, using the most sophisticated model imaginable, we're looking at one in at least two*

*hundred and fifty million to predict sixty consecutive games. Remember, there are only three games left. The insane improbabilities are behind him. Having come this far, I won't be surprised if Phil stays perfect. His chances are at worst twelve and a half percent—and probably somewhat better, having picked Virginia, the only remaining number-one seed.*

This last clause was voiced over a faux domestic scene, Phil helping Raleigh unload the dishwasher in full, if understated, Virginia regalia.

—Miles has almost the same belt, I said.

—Mm, said Raleigh.

—*I recently spoke with a statistician at Georgetown University,* Ron Tinaldi relayed to Phil and Raleigh, sitting next to Sunny Sanders in the living room in which I now sat, as if they were on some excruciating, public double-date. *And he said he'd no longer be surprised if you stayed perfect, having come this far. What is your mindset going into the last three games?*

—*I won't be surprised either,* said Phil. *I mean—have you been watching? This Virginia team is special, Ron. They simply will not be denied. And Texas Tech has been blazing hot. At this point in the tournament, it's all about momentum. I've never felt better about Texas Tech over MSU than I do now.*

—*What do you say to those who think you "just got lucky"?* Ron asked.

—*I don't believe in luck.*

Raleigh fidgeted slightly in her navy sheath on the screen as Phil spoke. It fit closely to her bump without any hint of clinging, somehow both more conservative and liberal than her usual attire at once. She looked less beautiful than she had in the interview with Tracy, the contrast to Sunny more direct and not to her advantage. Still, Crewe's "subtle tweaks" had made a difference. Raleigh looked, if not exactly tasteful, then at least like the sort of woman who, in a candid photograph with a golden retriever, would inspire a Republican constituency to vote for her husband. Maybe even a Democratic one.

—*You also favor coin-flip probability,* Ron continued. *You've repeatedly referred to the odds of a perfect bracket as one in some nine quintillion.*

—That's right.

Sunny frowned and moved to ask a follow-up.

—*Hang on, Sunny,* Ron eclipsed her. *Because I want to get Raleigh's take here.*

(I spared a thought for Sunny. She was a good reporter, who should have been speaking at least to Tony Bennett and De'Andre Hunter, let alone Steph Curry and LeBron; who could have held her own and more at the dude table on SportsCenter; who had played college ball herself at Penn State in addition to modeling. Why was it that the modeling had made her somehow less, rather than more qualified, forced into personal interest, the realm of hapless asshats like Ron Tinaldi? This is a rhetorical question, obviously. Sideline reporters are the political fundraisers of the sportosphere.)

—*I don't know much about basketball,* Raleigh said. *But we're so blessed by this whole experience.*

It was when I saw Raleigh feed this line to Ron on network television, rather than when she'd said it to me herself, that I realized she didn't quite believe it. Not, at least, that her husband had been—what? *Divinely inspired? Touched by God,* with a capital G? Her manner, so perfectly replete with innocuous cliché, that beloved vagueness of American commercial Christianity, was imperviously believable because it was a lie. She kept saying *blessed* because she couldn't—wouldn't—say the L-word. No, not love. *Luck.* But she knew it, same as me. That luck was Phil's true benefactor. Her refrain from saying it was born of neither delusion nor cunning self-interest, but a total fluency in the kind of cosmic compassion I'd only ever stretched to graze. Was it possible? Was this the full-glam face of philosophical fucking enlightenment? Why had the sheer visibility of her efforts always struck me as incompatible with such a concept? We all want our lives to be higher production quality.

I looked from the screen to the real person beside me, pulsing with another, doing so little to struggle against it: that maddening physical discomfort I had known so well. *About suffering they were never wrong, the old Masters.* How well they understood the whole pageantry: Awake, tingling, near. I gazed upon her high-maintenance equanimity as she took another bite of crab dip, with something close to awe, with something close to fear.

—*It's finally here,* said Jim Nantz, *one of the biggest days of the year not just in college basketball, but in all of sports: Final Four Saturday. Step aboard the Vikings Ship in Minneapolis, folks. We're in for a high-flying show.*

### ◻◻◻

I suspect the true reason for the NCAA tournament's violent brand pivot from *March Madness* to the *Final Four* can be divined through that great law of parsimony better known as Occam's razor: that among a prediction's competing hypotheses, the simplest is generally the best. Much like the very suitability of calling on old Occam, it is fundamentally a question of *when*. And *when* is the Final Four, you ask?

April.

There is, amidst spring's pageantry, its picturesque ploughmen and cavaliers—under the ever-heating sun, stretching to the edge of the sea—a dark crack running between them, March and April. March may be mad—*beware the Ides* of it, we soothsayers say. The weather's all over the place, neither winter nor spring, yet both. It is named for that wild god of war. As Phil pointed out: Women's History Month. But April? It's cruel. The cruelest, if you believe the poets—though April is also National Poetry Month, which rather suggests most people don't, the very act of demarcating a month for such things being a tacit admission of their exclusion from broader relevance.

Fortunately, this is a book about basketball. *Men's* basketball. But April's cruelty still applies. The four regional champions are given its first week to celebrate, parade around. But the great cruelty of the Final Four is that it isn't—*final*, that is, not really. You don't quite realize it until that first Saturday in April, the road leading up to it having been so squarely paved toward the Final Four itself. Fools! Only two teams can play for the national championship, and only one win it. There may be just three games left, come April, but there are still *three games left*. There is a specific, highly unsympathetic agony, an exquisite and, yes, some might say poetic cruelty, to reaching *the end of the road*, as they call it—*they* being the NCAA—and getting thrown from your horse. To thinking you've made it to the holy grail only to be stopped in its antechamber. It would never happen to Harrison Ford.

—*What Tony Bennett's team would have given last year just to make it to the second round*, Grant Hill mused. *But now, having gotten this far, being here isn't enough. They had an unprecedented loss, and they're out for nothing short of unprecedented atonement. Virginia wants redemption, Jim. Virginia wants to win it all.*

I'd started sweating again, that thick anticipatory sweat of feeling myself at the cusp of something, some novel greatness, a puzzle and a precipice, my wings raised and split.

—I'm nervous, Raleigh said, perhaps because she was, or perhaps out of reflective kindness.

—I am, too, I admitted aloud.

She held out her hand. Soft and swollen, her orange fingernails glistening.

It was true, I thought. Raleigh saw me. Raleigh *believed* me.

I grabbed her hand like the reins of a chariot, for dear life almost, with a force I was afraid she'd recoil from, but she mirrored.

And we watched.

The start was slow, not as in productivity but pace, Virginia controlling it, forcing a shot-clock violation on the first possession, getting solid shots off late in the clock on their own end. Layups off laser passes. Parabolic threes screaming across the sky.

—*This is how Virginia wants to play,* said Grant. *Long, drawn-out offensive possessions; good passing; efficiency; patience.*

—*To their patience, let's take a look at the stats, developed with Daedalus Cloud,* said Jim. *Statistically, Virginia plays at the slowest pace of any NCAA program. Out of three hundred and fifty-three teams this year? They ranked dead last.*

—*They'll put you to sleep if you're not careful!* Bill Raftery chimed in.

Auburn may have dozed, but never quite nodded off, keeping it close enough that—despite missing their star, recovering from ACL surgery back in Alabama—they were able to break through the pack line to take the lead six minutes in. Clark fed it back to Jerome, retaking. Then Auburn: on foul shots. Auburn on a nine-two run, until an uncharacteristic fast-break basket by Guy again shifted momentum. But we were still unable to create significant separation, up just three points at the next break in the action.

—It's our Buick commercial! squealed Raleigh, squeezing my hand even harder.

They'd recut the tail end of a current ad from their "that's not a Buick" campaign to feature Phil, riding in like some automotive augur:

—*Trust me,* says Phil, *it's a Buick.*

—*And I* like *it!* says Raleigh, sitting shotgun, the orange-plated fingertips now entwined with mine caressing the car's wood-paneled dash.

—He almost refused to do it, Raleigh told me after, until Crewe reminded him it would fund a new Audi. I think he wants a Tesla now, though.

—Mm, I said, thinking of our Model S outside.

Auburn took the lead again with four minutes to half, prompting the network to flash a shot of Phil's reaction. But he was unperturbed, deeply engaged in conversation—not with Miles, but with Sunny to his other side. I felt Raleigh tense before she reclaimed her hand to smooth her hair, like Phil's lightly reshaped. The "subtle tweaks" apparent in their pretaped segment and next to me in Raleigh somehow seemed even more glaring in Phil on live television, flanked by Sunny and Miles, a famous face and one I knew so well. I could already see Crewe's future metamorphosis in its present evolution, that specific series of changes a face undergoes as a result of too many people looking at it. There was already a difference in him from last week, though you couldn't quite isolate what made it.

Jerome hit a three, putting us back up with less than four minutes to half, but the Tigers closed out strong to go into the locker room up 31–28.

Jim went to Sunny for her now-obligatory check-in with Phil first thing—the network had apparently more or less assigned Sunny to "Phil duty" while Tracy and Ron manned the sidelines—so we decided to skip the roundtable in favor of seeing the nursery. Raleigh was eager to show it off, and I understood why. While the living room may have fallen short of her aesthetic vision, the nursery appeared to have been designed by the Instagram algorithm itself. Everything was yellow and white and gray—"gender neutral"—with twee watercolors of baby elephants lining the walls. Below them sat the four-and-a-half-foot giraffe it seemed impossible to escape contemporary parenthood without procuring (with twins, I managed ending up with two of them). A plush gray glider waited in the corner, its matching ottoman nuzzling up to a muted zebra rug.

—It's safari themed, Raleigh beamed.

Knowing, as all parents eventually do, that breast milk will spray on the chair, that teeth marks will be borne into the crib's white railings, that the sleek Scandinavian diaper pail will eventually smell like death itself, and that none of this early tumult close to compares to the chaos and destruction and total pandemonium of subsequent childhood development, it is tempting to approach such rooms with a twinge of irony and the urge to satirize. I recently—and this is factual—found a piece of day-old sushi on my Oxford Jane Austens, its fishy oils leaking between *Persuasion* and her minor works, marring the volumes' beautiful green covers. But then I looked back to Raleigh and was reminded of the ferocity of my own nesting instinct, the true pride that had shined through the curtains of my shame when I'd first showed off my own such room; the sincerity with which I'd believed the photographs in *Architectural Digest* with children in them, playing sweetly by themselves with one or two attractive wooden toys in nuanced colorways. Everyone of a certain demographic bent tells themselves they're not going to succumb to the neon plastic onslaught. But even the most privileged children in the world have bad taste.

—It's lovely, Raleigh, I said.

Downstairs, Charles Barkley was all-in on Raleigh's theme if not her team, not even trying to hide his partisan leanings, holding a stuffed tiger on set and joking the network was too cheap to let him have a real one.

—*Wait, wait, Aubie and I just need to say one last thing to Phil,* he said, interrupting Greg's attempt to wrap.

The network changed the angle, Sir Charles looking directly into the camera, pointing the mascot's plushy paw to his eyes and then away, as if to make direct contact with Phil.

—*I've been with you this whole way, Phil. Seriously, I love you, man. You've got a beautiful wife, and you're gonna have a beautiful baby. You are the ultimate bracketologist. But this is where your bracket busts. My Tyger Tigers are burning bright tonight, baby. We're up, and you know what I predict for the second half?*

—*What Chuck?* Said Kenny.

—*Some fearful symmetry.*

(I told you he was a generational mind!)

I laughed, and Raleigh joined me.

—You're a fan of William Blake? I asked, surprised but delighted.

—A fan of who?

—Never mind. Wait, why were you laughing?

—Because that's the reason Phil picked Auburn to make the Final Four, said Raleigh. I figured you knew.

—No, I said.

—Oh. Well, yeah, he just likes their mascot.

Hunter scored the first basket of the second half, and the next one to take the lead, which was extended by Clark on a fast-break steal. Our defense shut out Aubie's crew for the first five-plus minutes before, in a couple quick baskets, the Tigers tied it back up. Hunter heated up again. Still, like in the first half, every time Virginia, controlling the pace, seemed on the verge of breaking it open, their fatal flaw allowed Auburn to stay in it. The longer this continued, the more fearful Sir Chuck's symmetry seemed—though Phil looked contented enough when they flashed his image, Virginia up five with less than seven minutes to play. And then we doubled it.

A prophetic viewer of the Auburn game would zoom in on Ty Jerome's fourth foul—not a good one—in frustration after one on him went uncalled. They cut our lead to six, three. One, with less than three minutes left. A Tiger triple to go up two, a lead they were still holding on to with under thirty seconds, twenty. Timeout. Phil's ease ceased, though in contrast to his frantic excitement in earlier rounds he's motionless, clasped in dread, as if suspended midair. Would it be distant deeps—or skies? Miles's hand atop his shoulder, almost fatherly; a kindness meant to pull him up that only weighs him down. They split the screen, showing Phil head-to-head with Charles Barkley, stripped of all his gaudy paraphernalia—fire enough in his eyes, his heart beating wildly.

With two to give, Virginia has to foul three times to get the Tigers to the line. They hammer down the one-and-one. It's a two-possession game now: Auburn up 61-57, with less than ten seconds. Jerome feeds Kyle Guy in the corner and— the three is true. Charles twists away in agony, but with the ensuing foul Auburn tacks on one more. 1.5 seconds left, and Virginia trails 60-62.

—*Jerome to Guy—to win it—this one has wings! Dare*

*he aspire?* No!

But he was fouled. On a *three-point shot* down *two*, three free throws coming. With less than a second to go.

We have a preconceived notion of greatness that, for all their present irrelevance, probably traces back to the poets. We tend to ascribe immortal hands and eyes to high-velocity heroism; to a busy furnace, an anvil struck in the nick of time. We enshrine the eye-blink glory of Clark to Diakite, of Grant to Laettner. Of MJ. The taut muscles and fiery instincts. The strength. The speed. But symmetry, at least the kind to be most feared, is not actually a copy. It is a mirror. And sometimes poetic redemption appears not as a Tiger, but a lamb. Sometimes it is so quiet and slow and deliberate as to be nearly invisible—the scarier half of a shattered visage the one sunk beneath the lone and level sands. Sometimes, you see, *something amazing* doesn't fall from the sky, but plants his feet firmly on the ground. Sometimes, *something amazing* is the ploughman. Sometimes it's just a Guy.

And this time, "just a" Guy made them all. The three most expensive free throws in NCAA tournament history. To advance us to the national championship, making all the vales rejoice.

### 000

Phil and Miles missed the first half of Texas Tech–MSU, away from their seats due to a scheduling conflict with another timeless Virginian sport. I haven't spent much time plucking this particular vine of the athletic department yet, drunken revelry being one of those things far better experienced firsthand than second, and better second than third. Rest assured Phil had been doing plenty of it—partying—but it was only in the Final Four that his bacchanalia graduated to baccalaureate levels. For of all the vales rejoicing in the aftermath of our victory, few were merrier than the Viking ship's bar, so densely packed with Wahoos that it was, for many of them, hard to get their cups refilled on account of sheer positional physics. This particular problem was not, however, applicable to the Man with the Perfect Bracket, for whom everyone had a treat and a toast, offers heartily extended to his entourage—not just Miles, but also Sunny and her crew.

Giving the latter enough space to do their jobs, however, was another matter:

—*Madness has turned into ecstasy in here, guys,* Sunny relayed, at first in voice only. *We're having trouble even setting up to get an adequate view. But let me assure you Phil Fayeton is having a very good time.*

When they finally squared the video, coming out of the first break, Texas Tech and Michigan State tied at six, ecstasy looked like an understatement. The crush of bodies was so intense Phil had practically enveloped Sunny, the din deafening, his ear at her lips. Not that either of them seemed to mind.

—Do you . . . have a bottle of wine open by chance? I

asked.

She didn't, but Raleigh was nothing if not an accommodating hostess, and I let her open one. Unlike when she'd visited me, if I was going to survive her parasocial marital anguish tonight I was going to need a little something to take the edge off. (Sybils are not immune to the power of suggestion—and what flows under the bridge between madness and prophesy if not wine?)

With no one to share Raleigh's Barefoot cabernet sauvignon, though, I partook perhaps a bit too liberally. Raleigh loosened up herself when their Buick commercial aired again at halftime—Texas Tech was up 23–21, this game too shaping to be a defensive battle—and Phil and Miles returned to their arena seats, albeit visibly rumpled and Wagon Wheeled, the sweat of anxiety flushed with the sweeter sweat of release.

—Do you really believe it? I asked her, now fully supine on her sofa. That "Love Is Never Having to Say You're Sorry"? Or did you just like the font or something?

I thought I knew the answer, but I wanted to gauge her reaction. She'd surprised—alarmed—me several times over the course of the evening: with her blasé, almost aristocratic *mm* over Phil's and Miles's matching belts, her flashes of equanimity, her blessèd lie. The way she'd progressively softened my edges, my empathy overriding leeriness in the face of her captological nursery—even thinking she might like Blake. Above all: in the moment before she'd offered her hand, her own total lack of skepticism, my sense she had utterly believed me. Alarm in and of itself is not a familiar sensation to prophets, and in retrospect, I was probably looking to reinforce, to myself, my own identity. To assure myself that in the apparent lift of my curse with her I hadn't lost my gift besides.

Raleigh thought about the question for several seconds, considering it, giving it due attention and weight.

—I do, she said. Love is never having to say you're sorry.

Her face, staring at the television, reflecting its shifting glow, gave the impression of an almost trancelike state. Texas Tech was beginning to assert control. She elaborated:

—Not in terms of general love for humanity, necessarily, or even *love thy neighbor*. With people you don't know well, good manners often make apologizing necessary. But in terms of intimate love? The love you share in a marriage, the love you build a household—a life and a living room around? Yes. Because love is selflessness. If you truly love someone, you'd never hurt them intentionally. The reason it's important to apologize to acquaintances is because they don't know you, so they don't know your intentions. It's the selfless thing to do, in order to clarify them. But with your spouse? They should know you well enough to know you'd never mean to hurt them. And trusting that they love you back means knowing they'd never mean to hurt you, either. So when you are? Hurt, I mean? It's always a situation of misunderstanding rather than guilt. "Sorry" isn't what you want to hear, because it's only really appropriate if they foresaw their actions would hurt you and went ahead with them anyway. "Sorry" isn't selfless, then. It's not kind—it's not even polite. It's dishonest. All they really gotta do is listen. When both people know hurt could only be unintentional, they'll adjust their behavior as soon as you tell them, as soon as they know. And that's the thing you actually want, not an apology.

I stared hard at Raleigh, as bewitched by her enlightenment as she herself seemed. I'm tempted to say she sounded prophetic, except that clarity is more often prophesy's antithesis. The more lucid her logic, the closer she flew to insight's light, the blinder she seemed to be to what *I* could see it would inevitably come to illuminate with regard to Phil. And yet, when has blindness precluded sight? Did she foresee it, too? I turned my spinning head back toward the screen, where the Red Raiders were up significantly, and sinking deeper into Raleigh's sofa, let its warmth envelop me.

I woke up at seven a.m. to that wall hanging—and six missed calls and twenty text messages from my mother-in-law, who, on the back of our vexatious history of literary pickup failures, threatened to file a missing persons report if she didn't hear from me.

—I'm so sorry, Adrienne, I said to her impassively.

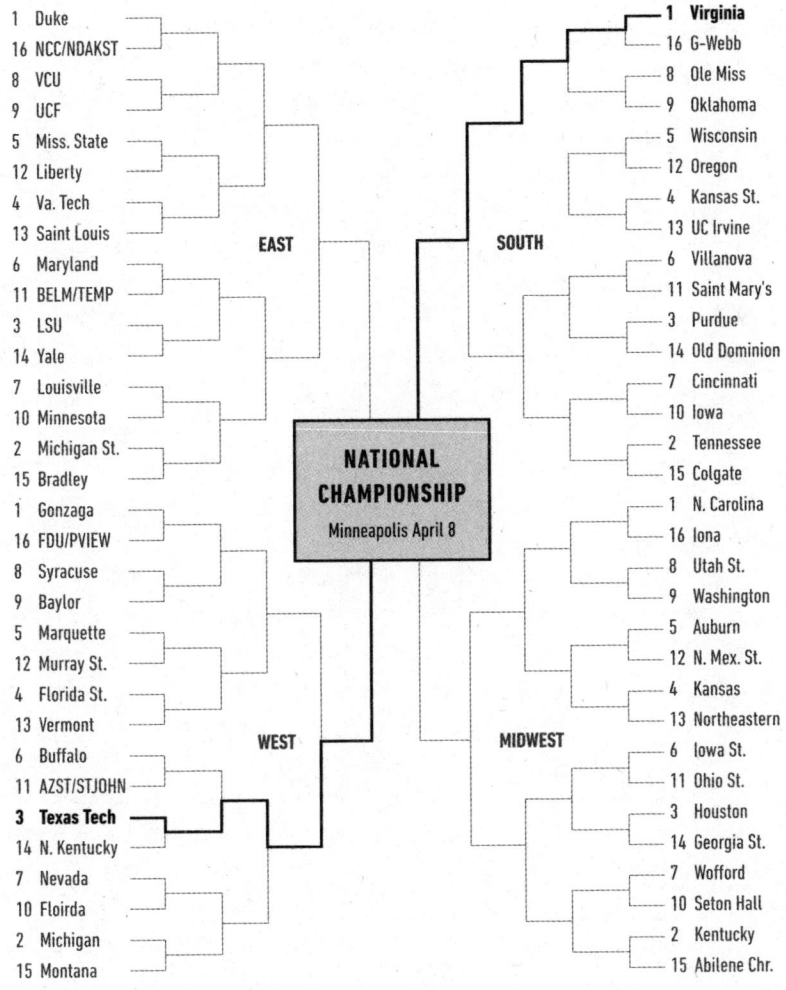

# NATIONAL CHAMPIONSHIP

## VIRGINIA (1) VS. TEXAS TECH (3)

While I blissfully, irresponsibly, slept on his wife's sofa in Arlington, Phil and his victory party migrated to a brewery across the street from the Vikings Ship following Texas Tech's win. Provided one didn't go outside, its crowd might have imagined itself transported to Charlottesville—until, at least, the Pabst Blue Ribbon and Natty Light ran out, at which point there was a downselect to the team's hotel.

It was one of those luxury downtown hotels so standard as to be simultaneously unremarkable, but on that first weekend in April, its bar and lounge had become the most exclusive venue in the Twin Cities. The only feasible mechanism for crowd control was to limit entry to those who were staying there—which, as guests of the NCAA, Phil and Miles were, alongside not only the team and coaches, but quite a few people from the network, including the one Phil most wanted to see off-camera. Yes, even more than De'Andre

Hunter and Kyle Guy and Tony Bennett himself, who, for all their gifts, simply could not compete with tits. I want to say Sunny's were at least 500ccs, high-profile—not so big as to be cartoonish, but flirting with the line; the kind of breasts a Beverly Hills plastic surgeon would readily agree to on a woman of her size, but advise against "going any larger." She mostly covered up on camera but had brought them out for the afterparty in a plunging burgundy dress with an asymmetric hem—shorter in front and almost wrap-like, like a curtain ready to part for the right actor.

Phil was hardly alone in vying to debut, the quality of his competition being part of her appeal—that first night, maybe even the better part of it. Phil's original goal was less to indulge in his fantastical desire to sleep with her than to elicit some confirmation of his social preeminence: to bank the cachet her more feasible, public attentions conveyed to the other powerful men. It was only after a photo of them "canoodling" appeared in the tabloids Sunday morning—a PG-13 exposé at best, heavily undercut by a companion article positing bracket conspiracy theories straight out of science fiction; after Phil assured Raleigh the speculation surrounding him and Sunny was as credible as the idea he'd used a time machine—that I think adultery entered his mind as any real sort of possibility. Denial can be funny like that: Sometimes it is in the act of dismissing something that we discover its viability. Having already been falsely accused, and his legitimate self-defense deployed in clear conscience,

Phil felt newly emboldened to pursue the indiscretion for which he'd been acquitted, as if protected by a kind of marital double-jeopardy.

He dragged Miles to the Mall of America in the afternoon, buying lavish gifts for Raleigh and the baby (not apologetic if preemptive!) and a number of astronomically expensive plain, light-blue button-downs for himself. When I saw these later, they seemed an almost comical mélange of JFK and Gatsby and Arun Patil, with his famously unwavering uniform of four-hundred-dollar T-shirts from Brunello Cucinelli. Phil was recognized and stopped several times on the outing, including by two guys at Pita Pit who asked for his signature. He agreed, but they didn't have a pen. Phil realized too late that following them to find one undercut his air of celebrity, and he vowed to Miles he'd never make such an accommodation again.

The plan for Sunday, known to every person under forty years of age associated with the University of Virginia in Minneapolis that night, was to congregate at a bar and nightclub in the Warehouse District called Sneaky Pete's. The name was so transparently debauch—so, shall we say, *cavalier* in its rakishness—as to suggest nothing seriously untoward could happen there. And yet, transparency can be its own kind of mask. Plain sight is often the best place to hide because it is the last anyone thinks to look. And if witnesses pose a problem for explicit wrongdoing, in grayer areas their presence offers a counter-conveyance: implicitly, of having *not* crossed the line. Of performing a public service almost, in beating the line back a bit for everyone. It is adjacent to the promise embedded in sin cities everywhere, and quite explicitly in Las Vegas: *what happens here stays here*—and so, while you are here, freedom is yours.

Phil made extravagant use of his, courting Sunny in the same collegiate, Spring Breaky way half the bar was of someone—in the same way several other women were courting him: body shots, grinding, mangled words to the ear. None of this attracted much attention, everyone focused on their own extracurricular pursuits. Miles was having his own fun, I assure you—which I was basically fine with, provided it stopped short of pregnancy or venereal disease. And Phil was not the only celebrity. The players were there, other high-profile alumni and fans. No, it wasn't until later. Sneaky Pete's actual slip was an internal passageway to a distinct yet affiliated strip club—still very open as Pete's was shutting down—through which guests were forced to pass in order to exit the complex. A slew of photographers were ready for them. That Miles appeared in several pictures only served to emphasize Phil's absence. He wasn't there. And neither was Sunny.

—Raleigh's upset, I told Miles on the phone the next morning, the morning of the national championship.

—I don't understand, he said, she's upset he's *not* exiting a strip club on the gossip sites?

He was hungover and irritable.

—Well, and because he's not answering her calls. You don't think it's strange he left last night without saying anything to you?

—I don't know, said Miles dismissively. Today's a big day for him. He's probably still asleep.

—Mm, I said.

—Don't *mm* me, Cass. It's no stranger than that shit you pulled with my mom Saturday.

—I want to see Daddy! said Tate.

I switched to FaceTime, letting Miles see my eyes roll before handing the phone to Tate, pushing back his curls and kissing him.

—Are these my intestines? Percy asked me.

—No, honey, those are your testicles.

—Put your pants back on, Perce, said Miles, as Tate held the phone up to his brother's bare ass.

—What good advice! I said, leaving the room to pack their lunches.

I knew Phil hadn't taken it, that particular advice. That even as Miles said it, Phil was still in bed with Sunny, his limbs flying over her heavenly body, diving into its orbs and crevices, sucking on her solar discs. She'd be turned on by his desire for her, and shockingly, torrentially wet. Preposterously wet for a woman so impossible to imagine secreting anything, who looked, in spite of being the pinnacle of femininity, somehow also devoid of hormones. Hairless, poreless in the dim light—but now unbelievably smooth and slick. Astral and oceanic at once. Slipping inside her black hole is a firestorm and a bath. He dissolves, melts, molts into her, falling down, down, down with every clench and thrust. And the explosion comes with a little splash.

I returned to the living room with lunches in tow, and, preoccupied with thoughts of Raleigh, steered the double-stroller to Montessori school.

○○○

That we would watch the championship together was never in doubt—we didn't discuss it; it was just understood. But the details were another matter. After the dust-up with my mother-in-law, Raleigh had agreed to come to our place. The plan was to order takeout around five-thirty and let the twins watch the first half. And so I was surprised to see her name flash across my phone two hours earlier, on my way to pick them up. Was there any chance I could pick her up, too? She was having Braxton-Hicks, and frankly just didn't want to be alone. I was mildly annoyed by the prospect of crossing Key Bridge so close to rush hour, but also still reeling in vicarious guilt for Phil's betrayal. Besides, there was at least a 50 percent chance she'd close out the night a woman of the sort of leisure I'd be keen enough to partake in that, sympathy aside, I deemed it a reasonable sacrifice.

—We're on our way, I said. But when Phil wins the billion

dollars tonight, you better invite me aboard your yacht.

Raleigh began to laugh, then stopped.

—Raleigh? Are you okay?

—Excuse me, she said. Just another Braxton-Hicks.

But she looked pale, swollen, almost cetacean getting into the car, buckling her seatbelt with difficulty. By the time we crossed back into Georgetown I was beginning to think those contractions might not be Braxton-Hicks. By the time I pulled up to our townhouse, I was pretty sure they weren't. And by the time I'd gotten Percy and Tate out of their car seats, it was clear I was going to have to put them back in again. Reluctantly, but inevitably, I got out my phone.

—Hi, Adrienne, I said.

My mother-in-law was waiting out front when we pulled up, all plucky encouragement for Raleigh and *oh, don't worry, Cassandra, it's fine*, but I could see her annoyance hiding behind those chic progressive readers, enveloped in her cashmere wrap. As if I was saddling her with the twins again to go write or because *I'd* booked a last-minute trip to the Final Four. As if Miles and I hadn't bought a house six blocks away from her expressly for this purpose! Returning to a car with a woman in preterm labor was almost a relief.

—It'll be okay, Raleigh, I said, making a U-turn. You're going to be okay.

—Wait—where are you going?

—Uh, *to the hospital*, I said.

—But George Washington is the other way.

—We're three minutes from Georgetown.

—But I don't know anyone there.

—But also, they still know how to deliver a baby. I gave birth there. Believe me, it's fine.

—Please, Cassandra!

—You're out of your mind—it's after five.

She started to cry.

—I'm not going tell you I'm sorry, Raleigh, I said, very firmly, very calmly. I think we're passed such politesse, don't you? It's the right decision. Are you going to call Phil?

I heard it ring and ring as I entered the Emergency roundabout.

—I'll be back as soon as I've parked the car, I said, passing her off to an EMT.

Phil and Miles were en route to the Vikings Ship in the Minneapolis Skywalk, which does have cell service, but it took a while to get a hold of either of them because they were walking and talking with the University of Virginia's president. By the time Miles answered, they were approaching stadium security.

—*Jolly?* I'd say it's more than "a little."

—No, I said, louder. Not jolly, *Raleigh. Ra-leigh's at the hos-pi-tal.*

—What? Is she okay?

—I think she's going into labor.

—Yeah, I can't hear you either.

—*I think she is in la-bor*, Miles! Don't go through security. You guys need to get to the airport stat.

—What? Are you sure?

—Oh my god, just put Phil on.

Miles handed the phone to him.

—Hey, Cassandra.

—I want you to listen closely, I said, very firmly, very calmly. Your wife is at Georgetown Hospital. I'm headed back there now to see if I can get more information, but you need to get here as soon as you can. I think she's in labor.

Phil paused for long enough that I wasn't certain my words had reached him. When he spoke, however, it was with remarkable clarity.

—Do you really *know* that, though?

—No, but she—

—has been having a lot of Braxton-Hicks recently, he said. She's not due for a month.

(She was due in three weeks, actually. Thirty-seven down that day.)

—I'll give her a call, but this is the national fucking championship, Cassandra. I'm on the precipice of history. We're not leaving until we know there's something wrong.

It would have been tempting to tell him I *did* know something was wrong. But it is an assertion that would have so inevitably elicited that cruel, haughty follow-up: *well, what?* And that, I didn't know. I couldn't attach a long, Latinate name to it, or tell him whether or not it meant she'd need to deliver. (I'm an oracle, not an obstetrician.) Still, I did know *something* was wrong. I was certain of it. I would have bet Phil a billion dollars. A waste of breath to insist, though, without a medical degree and authoritative prognosis, preferably delivered in a drawling baritone. Phil didn't trust my maternal intuition. There was nothing I could have said to make him believe me, because the problem was *me*. I was an unreliable narrator. I told you that on some level women always are.

And so I didn't try. I saved my breath for Miles, for what I could imagine the two of them considering more "rational" instructions: *don't get too drunk, keep your fucking phone on.*

—Oh, and make sure Phil calls Raleigh, I said. Now, please.

He did, Miles confirmed via text, but Raleigh hadn't answered—it's hard to, when you're under general anesthesia. I didn't know that yet, though; the nurse wouldn't tell me anything after I admitted I wasn't her partner.

—Is the dad on his way, then?

—No, I said, he's on national television.

I flipped my phone toward her, streaming the game—they had just tipped off, though it was still scoreless. *Defense.* I thought. *How exhausting, always being on defense.* Diakite scored, and they briefly flashed Phil's reaction.

—That's him, I said.

But she only grunted and pointed me to the waiting room.

○○○

I watched the first half on mute. The last two teams, titans of sport, collegiate gods. Men six and a half, seven feet tall, already towering, now at the apex of spectacle. Anointing fans celebrities. Rendering celebrities fans. And yet also so small onscreen I could have fit them all in my pocket. I was almost tempted to, to turn the game off entirely. But something had happened over the past two and a half weeks. Not to Phil, or Miles, or even to Raleigh, but to me. I had already known that if you want the world to pay attention to an extraordinary woman, you have to tell the story of an ordinary man. But for all my confidence, I had underestimated my narrative gifts. I'd constructed so fine a labyrinth I'd become caught in it—in the horse's belly I sat atop. Yes. There was no way to deny it. I, Cassandra, had fallen in love. Separately, individually, alone and of my own free will, utterly and completely. Cruelly. Madly.

I loved basketball.

Specifically, I loved *Virginia* basketball.

I loved their signature style of play. Their vicious pack-line defense—how they pushed through the exhaustion, *playing continuous*; that they never took off a play. I loved their long, drawn-out offensive possessions. Thoughtful, smart, situational; waiting for the sort of high-probability shots they so effectively took away. I loved their passing—it wasn't just good, it was great. Unselfish. A *team's team* was an understatement.

I loved De'Andre Hunter and Kyle Guy, Ty Jerome, Jack Salt, Kihei Clark, and Mamadi Diakite. I loved the players who mainly sat the bench, and the ones who always did. And Tony Bennett—I'll admit, I had a little crush on him. I loved the way they all loved each other. It was the key, I thought, to their efficiency: that they moved as one, their choreography tight, balletic. Above all, alone in the hospital waiting room, I loved their patience. Not just within the game, but outside it. They'd overcome the most embarrassing loss ever in college basketball—perhaps in all of sport. And the prevailing image of their fall to Cinderella? Not sound and fury and stepsister scorn, but a still image: of Hunter's arm around Guy. Hunter, who had been injured, had not even played, comforting his distraught teammate. It is an image of devastation, but also of resilience, of care. Of love. As Kyle Guy hit a jumper to retake the lead, I saw it clearly. My Trojan horse bore a new, glass-slippered Cavalier. You know why? Think about it. Defense. Unselfishness. Efficiency. Patience. Resilience. Care. Love. *Not the most exciting team to watch*, people complained. People always would, even in fairytales. Because the real reason Virginia was so damn good was *they played like women*. That's what Tony Bennett was teaching them. That's how he was making them great men.

In that moment, I couldn't give a shit about Phil. I wanted them to win because I loved them. I wanted them to win for themselves. I wanted them to win for one another.

Virginia didn't let the Red Raiders score from the floor

for seven minutes and twenty-two seconds, going up 17–7 in the first ten. Tech responded with three quick triples, though, intercut only by a midrange jumper by Jerome. The pace was quickening—and the faster we let them play, the faster our lead slipped: Within two minutes, it's one-possession. In three? Tied. We're trading twos, then the Red Raiders get an extra, putting us down four with less than five minutes in the half. We rally to tie it back up, preserving the last shot. Jerome to Hunter, back to Jerome, who lets it fly with three seconds from the top of the circle. The shot is true, off a brilliant pass. He was wide open. 32–29.

The camera cuts to Phil, other hands all over him, slapping his back, the brim of his hat. Sunny struggles to get close enough to interview him until Miles helps her, ceding his space—gallantly, I guess. My phone's still on silent, and as the microphone passes between them, I dub perforce the words I cannot hear.

—Hey Phil, I gotta say, this has been an impressive performance. How are you feeling?

—Pretty good, Sunny. Nice to sink a deep one at the end there. I was worried for a second we'd been boxed out, but that was some impressive ball handling.

—Straight through the rim, amirite?

—Yeah. It was an excellent *rim job*.

—Oh, baby, you're gonna make me double-dribble—

—Excuse me, Cassandra?

—Hi—yes.

The doctor was in her middle fifties and exuded skill, experience, and (I viscerally sensed this) adeptness in calmly managing situations where her skill and experience were baselessly called into question.

—You're Raleigh Fayeton's friend?

—Yes, I told the doctor, with no hesitation at all.

Preeclampsia is not understood well—I'll give you one guess as to why—but it is thought to be an autoimmune reaction, marked by high blood pressure, swelling, and nausea. It is, almost, like an allergy to pregnancy itself, the only cure "depregnatization"—a little joke among specialists of maternal–fetal medicine for ailments alleviated solely by birth. Raleigh's had caused an acute placental abruption—internal bleeding—which was why she'd been rushed to the OR for an emergency C-section. I couldn't see her yet, the doctor explained, she was in recovery, still waking up. But she'd asked them prior to surgery to update me in Phil's absence. They'd tried to reach him, unsuccessfully. If I was able to, I could tell him his wife was going to be all right. And she'd had a healthy baby. A healthy baby girl.

—I don't want to downplay what they've been through, though, the doctor said. It's good you got here so fast.

—It's lucky, I said.

She nodded.

—Yes.

I tried Phil, then Miles, composing texts to both, overflowing with the kinds of words I'd needed earlier—*preeclampsia, placental abruption, caesarean*—as I walked to the hospital food court. Nothing was going through. I purchased an evangelical chicken sandwich and turned up the audio as Kyle Guy nailed a three to start the second half.

— *. . . and Hunter's fouled. . . .*
— *. . . but he fouled Guy. . . .*
— *. . . Diakite draws another foul. . . .*

It was back and forth on the floor, our lead hovering around seven. As few as four. As many as nine. I was entranced in the true sense of the word, time reduced to the shot clock, my food gone before I knew I was eating.

—Are you alright, ma'am? One of the chicken ladies asked me, with a tentative touch to the arm.

I'd seen Jerome find Guy in the corner, the beautiful arcing three, but I hadn't realized I'd screamed. I smiled at the woman dementedly, which she somehow took as assurance. Still, I saw this as my sign to return to labor and delivery. Virginia was ahead by ten, with ten minutes left. Still up eight at five, back in the waiting room. Then Tech sinks a two. A three. All of a sudden: one possession. Jerome misses, and the Red Raiders get a layup—and one. Three minutes left. Fifty-nine all. Diakite makes a pair of free throws, and Tech matches them. A huge jumper from Hunter; Guy in the paint—but a fast, long-range three goes for them. At 1:08, a questionable possession call goes Texas Tech's way.

They show Phil and he's lost any sense of possession himself. Flashing eyes, floating hair—his hat lost somewhere. A reckless madness, distraught of wit. Moon-struck. It's dreadful to look at him. More dreadful still when Tech takes the lead with a layup. On the other end, ours bounces out. Twenty-two seconds. We have to foul.

They make the first.

They make the second.

For all the virtues of defense, patience, teamwork—sometimes, you need to score, and fast. That's *situational basketball*. Sometimes, the situation calls for a star.

Jerome got the ball to him, down three, twelve seconds left. There in the right corner. De'Andre Hunter, open again. I saw him receive the ball, control it. I saw him set and leave the ground, the flick of his wrist as it broke contact with his upper hand. I saw the ball airborne, climbing, flying, at the height of its parabola—and then I saw only Phil's wild, flashing eyes.

Except they weren't Phil's, they were mine. In the reflection of my blackened screen, because my phone had died.

—Mother*fucker*, I said aloud, rushing to reception. Excuse me—hi. Do you, by any chance, have an iPhone charger?

The nurse looked at me like I had two heads, shaking her own. I reassessed the room. There was a mounted television, playing a video demonstrating breastfeeding techniques and touting Georgetown as a "baby-friendly hospital"—a troubling phrase to me, with its implication that any hospital possibly wouldn't be.

—Okay, well, do you think you could—just for, like, thirty seconds—put the game on that TV? It's the national championship.

—The national championship of what?

—March Madness.

She looked at me with the wary pity reserved for the insane.

—It's April.

Cruel!

I put my face in my hands, trying to think. Did I have time to go back to the car? I couldn't—wouldn't—risk it. There was no one else in the waiting room, no one to ask for a charger.

—Cassandra? Are you okay?

It was the doctor. I realized I'd started pacing like a lunatic.

—Mm? I said, smiling at her.

—Would you like to come back and see Raleigh?

She led me through a quiet hallway with numbered doors, a cross between hospital and hotel, past sixteen, eight, four, and two, to one. Raleigh was drowsy, but awake, propped up with a direct view into the little Lucite roller-bin where her daughter, wrapped tightly in a muslin ball, slept.

—Congratulations, Raleigh, I said.

—Thanks to you.

—She's beautiful.

—She is.

For a moment, I reflexively fought against them, the tears. But why? Because I'd been taught, implicitly, they were a sign of weakness? To mistrust them? That they were incompatible with intellect? With irony? Lies. I let them fall, and took my friend's hand, smiling maniacally.

—They still can't reach Phil, she said.

—I know. I couldn't either.

—Did we win, Cassandra? UVa, I mean.

—I don't know. My phone died.

—Well, do you want to turn it on? she asked, pointing to the television behind me.

—We don't have to—

—I want to turn it on, she said, smiling up at the gilded Jesuit crucifix hanging above her bed. If you don't mind. Could you please?

I could, and I did—quietly, so as not to wake the baby. Hunter's perfect, parabolic three had gone in. *Not the most exciting team to watch*, I thought, inflamed. *What a load of Trojan horseshit*. The championship game was going to overtime.

### 000

—*Overtime in the national championship is brought to you by: Daedalus Cloud*, says Jim. *And I tell you what, that man right there, Phil Fayeton, is going to be riding mighty high on Daedalus Cloud if Virginia pulls this out.*

—*He'll be on Daedalus Cloud nine!* says Bill.

Virginia gets the ball, and Hunter's fouled, makes his free throws, but Tech banks a quick three, then a bouncy jumper. A couple more free throws for Guy. Hunter drops the exact same right-corner triple he made to force overtime to retake the lead, up two; he's burning hot. Two minutes left. A scorching block from Diakite. A defensive stand.

We slow it down, missing a shot, out of bounds in transition, but replay confirms it: UVa ball.

One minute now. Jerome's fouled and delivers to go up two possessions.

Thirty seconds. Two more free ones from the Free Throw Guy himself.

Another two for Diakite.

Tech scores a quick layup, but ahead six with seventeen seconds? I wasn't the only one who could see it.

A timeout, and Raleigh tried Phil. Straight to voicemail, but when I borrowed her phone to call Miles it rang as we inbounded, Jerome finding Braxton Key, who'd had a stellar game off the bench, for the lights-out dunk.

—Raleigh? Is everything okay? said Miles, yelling, but not rudely, just out of necessity.

—Hey, it's me—she's okay. Tell Phil—no wait, I have a better idea. Tell Sunny. Here's what you need to tell Sunny.

### 000

I could see her discomfort after Hunter secured the final

rebound; after the clock showed 0.0, the scoreboard Virginia 85 and Texas Tech 77; after the initial euphoria and streamers and white, snow-like confetti blanketed the April court; after Jim and Grant and Bill marveled at the redemption narrative, at the minting of the perfect-bracket billionaire. Not Raleigh's discomfort—she was on a delectable mix of oxycodone and oxytocin. No. *Sunny's*. For all of Sunny's exquisite professionalism, which I'd relied on, I could see the traces of her personal entrapment as she told Phil, alongside all of America, that he'd achieved a feat of incomprehensible rarity and, with a wink, should get an invoice ready to send to Arun Patil.

—*All this you know, Phil,* said Sunny, *but there's something else you don't. I learned minutes ago that during the game, you became a father. Mother and daughter are both doing well—yes, it's a girl! Congratulations!*

She paused to let Phil react, for the audience to, to maintain her own composure, folding narrative on narrative, like an onion mille-feuille, as she prepared for the pinnacle of her career, to deliver the signature, climactic line I'd incepted.

—*And one final thing, Phil. Your wife, Raleigh? She already went ahead and named the baby. But I think you'll agree it's the* perfect *choice.*

The photo I'd texted Miles—her teensy little profile, sandwiched between burrito and hat—filled first the Jumbotron, then half the hospital TV screen.

—*Meet Virginia,* said Sunny.

# PART 2: POSTGAME SHOW

# MAY

**H***ide yo kids hide yo wife*, it's Big Barry Wood with some Chocolate Rain sending David after the dentist. Send Charlie, too—he bit my finger—and the teens eating the Tide Pods. Yes, fame's Gritty Evolution of Dance has Rickrolled us with questions, people: Rebecca Black and blue, or white and gold? Yanny or laurel? We're all so William Hung up on it we've fallen into Harambe's cage, Gorilla Glue in our hair. It can happen when you try Kombucha and make a funny face, or join the senior staff of the president of the United States. So easy to come by and so hard to orchestrate, fifteen minutes of fame. It's pretty Scaramucci. And a dime a dozen, a cliché. So you'd be forgiven for adding Phil Fayeton, basketball bracketologist, to the list, maybe with a little pun on "fill."

But Phil was different. He hadn't sung or danced. He wasn't particularly cute or cringe or controversial or (to my knowledge, anyway) giant-cocked. He wasn't a superlative moron, either; he hadn't vied for a Darwin Award. No. It was something else, a far more powerful gift, or at least the perception of one, flying Phil past fame's inflection point, that elusive, magic line between *what* and *who*, distinct from absolute fame, whereby a figure—he often goes by the name *genius*—derives his power not from the value of his achievements, but from his being. From his very self. Everything that he touches, that touches him, turns to gold—especially money. And that was certainly a part of it, the money. The *profit*. The media frequently referred to Phil as a "billionaire," though it wasn't strictly true. Even after the funds cleared, the nature of Phil's earnings was closer to those of lottery winners than titans of industry, foreclosing many of the latter's tax-avoidance schemes. But his Midas touch was secondary, not the cause but an effect of the real prize.

I speak of prophesy. A gift to beware, I'm afraid. *Among all forms of mistake*, Eliot says, *the most gratuitous*. Not that you'll heed our warnings. In this case: I don't blame you. We can't heed them ourselves. Soothsaying is too seductive, too existential. The moth-light of humanity, the quest that unites bracketologists and search-engineers, theoretical physicists and investment bankers, with their *options* and *futures*. Artists, too. Narrative artists above all, honestly, our every warning styling a self-transgressive act. Prophesy is the impetus and the outcome of genius and narrative, of narrative genius. *The idea of the divine possession of the poet sprang from religious practice*, the scholars tell us. *It is an offshoot of the belief that the predictions and auguries of priestesses and prophetesses are fulfilled by*—wait for it—"*divine* madness."

Phil was famous thanks to basketball in March, in April.

But it was prophesy that kept him in the spotlight, that drove the Madness into May(hem). Prophesy—and credibility. I envied him that. Phil had visibly predicted the future. Whether or not people cared about basketball, they cared about that. Because implicit in even the apparent gift of prophesy is not only profit and fame and genius, but the godlike affect of apotheosis—of immortality itself. This is at least partially an illusion. (Seeing the future is separate and distinct from the power to change it.) But it is a sticky, seductive one, which tends to blossom in optimistic minds at the height of spring. Phil basked in its rosy light, carefully tending to the garden of his fame—more carefully, I assure you, than to his newborn daughter. The insistence on coin-flip math, his crusade against luck, how he spoke of his family—his obdurate cognitive dissonance was all, though perhaps not consciously, calibrated to reinforce the twin themes of his personal brand: prediction and rarity. He was a rare medium.

—*They're calling him "Medium Rare,"* said Jimmy Kimmel, *he's the man who filled out a perfect March Madness bracket this year, the only person who's ever done it, predicting sixty-three consecutive games in what was a wild tournament won by the University of Virginia. Please give him a warm welcome: Phil Fayeton!*

And he emerged, yet again, in his expensive, light-blue shirt. I saw now how much work it did for him, bringing out the blue in his eyes. It was a trick I recognized, straight from my personal arsenal.

Don't get me wrong, Crewe helped, too. It was thanks to Crewe that Phil got to preen on Jimmy Kimmel in the first place, to lip sync on Jimmy Fallon; to talk pack-line defense with Seth Meyers and grains of sand with Stephen Colbert. He was on the cover of *People* magazine (with Raleigh and Virginia) *and* profiled in *Rolling Stone*. He was profiled everywhere, public interest in him insatiable, relentless. To Phil's ambivalence and Raleigh's postpartum horror, paparazzi began descending on their house in Arlington. Between Virginia's arrival and Phil's press circuit, they hadn't had a chance to start looking at new "houses" yet (read: estates, plural), which Phil was firmly resolved to acquire. They were forced to hire a security detail, and every day that passed before Arun's payment cleared privately deepened their cash-flow challenge, until Phil fessed up to his new accountant, who helped secure a short-term low-interest loan.

I saw little of Phil during this period, aside from on television, but a great deal of Raleigh. He was on the road, in New York and—especially—Los Angeles. LA held particular appeal for him, not just for its narrative, Manifest-Destiny qualities; the Hollywood glamour and Kerouacian freedom and Crewe's attentions, but also for its being the permanent residence of Sunny Sanders, with whom Phil had firmly eclipsed the realm of drunken indiscretion into that of a full-fledged affair.

I said nothing to Raleigh, much as it pained me. How could I? I knew it was true, but I had no proof. The higher truth was I saw no benefit to her in interfering. My collegiate warnings had already failed catastrophically. And where those had been wrapped in what seemed to me actionable revelation (easy enough, theoretically, to walk away from a noncommittal frat boy), their reincarnation would implicate the father of her child. Raleigh, meanwhile, was hyperfocused on the baby, and largely without the infrastructure of ultra-privileged parenthood you might expect. Between the surprise of Virginia's early birth, Raleigh's own extended recovery, the more modest plans they'd made prior to Phil's windfall, and the startling upfront time and effort it generally takes to put reliable outsourcing in place, Raleigh needed an altogether different kind of help. She didn't have a night nurse yet, and was exclusively breastfeeding anyway. Even when Phil *was* home, though he'd quit his job at the AASSS the day after the championship, he was pretty useless, especially in those wee hours new mothers—even well-supported ones—often come to dread. This was the treachery that weighed on Raleigh's mind. I helped where I could. More than I'd ever helped any other friend, certainly.

Because something amazing had formed between us over the course of the tournament. I hesitate to use the word *sisterhood*. It's too ironic; too firmly linked in my mind with the stupid gold pins and candles and expensive jeans, the songs and ceremonies and general pseudo-cultishness, like we were some kind of illuminati for social superiority. This had nothing to do with that. *Kinship*—or really *partnership* would be closer. The kind of intimacy that can usually, almost definitionally, only exist between two people, though Virginia was a part of it, too. I felt an extraordinary connection to her, akin to my bonds with Percy and Tate; the only child I've ever been drawn to like that, aside from my own.

I've mentioned my maternal instincts and lack thereof a few times, but sparingly up to this point: only to the degree it was strictly essential—which, unfortunately, a deeper foray has now become. I say "unfortunately" because the majority of novels about motherhood are aesthetic disasters, being frequently laced, as they are, with bitterness about the incompatibility between the author's own childrearing and the creation of the very project in which they make this tension its subject. Blah, I get it, *structural inequities*. I'm deeply sympathetic—truly—but most people don't want to read about structural inequities in their spare time. Never confuse guilt for desire, not to mention activism. *About suffering they were never wrong, the old masters.* But what they knew, what is now too often forgotten, is that for suffering to be worthy of art, truth is not enough. It also requires beauty. To serve an aesthetic purpose beyond the suffering itself.

I never confused practical maturation with artistic compromise, but I probably *did* confuse the desire for a child with that for a cat. I wanted to cuddle with something small and warm and alive, to look into big, round eyes, and was tricked by my biological clock into an insistence those eyes resemble my own. I'd only planned on having one, having grown up with too many siblings for my liking. But twins run in my family; I hadn't been surprised. Another of the many reasons my preparation for motherhood's responsibilities disproportionately involved the careful planning of their offloading—not to say luck wasn't involved in my success. But this was why I'd pursued Miles and submitted to Georgetown and put up with Adrienne's petty shit. My dislike for her probably sprang from her total integrality to the life I enjoy, if also her persistent presumption that I alone—and not her son—drink a little too much freedom on her tab.

I don't feel guilty. Between the demands of my job and my literary pursuits, conventional wisdom might accuse me of providing a "chaotic" home environment—goodness knows my mother-in-law has—but despite the state of the bathrooms when the housekeeper's sick, never having snacks in my bag, and a total inability to feign interest in fire trucks; despite having—until Virginia—not the slightest interest in children more generally, in a way I do still consider myself a natural mother, an intuitive one. What I lack in that selfless form of love manifest in laundry I more than make up for in the selfish one. I love my sons the way I love myself, the way I love my own existence, my capacity to create—even as I value their distinct humanity, their own dazzling creativity, their independence (Montessori!). I've always, since the moment of their births, had close, individual bonds with them, borne of the things I can share honestly, without a shred of orthogonal resentment, with active joy. Generous physical affection, excellent take-out, naps. Blake and Saint-Exupéry. Sartorial delight. Now: basketball. I've found, you see, for all my shortcomings, and all their wildness—with a combination of planning and luck, skill and randomness—my own way to tame them, and they me.

Still, you can see how Virginia's pull would have formed another data point in the alarming trend I was coming to associate with Raleigh—that is, her unprecedented capacity to alarm me. It gave her the sort of inflective Midas touch for me that drove everyone else to cling to Phil. That helping Raleigh through motherhood's early days gave me unusual access to his story was a boon, to be sure, but, in retrospect, proximity to Raleigh herself was the goal and the catalyst, the reason I volunteered for the sort of labor I've historically so adroitly resisted.

And so when Phil was out of town, and even sometimes when he wasn't, I'd often head to Arlington after picking up the twins from school, bearing whatever Raleigh happened to need that day and dinner from Whole Foods. We'd eat on the sofa while Virginia slept in my arms—or screamed. She had a howling, powerful voice, louder and more insistent than I remember Tate's or Percy's being, her vitality so urgent I could see it pulsing through her even as she slept. I had the sense, in the serious, rapt knowingness of her gaze—giant eyed, piercing, already somehow feminine—that she truly possessed the dangerous gift her father merely postured; that she was, in this way, plus in the amount of time I spent with her, more my child than his.

By the time the boys' school let out mid-May, Virginia was no longer a newborn and Raleigh herself had healed enough to be anxious to get out of the house. I'd already taken a week off to respond to initial edits from my agent while filling the childcare gap between school and camp, and we decided, more or less on a whim, to escape both the paparazzi and any further debt to Adrienne by decamping to my family's place in Maine. It would be more than large enough for the five of us, especially with my parents still in New York until Memorial Day.

Maine is the last vestige of real New England. Its coastal charm still has a rough, puritan authenticity about it, unlike the famous, flexing peninsula and islands to the south, which social media and money have increasingly transformed into a sort of cedar-shingled Disneyland, the hedges too straight, the hydrangeas too blue, often so overrun with people wanting to be seen there as to verge unenjoyable, a matte cesspool of mimesis increasingly discernible from the glittering Hamptons only on style's flimsiest nuances. Not that my parents' meandering Victorian wasn't exquisite in its own way, but its shabby chicness was not contrived. It was shabby. My father had, even in my childhood, an air of rotting luxury about him, a last-scion-type vibe, and this was reflected in the aesthetics of all our family's properties, though the wildness of Maine made it particularly true of that one. There was no pool, cess or otherwise, despite the finicky plumbing.

It was rustic enough I worried Raleigh might be disappointed, or worse still, uncomfortable, but we managed brilliantly. Late May in Maine is like late March, early April in Washington, and the landscape teemed with the refreshing possibilities of spring. We watched a couple of Phil's appearances on television, but skipped more of them, passing the days on the lawn, the rocky beach, eating premade lemon pasta salad from the co-op. Percy and Tate had recently stopped napping and went to bed early enough for us to enjoy quiet sunsets from the veranda—reverse sunsets, more precisely, which were often, somehow, more beautiful for their subtlety, lavender and yellow over the Penobscot Bay.

For all my truth-telling, we talked with a candor I'd never before experienced. About fame and money, social media, child-rearing. I asked about her maximalist approach to appearance, what she felt it gave her, who exactly it was for, and learned it stemmed from politesse.

—Making an effort shows you care, said Raleigh.

—Care about what, though, patriarchal standards?

—It's no more patriarchal than "the natural look," Cassandra. It might even be less so.

She was right.

—You're right, I said. But please know you don't have to make that particular kind of effort for me.

While Raleigh never abandoned her vigorous skincare regimen, by the end of the week, she was wearing less makeup, allowing her hair to air-dry. Her relaxing beauty practices were independent of mine, tied only to my words, to reallocating her time so we might spend more of it together. It was in these days that I fully, explicitly realized her malleability was born not out of self-abandonment but an active quality: her remarkable, protean positivity. I wondered why I hadn't noticed this about her sooner; why she'd seemed to me such a fixed sort of woman—the sort of woman I didn't want to be, that I wanted nothing to do with, aside from defining myself in its opposition. Ours was nothing like the (rare) close female friendships I'd experienced previously, which had uniformly possessed a *My Brilliant Friend*–type intensity. I didn't envy her. She didn't envy me. The mimicry I'd observed had not been her doing, but Crewe's. Raleigh and I enjoyed each other's company in its sheer present pleasure, our reciprocal curiosity devoid of that primordial will to copy, the undercurrent that so often defines rapt nonsexual proximity.

I was, however, envious of Phil—in a two-tone, paradoxical kind of way. I was envious of his fame, resentful of the country's vast, face belief in apocryphal augury; of how even the promise of dollars he didn't yet have lent him unearned credibility. The way he passed off his cognitive dissonance as paradox. The status and power his false narrative was yielding—the structural advantage of false narratives overall. Not that I wanted quite the same kind of fame he was courting.

Stratospheric celebrity melts the wax of mortal wings: It is not only dangerous, but dehumanizing—and a logistical pain in the ass. I was more interested in the middle course, myself. In the sort of authorial gravitas that tends to be a slower burn, that keeps you airborne longer; that would, ultimately, be far more likely to outlive me. I still envied him his celestial position, though, in spite of its inevitable brevity—and even as I understood the higher he flew, the more assuredly he charted my course toward artistic immortality.

My second envy lay in his formal relationships with Raleigh and Virginia, even as they spent more time with me. It was, I thought more than once, extremely inconvenient that Raleigh and I didn't want to sleep with each other. It might have happened naturally enough that week if either one of us had possessed the remotest inclination. But then, the extraordinary nature of our friendship would have, with sex, been rendered far less extraordinary, been tied implicitly to a quid pro quo that, as it stood, we were free from. You see, by the time we were in Maine, Raleigh had, almost without me noticing, started helping with Tate and Percy as much if not more than I helped with Virginia. She understood the worlds of fire trucks and monsters, of rock collecting and insects, in practical and pedagogical ways I couldn't touch. Children nearly always listen better to adults who are not their parents, but Raleigh's word might as well have been the voice of a god for the way they obeyed her—instantly, like she'd bewitched them as she had me.

—Teach me your magic, I begged one night after a particularly efficient bedtime.

—I can't.

—Why?

—Cassandra, you're not the only one with special gifts.

She'd said it with a wink, but it chastened me.

—I fear mine have sometimes hurt you, I said.

—Nonsense, said Raleigh. I've always known you meant well.

—I'm not sure that's as true as I'd like it to be.

—You're proving my point, she said, squeezing my hand, almost mothering me. I *love* your candor. Where I'm from, it's a pretty rare trait. And you were right about Phil in college! It did take him a while to grow up, now didn't it?

—Raleigh—

I was on the precipice of telling her.

—Your discretion *has* improved by the way, she added. But I shouldn't have interrupted you. What were you gonna say?

Her eyes: placid. Her smile the same. The reverse sunset; the deep wind chimes. The porch swing's subtle creak. *Your discretion* has *improved*. I hesitated—smiled back at her.

—How are we going to survive without you, after this week?

But it turned out we didn't have to. The day before our return to DC, Phil called to say he'd be delayed in Los Angeles. Crewe had booked him on *Ellen*, and his real estate agent had several properties lined up that she expected to move quickly. So Raleigh came to stay with us in Georgetown for a while—to Miles's pleasant neutrality, and *much* to my mother-in-law's indirect appreciation.

# JUNE

Phil did not return to our nation's capital until June, and only then because he had an unmovable appointment—by him at least—with the president of the United States.

It was set to be a consolation-prize, silver-medal-type affair, though Phil would never have admitted as much. He'd been invited after Tony Bennett respectfully declined a White House visit on behalf of the Virginia team, the optics of which would have been impossible after Trump's behavior vis-à-vis the Charlottesville rally less than two years earlier. Few if any of the players would have deigned to go anyway. Basketball is a famously liberal sport, politically: the polar opposite of golf on the right. But Phil, as an individual—and what are "moderate Republicans" if not *individuals*—had many fewer qualms about visiting the Oval Office than he'd had about Trump weaseling his way into it. The draw of raw power was simply too great. Phil accepted the president's invitation with the same gusto he'd shaken the Democratic Speaker's hand.

Phil dressed carefully in the Presidential Suite of the Trump International Hotel, a move he'd sold Raleigh on between the White House visit and the impending sale of their Arlington townhouse. Their equity would cover five or six days in these new environs, not that Phil was paying much attention by this point. Arun's payment had cleared, and—aside from Virginia's cries—he was feeling very at home indeed, blending seamlessly into the opulent décor with his now trademark shirt and the darker blue suit he'd had made in Los Angeles expressly for this occasion. Only the red tie set him apart, and not with incongruity, but distinction.

—Is she all right? Phil asked his wife's reflection in the mirror. How do I look?

—Yes, she's just . . . insistent, said Raleigh, lifting up her shirt.

Phil turned like a peacock, begging an answer to his second question.

—And you look very presidential.

It was a mere three blocks to the White House's East entrance, but Phil took a car, wary of sweating, and intent on the optics besides. You would never see a dignitary arrive on foot. An attractive woman from the Office of the First Lady—more or less the White House equivalent to a Congressional fundraiser—met him past security in the East Wing. She looked a little like Melania, Phil thought, only younger and less beautiful.

—Melanie, she introduced herself, making Phil do a double take, but there was no sign of the First Lady. Welcome to the White House. I know the president is looking forward to meeting you. I'll be with you for the duration of your visit today, so if at any point you have questions or need anything, please just let me know. If you'd follow me this way?

He did, through a finely appointed hallway alongside the First Lady's Garden, through the arched Ground Floor Corridor. Melanie permitted a brief stop in the Vermeil Room for Phil to pay homage to Shikler's portrait of Nancy Reagan (personally I think it makes her look like more of a Goneril), before passing the other ceremonial rooms into the Rose Garden colonnade. She led him up the ramp built for FDR into the West Wing's side entrance, past the press secretary and into the lobby, where Melanie announced his arrival to another attractive young woman.

—Welcome to the West Wing, Mr. Fayeton, the receptionist said, gesturing toward an ornate cornflower-blue settee. Can I get you something to drink?

—A Diet Coke would be great, thanks, said Phil, now well-accustomed to taking advantage of little hospitality perks without the slightest hesitancy.

Leaning back toward Melanie, he pointed to the Oval Office.

—It *is* true the president installed a Diet Coke button in there, right?

—It is, she confirmed.

Phil slung a dangling ankle over his opposite knee. When the receptionist returned, he reached across it to claim his beverage, turning to Melanie with a wink.

President Donald Trump was fresh off a state visit to the UK and all hopped up on monarchy—at least blithely impervious, if not properly ignorant, to the irony that the country he led had been founded in direct opposition to it.

—I love having a winner to see me, it's terrific, just terrific, said Donald, turning to the cameras while he shook Phil's hand. What, are we gonna do pictures first? Let's do pictures first. Yeah, we can do the chairs, but I think we also need to do the desk. The queen told me—you know, I was with the queen last week, we had a tremendous meeting, me and the queen—the queen reminded me the desk was a gift, an incredible gift. It was a gift from Queen Victoria. Believe me, we gotta do the desk. You want a desk picture, right Phil? See? He wants one behind the desk. Let's do the desk.

The press bunched closer together, bulbs flashing as the president took his favorite seat, smiling maniacally. Phil lorded over him to the side, like an afterthought in a matching tie.

—You get it? We got it? Good. Good.

They moved back to the chairs by the fireplace, plunging straight into the pool spray, the reporters shouting questions over one another until the president began to speak:

—Well, I think you all know Phil's story, why he's here.

It's incredible, something amazing. He won March Madness, the first person to ever win March Madness. He filled out a bracket, and he won a lot of money. Millions and billions of dollars from Arun Patil—you see? I told you Arun was a loser—but Phil? Very impressive. He's also worked in government. I've heard he's a Republican. Is that true, Phil?

—Yes, but—

—Tremendous, said Donald, turning to the press. What a classy guy. We're happy to have him. Very happy to have him here today. What do you think of the Oval Office, Phil? Everybody likes the Oval Office. Everybody.

The din of questions rose again.

—All right, Doug, go ahead.

—Mr. Fayeton, said the reporter, you've previously asserted luck had nothing to do with your perfect bracket. I'm curious if you still feel this way?

—I—

—He made his own luck, Donald interrupted. That's what I always say, I've always said that. What they call luck is just hard work—you'll see if you try it, Doug, believe me. And I think it's a shame, really. A huge shame. A guy has an incredible achievement, and they say it's luck. Okay, Brad.

—Thank you, Mr. President, said Brad. I'm interested in learning more about how you approached the selection process, Mr. Fayeton. You went to Virginia, and your father graduated from Texas Tech, correct? How did your personal ties inform your selections?

—I—

—These are really very unfair questions, Brad. Very unfair. A guy does something amazing, and all anyone wants to talk about is his father. No one asks about the queen's father, by the way. Who cares where his father went to college. Where did your father go to college, Brad?

There was a pause; Brad—everyone—unsure whether the question was rhetorical. But the President waited.

—UMBC, said Brad.

—Never heard of it, said Donald. Go ahead, Kai.

—Mr. Fayeton, did you know Representative Maria Muñoz would be running for the open Senate seat in California prior to her announcement yesterday?

—I—

—What does *that* have to do with anything? Why would he care that some nobody's running for Senate? Nobody likes her, you know. Never gonna win. She's a very nasty woman.

—I asked because Mr. Fayeton attended a basketball game with her, Mr. President, said Kai.

—Lots of people go to basketball games. Many people. Next question. Moses.

—What *other* predictions do you have, Mr. Fayeton?

Phil was more than happy to defer to the president on this one, but Donald turned toward him, eyebrows raised, chin up, making that ridiculous, gooey pout he so often made, and Phil realized he would be forced to say something.

—Tune in next season to find out, he said.

Donald nodded approvingly.

—You know what you should do until then, he offered. Get into real estate. Real estate is a tremendous business.

Phil smiled, looking forward to mentioning his current accommodations, but the reporter preempted him.

—Follow up, said Moses. Are you saying, Mr. Fayeton, that you think you can do it *again*? Fill out *another* perfect bracket next year?

—Well, I—

—Of course he can do it again! I wouldn't bet on Arun Patil offering more money though. Then again, Arun's so stupid he might not learn his lesson. All right, that's enough. We've answered your questions. We've answered all the questions. No more questions. I want to talk to Phil.

The reporters shuffled out, staking out their own real estate in the briefing room. The Oval Office filled with a grandiose, bloodcurdling silence. Phil could hear Donald's hamburgery breathing. It crescendoed into a little, self-satisfied sigh as he turned toward Phil, his face relaxing into a new expression infinitely more horrible than the chinny pout. It was only when Phil saw this new face that he felt its distinction from the previous one, from all the previous ones, those being akin to the set of expressions we all reserve for ourselves when looking in the mirror. This was different. Sharper. Conspiratorial. His gaze intent and penetrating, focused on Phil, as opposed to the performance of focus. They were utterly alone.

—So how'd you do it? Asked the president of the United States.

—What?

—C'mon, you can tell me. How'd you do it?

Phil shifted in his seat.

—Well, I watched a lot of games, said Phil. I'm a pretty big fan, and—while I do keep up with Bracketology and stuff—I analyze the stats my—

—No, no, no, I mean what did you *really* do. I won't blow your cover. But I need to know.

—Mr. President, I didn't do anything unusual.

—Money? It was money, right? Which games did you throw?

It felt to Phil like an accusation, an attack, and yet the question came not in admonishment, but admiration, a wet little smile crossing the president's lips.

—No—I mean, I barely had any before the tournament—

—Yeah, but the prize was pretty big after.

—Mr. President, I didn't—

—What then? What was it? You know people?

—No—

—I know people too. Many people. A lot more people than you . . . Never mind, never mind. I'll find out eventually.

—But Mr. President, I'm telling the truth!

Phil wasn't sure why it seemed so important for a man he neither liked nor respected—a revolting man, frankly—to believe him. But Phil no longer had Donald's attention, in any case. The door was already opening. Phil's entire experience in the Oval Office had lasted a quarter of an hour.

That's right: *fifteen minutes.*

Melanie showed him to the West exit, back into the pool spray. He could feel its flashing splash; the press's water pressure.

—Mr. Fayeton, how did—

—Mr. Fayeton, why did—

—Mr. Fayeton, what did you and the president discuss?

—Um, said Phil, dazed, blinded by the flash not just of the bulbs, but of the Donald—his lurid, horrible brightness—even as he began to drown. *Golf?*

The answer drew appreciative chuckles from the reporters, which Phil acknowledged with a grin, recovering himself.

—And basketball too, of course.

Phil muddled through a few more questions, enough that he wouldn't seem either riled or aloof, using the late-night-show answers that had come to form a sort of stump speech.

—It was such a pleasure to host you today, Melanie said as they dispersed, mechanically, Phil now realized. I know the president was delighted.

—Take care, said Phil, a new closing he was testing out to see if he should make it a signature.

—Oh! said Melanie. And I almost forgot—official Presidential M&M's.

She handed him a little box, reminiscent of a cigarette pack, with the presidential seal and Donald's signature on the front, an anthropomorphized red M&M waving an American flag on the back.

Had Raleigh been there, she would have insisted Phil save them. But she wasn't, and he opened them automatically in his perambulatory daze.

They tasted exactly like regular M&M's.

# JULY

—Mm, I said, looking at the lead image for the listing of Phil and Raleigh's new Beverly Hills estate.

It was white, glassy, aggressively rectilinear; shot from the other side of the cyan pool, the bottom halves of a row of minimal white loungers visible, as if taken in a wide-angled shot from the comfort of the middle one. The house reflected palm trees. The pool reflected the house. I swiped to see the second photo; it was of the massive, steel-and-frosted-glass entry gate, closed.

—This is good for keeping the peasants out, I said.

—*Cassandra*, Raleigh chided, though she also blushed furiously. We actually need this sort of security now.

I swiped again to find a photo of the "front door," if you could call it that, a recessed square of disorienting, tessellated mirrors, flanked by marble lions and canopied by a sharp-cornered arbor, like a midcentury-modern labyrinth crossed with the New York Public Library.

—Those guys look like they'll protect you, I said, pointing to the lions.

Phil had been highly offended, infuriated by the president's assumption he was a con man—but not enough to disregard his advice on the matter of real estate. By the end of July, the Fayetons had purchased or were in the process of purchasing not only the Los Angeles library-labyrinth, but properties in New York, New Orleans, Nantucket, Charlottesville, and the Washington, DC Beaux-Arts mansion in Kalorama where I then sat on the back terrace in a scalloped bikini, looking at pictures of the others.

For all the Kalorama house's blanched glamour, it was the aesthetic antithesis of its new sibling in Beverly Hills. Though it had been built more than eighty years later, this one was arched, flowery, intensely symmetrical. Its facade looked, I couldn't help but notice, with its two-story Corinthian columns, like a smaller, more ornate version of the White House. Phil and Raleigh's had Ionic columns, too, but interiorly— and Doric ones. If I turned to the right on my striped lounger, I stared down a Doric colonnade to a wall lined with the Beardsley prints from *Salomé* we'd given them as a housewarming present. It was a nouveau Musée des Beaux-Arts in the truest sense, save its being closed to the public: indiscriminately luxurious, a fancy style soup: Greek and Baroque, Federal and Louis XV, the kitchen almost Modern. Decadent wrought-iron railings snaked throughout, the whole thing a precarious balance between imposition and fragility.

I'd practically been afraid to allow Tate and Percy in the front door. But Frances, one of the *three* nannies Phil and

Raleigh now employed, swiftly whisked them to Virginia's nursery on the other side of the house.

—Here's the apartment in New York, Raleigh said, texting me the link.

It was a duplex penthouse in a brand-new Hudson Yards building, akin to the Beverly Hills place in a way, luxuriously minimal almost to the point of inhospitability, but curved where that was rectilinear. Its twenty-six-foot glass edifice warped ovally toward the Hudson River, like it was being drawn as far west as possible without leaving Manhattan. Like an aerial West Egg.

—The views of New Jersey are breathtaking, I said.

Raleigh frowned.

—You can see downtown, too, she said.

—It's stunning, Raleigh.

And it was. Not just the view, but the elegantly sloping white furniture, the monumental Twomblyesque art, the lacquered kitchen, its marble island wrapping all the way to the floor. The lofted glass hallway offered a view almost straight down the Vessel, the haute new public structure the city would close less than two years later after too many people jumped to their deaths from it.

—Are you getting annoyed, Cassandra? You don't have to look at all of them.

—Oh, but I want to, I said.

Raleigh took me at my word.

—Here's the one in Charlottesville, then.

*Chiswick Farm,* I read.

—They misspelled *manor*, I said.

. . . *the only residence still in private hands known to have been designed by Thomas Jefferson.*

—Holy fucking shit, Raleigh.

—I know. . . . Phil says it's an "investment." He says that about all of them, actually.

It was an exquisite white Palladian with blue-black shutters at the foot of (yes) *Fan Mountain*; impeccably balanced, practically the definition of balanced, its manicured gardens tumbling into rolling hills; its brick walkways reflected skyward in the stately twin chimneys. Modern comforts—guest house, pool, tennis court—had been integrated seamlessly, preserving all the property's historical charm. Inside, gamey, Stubbsian oils dotted the walls. The upholstery invariably matched the drapes. This was the sort of house that not only comes with a formal, given name, but where every room within it has one.

—We haven't actually closed yet, Raleigh reminded me, but Phil's hoping everything will be settled by basketball season.

—I see.

—Will you come down for some of the games?

—You know we'd be delighted, I said. Though I may need to put Tate and Percy on leashes.

—Cassandra, you're horrible—

—Metaphorically speaking! Let me see New Orleans.

—All right, she said, sending me the link. Remember, Phil's father's going to live here year-round. . . .

It was every bit as palatial, though a fraction of the price of the others. A white French Mediterranean on Swan Street, by the lake, with another lofty columnar portico, arched gables, and double French doors. The interior was somehow even whiter: the furniture, upholstery, drapes, countertops—even down to the marble floors. To the textural, Robert-Rymanian canvases framed by ornate boiserie. It was so tonal as to be almost uniform, besides the odd flash of Ionian gold.

—What an inspiration for your father-in-law to remain . . . continent, I said.

Raleigh's mouth dropped open, and I waited for a firmer admonishment, but by the time our eyes met she was smiling, laughing, and then we both were, falling back in our loungers, close to tears and short of breath.

We took a dip in the pool and grabbed a pint of kefir from the kitchen before settling back into our chairs, taking turns whirling the white frost into our mouths with gilded spoons. The head of Medusa was carved into their temples, and it struck me that, for all her symbolic mutability, these particular spoons wouldn't have quite fit at several of the other new homes; not in New York or Los Angeles, certainly not at Chiswick Farm. Each property was representative not of Phil and Raleigh but its own geography, each a quintessential specimen of a distinct, localized flavor of

American luxury—the consistency in their colorlessness a little like Phil's blue shirt, less an anchor than an ever-blank canvas.

I looked again at the Los Angeles house, the De Stijlly leonine labyrinth where Phil was now. It was so easy—effortless, really—to imagine his blue shirt open, sitting by the pool next to Sunny. But just as easy to imagine him leaving her there. Phil was buying freedom, yes, but also something more. He wasn't wrong, exactly, to call these places *investments*. They were investments in other selves, in other lives. A well-resourced workaround to *you only live once*: you only live once *at a time*. He wanted these places for the same reason I wanted his story, for the same reason the sibyl at Cumae asked to live, disastrously, for as many years as the grains of sand in her hand. Even prophets—*especially* prophets—don't want to die.

—Okay, how many more are there? "Houses," I mean.

—Just one, Raleigh said, flushing, aware of the ridiculousness of the word *just*.

It was the most insane yet, on the 'Sconset bluffs of Nantucket. A veritable castle with bubbling porticos under an Escherian roof; so big it had multiple addresses, an aerial slide showing their legal division, two of them bisecting the tennis court. It was sided in the island's traditional cedar, and yet the primary function of its weathered shingles almost seemed to be to emphasize the extremity of the trim's whiteness. The interiors were brightly matte, too, aqua and sage and sand with nautical little pops of navy and vermillion, mottled wood—everything roughly precise and engulfed in violent white trim.

—Unfortunately, we're not going to have a chance to go *this* summer, Raleigh said. Because . . . well, Phil also bought a boat. I know it's short notice, and I would have asked sooner if we hadn't just finalized things yesterday, but we'll be in the Mediterranean for the next couple of months and we'd love it if you guys could join us for a week or so—however long you can get off work. And we'll have Frances and Debbie on board, too, to take care of the kids.

—It's a very generous offer, Raleigh. Let me talk to Miles and look at plane tickets.

—Oh, no need! she said, delighted to be able to lower the threshold for confirmation. We can send ours to pick you up.

—You bought a private jet.

—Two, actually. Phil just thought they would make it easier for us to get around.

—Yes, I said, with an airy little chuckle. I imagine that's the case. But what do *you* think, Raleigh?

—Oh, I don't know—the same thing you think about all your parents' houses and fancy things, I suppose.

—My parents! I said. This is a different order of magnitude.

—Is it? Or is our money just newer?

—Raleigh, I didn't mean to—

She smiled reassuringly.

—I know. It's okay. And I do feel twinges of guilt sometimes—don't you? We're so lucky; it's crazy. But you can only be generous if you have something to give, and I *love* being able to give generously. It's so nice being able to treat your friends, you know?

# AUGUST

We met the Fayetons in Greece.

I would have preferred any of the previous stops on their itinerary. The Balearic Islands—Ibiza, Mallorca. The glittering sands of Cannes and pebbles of Nice. The bastion of luck that is the Principality of Monaco. The Amalfi Coast. Capri.

Even the isles of Greece are overheated in August. But this was what schedules allowed, and it's hard to argue when you're being ferried by private jet to Mykonos.

The superyacht was at least four or five times larger than the boat we'd been on the last time we were at sea with them, that other *leisurely Saturday on the Potomac* all those years ago. And yet, for all its capaciousness, the mood on board was stifling, irascible. The gods were hot and restless, like the decommissioned windmills no breeze could turn onshore.

—What do you want to do first? asked Phil in chipper overcompensation. We could take the tender into town. Or find an inlet and get out the toys. There's an enormous inflatable slide, you know. And jet skis. You like to jet-ski, right Miles? Everyone likes to jet—

—They just got here, Phil. They're probably hungry and tired, said Raleigh, looking to us.

Even as she said it, though, libations appeared, delicate morsels to match. Truffle bruschetta, salmon nigiri, puff pastry stuffed with pistachio crème. Strawberries and nectarines adorned everything, cut into fanning pinwheels.

—This looks marvelous, I said, my professional opinion.

Phil studiously dismissed my praise with a handy flick, as if misapplying some newly acquired sense that *being impressed* was gauche.

—I fear we've gotten spoiled, Raleigh said with a blush.

—Or, we could go to Delos, said Phil between bites, ignoring her, it's only like half an hour away. We haven't been yet. And I've been meaning to consult the oracle. Ha ha.

—That's Delphi, I said.

—What?

—Delos is the island just west of us, but the oracle was at Delphi, on the mainland. They're two different places.

—I don't think that's right.

—They're frequently confused because both are associated with the god Apollo, I explained.

—Where on earth do you get your confidence? asked Phil, consulting Wikipedia.

—Greece, in this case. But I object to the question. It implies my confidence is misplaced.

Phil flung his phone to the side and scoffed.

—God, Cassandra, you're so pretentious, he said with a nonchalance that could not entirely conceal his contemptuous embarrassment.

It was a manner modeled on the negging of intimate friends, and I considered how unlikely he would have been to use it on me just a few months earlier. There was something deeply gratifying in it, even as it felt like a concession to him. For it was a concession I had beckoned, courted—willed. My story rising alongside his station, our confidence our lighter fuel.

—Thanks, I said, smiling.

—If Phil's been wanting to go to Delos, let's do it, said Miles—diplomatically, but failing to register I'd undermined his impetus.

—Oh yes, let's! said Raleigh, eager for the resolution of a plan.

Delos: birthplace of Apollo, god of the sun, of art and knowledge, of straight shots and laurels and swans. Of poetry. Of prophesy. Beautiful, too: youth's very ideal. You'd think I'd like him—and I do, actually; we have a good deal in common. Still, even allegorically, I am leery of courting his patronage; too aware of his storied conduct toward women like me—of "godly" men more generally, ever ready to credit themselves for women's gifts then demand a quid pro quo. He either rapes you, or you get to be a tree? No thanks, dude. We're *colleagues*. Fellow artists, you see? It's not appropriate; undermines your famous rationality, your self-control. Your *very stable divinity*. Go ahead and call us mad. You're only proving our point. The taproots of divinity, of genius, are *in*stability.

This is what I told myself silently as we disembarked, climbing up the coast past the crumbling temples of Isis, of Artemis, of Leto—of mothers and their Olympian friends. Though tiny, the island was once immensely rich, a "free port," a center for trade, the home of the Delian League treasury until the age of Pericles. There may have once stood many marble lions on its famous terrace, where we saw only five now—and these fragments replicas, the originals moved into the nearby museum.

—Just like your place in Los Angeles, I said, taking a photo of Phil and Raleigh between two lions.

Raleigh insisted on taking one of us, too, and I nestled under Miles's arm, smiling behind my shades. But when I turned for a final look at them, at the lions, casting long shadows in the waning light, with their erosion, their weathered pitting, I thought they looked more like giant, emaciated lambs.

We looked in on the children en route back to Mykonos, where Phil was intent on a night out with Miles before we left the area. Raleigh and I were invited as a courtesy, but everyone knew we'd stay on the boat after dinner, that we'd infinitely prefer to watch the lights twinkle in the harbor, maybe from the jacuzzi. Above all: without them. There was, indeed, a palpable sense of relief with Phil off the boat; I expect this was true in the tender, too, as it whizzed ashore. I waited until the stewardess refilled the wine and left us, among the mountainous white pillows of the bridge deck's sectional, and posed it as a statement, not a question.

—What happened.

Raleigh turned toward me, our first true breeze catching her hair—now a golden balayage, impeccably blended.

—It's that obvious?

—Maybe not to Miles.

—But to you.

—But to me, I said.

She freed a golden strand from her lips.

—I think he met her in Ibiza. Sunny, I mean. He's been in LA constantly, then on our second night he never came back to the boat. He swore he didn't see her. Called me a lunatic. Said he just lost track of time at Pacha because it's an "iconic experience" and—he admitted this later—because he took molly with the DJ. Molly! Does that sound like *Phil*? I don't know. Maybe I'm wrong. He hasn't done it again, exactly, though he's also made excuses to go to shore alone a few times and been "delayed." I half think she's in Mykonos now.

I looked at her darkly, my suspicions shining through.

—We'll know tomorrow.

—How?

—Miles.

—You're sure he'd tell you?

—It doesn't matter, I said. I'll be able to tell.

### ◻◻◻

The Naxian dawn glowed pink through the Portara on Sunday morning, like the preternaturally beautiful background of a colossal iPhone. Phil and Miles hadn't stayed out very late, Miles pleading jet lag, and from the way he crawled into bed alone I could more or less confirm the Sunny truth.

—Run into anyone you know? I asked, just to be sure.

—What? Is this about Sunny again?

—That you brought her up justifies my question.

—Relax, Cass. Phil said she's filming, in Pebble Beach or something.

—That *he* brought her up justifies me more!

I also thought, but did not say, that this was probably why Phil had wanted to spend August in the Mediterranean in the first place. Raleigh had been correct in spirit, but specifically mistaken; she'd asked Phil the wrong questions, and received the right answers to an irrelevant test. A factual result, and yet also a false negative. Sunny hadn't been in Mykonos, or Ibiza, or anywhere else along their route—but Phil was absolutely fucking her in Los Angeles. And so he could adamantly deny seeing her in Spain, could plausibly paint Raleigh a lunatic. Even pursue other women, maybe— all while feeling himself unjustly persecuted. Not because his wife was properly wrong, but because she wasn't precisely right.

Raleigh didn't have to rely on my intel, though, because overnight ESPN also ran a story detailing Sunny's stay in Pebble Beach, where she was hosting a reality show for the Golf Channel. By the time we saw them the next morning, Raleigh had already tearfully, profusely apologized to Phil.

—It's okay, babe, he said. "Love Is Never Having to Say You're Sorry," remember?

—I know, I'm furious with myself. I can't believe I doubted your intentions. That's not love. And it's not right. I won't do it again, Phil.

—That's all I ask, he said.

Easy enough to forgive a technical foul in a game you've rigged. It almost serves to bolster the broader illusion's credibility. It certainly bolstered the mood on the boat—which perhaps you'll likewise forgive me not for rocking. The omelets were too good. The service too prompt. The pool too refreshing. Everything too unbelievably clean. The children often in our arms, but without an ounce of responsibility for them. The ounces were all in caviar, heaped on top of the omelets. I wanted Raleigh to enjoy herself, and after three weeks of paradisiacal misery, she finally was. I wasn't about to spoil that. She wouldn't have believed me in any case. Not because I'm me, but because she wouldn't have believed anyone. There are some illusions one can only break for oneself.

Besides, I told myself, it's hard to get too worked up about infidelity nowadays. There was a time when it could get you killed. But the stakes are so relatively low now it's tough to find a compelling narrative angle—mighty impressive when somebody achieves *that*. Rags to riches is more reliable, statistically speaking. And generally more fun, I thought, as I glided down the jumbo slide it took three deckhands to inflate, into the wine-dark sea.

I thought so again on Monday, as we drove a convertible up (yes, yes) *Mount Fanari*, as we lunched at a cliffside café, as we trod the white marble streets of Apeiranthos, so well preserved as to nearly convince me Phil and Raleigh's new collection of kitchens and bathrooms would never grow dated. As we snaked back down toward the water, stopping at a magnificent hotel I would have liked to explore more thoroughly but had been reserved merely for us to freshen up and change in, our clothes hung in the wardrobe neatly. We were at the Portara by magic hour, a professional photographer waiting—soon crowded by many amateur ones, snapping voraciously.

The photos were in the tabloids the next morning, and we looked wonderful in them. Effortlessly so, with the breeze rippling our clothes. The light was otherworldly. I'll admit it: Apollonian.

We scrolled through, drinking fresh pomegranate juice as the sun rose again, this time over the caldera of Santorini.

There are some gods, like some stories, so culturally

existential they bear not only imitation but iteration, like the evolution of two distinct species from the same ancestor; like fraternal twins, or islands of the same archipelago. Apollo, for instance, has not only silvery Artemis—*Diana*—that foiling chaste moon, but the Titan Helios: Sol, another god of the sun, less its patron than its personification. The Sun with a capital S. The celestial charioteer driving four white horses, who doth permit—or not—the base contagious clouds to smother up his beauty from the world.

If there is anywhere on earth the Sun pleases to be His most wondrous self, it is in Santorini. Those wished-for white houses, blue domes. It is a rare accident of an island. The ideal idle idyll isle. No other has attracted more I's, has become more overrun in service of the modern world's most offensive skill: solipsism. Playing holidays all the year on social media, real ones tedious as work. Oia's winding backstreets yoked with cruise-ship crowds, ploughing through one another's sweaty shoulders for a glimpse of Sol at sunset—or, not quite of *Him*, exactly, but of His image on our phones. Of ourselves in his company. The face that launched a thousand clicks: your own. Expensive, delicate ships dotting the background, sure—but otherwise cropped, if possible. As if otherwise alone.

I didn't want a picture. I meant to focus on Him, unfiltered. But my eyes kept darting over to Phil, whose eyes kept darting to the cliffs, his shiny face raised, watching the sea of craning glass reflections brighter than the actual sea. Brighter than the actual Sun. As if backlit with his knowledge of basking separate and apart from the ploughmen. I could see Phil calculating his market share in their minds: the degree to which his superior view offended their present enjoyment; the degree to which his boat enhanced the pictures they'd use to reconstruct their stories of it, redeem their time in later shadows.

I could see Phil deem it insufficient: to be merely *in* the photos, not their subject. Imitation wouldn't cut it; son with an "o" not close enough. He turned again to the fiery ball, now sinking low, the sea licking its pebbly orange surface with smooth black ribs, and I could see him long to take its reigns. That he'd be willing to risk everything to drive.

### 000

—I had a call from Crewe last night, said Phil a couple of mornings later in the Sea of Crete. They're working on a television pitch for me, and I need to get back to LA, so I think we'll head back with you guys on Saturday.

This was a change of plan; theirs had been to continue on to the Peloponnese and Athens.

—Holy shit, Phil, said Miles. *Television?* Have you been taking acting classes out there?

—Nah, this would be Reality.

—Well, he did quit his job, I said, taking a sip of strong black tea and turning to Phil with a smile. Are you going to be a Real Housewife?

—Funny, he said humorlessly. No, it would be a new show, designed around me. There have been a number of ideas, but this is why I need to get back. To understand all the options and figure out what I want to do.

—What about you, Raleigh? I said, turning to her. What do you want?

Phil's shoulders visibly tightened.

—I think it'll . . . depend on the concept, she said, gauging Phil's reaction. I'd be a little nervous, of course, but I'd be on it if Phil wanted me to be.

With effort, I avoided rolling my eyes. As pleasant as the past few days had been, Raleigh's contrite deference to Phil had reached new heights of absurdity. I might need, I saw, to give her a little nudge into the room with Crewe, to help her navigate the maze of Hollywood. (For all luck's power, it is not wise to rely on it.)

Not that I had any direct familiarity with that particular social world. But it would be populated by people like any other. People with needs and desires, incentives and disincentives, cognitive biases and cognitive dissonances. And often—so very often—the same ones. Psychological sleights of hand we fall for again and again and again (yes, even me). For wealth as a proxy for freedom. For power as a proxy for purpose. For fame as a proxy for immortality. For admiration as a proxy for love. For religion, obviously, let alone art. O fatal art! Even art's a proxy. A proxy for beauty and truth. And for all the others—for freedom and purpose and immortal love. For life itself. What makes them so tricky, these proxies, is that they often work to some extent. But they work in the same manner as stereotypes and clichés: not founded on nothing, but still fundamentally untrustworthy. Even lay statisticians understand correlation is not causation.

On Friday we took the tender to Heraklion, a car up to Knossos. Phil had booked a "private tour" that proved only a tourist trap. Our day: dusty parking lots and trinkets. It was almost so appropriate I was tempted to forgive him—not that he apologized. To be fair, he also disproportionately bore the consequences. Phil had neglected to bring a hat, forgotten sunscreen, and it was the sort of intense, solar day that can scorch you even with it, even at four, let alone high noon. The back of his neck glowed hot by the time we got back to the boat, the tips of his ears darkly singed. By dinner you could see little boils—it was going to peel—and the burn had spread to his limbs. When Percy lightly brushed the back of his calf, playing under the table before dinner, Phil screamed so loudly I worried the boy had fallen. Percy had been frightened enough by the sound for me to follow Frances to the cabins to help calm him down, which he did, soon enough—unlike Phil, who was miserable the entire night. Sleepless, too, and tragic the next morning, huddling in the shade of the main deck as the rest of us enjoyed a final swim. A giant towel draped over him on the tender to port, protecting his ragged skin. Not even the plush seats of his private jet seemed to comfort him. He only sat very still, emitting little periodic groans. Getting up only when we refueled at Stanstead; speaking only when we deplaned in Washington.

—Take care, he croaked with effort.

It wasn't until after Miles and I got home, while we were unpacking, that I saw it, nestled in the little folder that had also held our customs forms. A brochure for the company Phil used to crew his planes, touting *excellence in safety*. I saw the little winged logo, the orange branding, and had to laugh. Who could have possibly named such a business *Icarus Jet*? Reality was bonkers. Even I couldn't have predicted that.

# SEPTEMBER

I'm thinking *American Pickers* but for college basketball, said a redheaded junior agent. Phil travels across the country to college towns, digging up legendary sports stories of yore. It's got nostalgia, Americana, sports; plays to the blue-collar crowd—

—No, said Crewe definitively. We want to go a bit more upmarket than that. Have you ever seen Phil wear flannel? No flannel.

—What about leaning into the bracket concept, said another, bespectacled man, younger still. Maybe with a romance angle to it? Highly sellable—like, *The Bachelor* but it's a bracket, with games and rounds and direct matchups. Phil could host and provide counsel—the "married sage on the other side," so to speak, having made such a great match himself.

He smiled obsequiously here at Raleigh, who had successfully claimed a seat in the room, if not exactly a voice in it.

—So you want to pit women against each other head-to-head over a man, said an attractive producer in her forties with a violently smooth brow. In the year 2019? I don't think so. Have we explored food? Do you like food, Phil?

—Yes?

—You're right about the bracket *Bachelor*, Amy, but I'm not seeing a food angle either, said Crewe. Doesn't take advantage of any of Phil's brand equity.

—Real estate? Amy tried. Phil and Raleigh have a bit of a Chip-and-Joanna-Gaines vibe about them, don't you think?

Phil liked this idea.

—We've recently purchased several properties—

—Are any of them run-down? asked Crewe.

—No.

—Are you secretly a real estate agent?

—Uh-uh.

—Then it'll either veer too MTV *Cribs* or you're basically just looking at a family drama.

—I mean, a family drama's not the worst idea, said Amy.

—What's the hook, though? The bespectacled guy questioned. That he filled out a perfect bracket? That he's rich? Where's the rest of the cast? We might as well just try to get them on *Real Housewives*.

—We're *not* doing *Housewives*, said Phil adamantly.

—How about *Pawn Stars*, but—

—Jesus, enough with the *History Channel* shit, Charlie, said Crewe.

—I still think there has to be something we can do with the bracket, insisted bespectacled. What about a true, old-school gameshow? Play up the whole Ken-Jennings savant thing. Could have a sports angle—or not. You could make it more about prediction.

—That's it, Eric, said Crewe.

—*Wheel of Fortune* except it's a bracket—

—No, *prediction*, Crewe clarified. An unscripted medium show. Like, *Long Island Medium*, *Hollywood Medium*.

—I love it, said Amy. *DC Medium*?

—*Basketball Medium*? said Charlie.

—*Millionaire Medium*? said Eric.

—*Medium Rare*! said Raleigh, the first words she'd spoken.

*Medium Rare*. It was perfect, leveraged every bit of Phil's "brand equity," Hollywood gold, save a single showy crack: Phil couldn't predict anything. And I don't just mean he wasn't a bonafide prophet. Obviously he wasn't a prophet. But he also utterly lacked the deft propensities for hot and cold reading—the combination of research, observation, vague probabilistic couching, and outright deception—that allowed other celebrity mediums to affect clairvoyance. That is: He couldn't even fake it. Not that he was willing to try. If anything, Phil clung more tightly than ever to the purity of his mythology, his insistence on skill and analysis, as if blinded by transcendental temptation except the "higher cause" was himself. He didn't bristle so much as seethe at the word *luck* now. And yet he proved equally unwilling to make his own, afraid this would carry the implication he hadn't already. He categorically refused the psychological coaching Crewe wanted to get him.

They tried other angles. Scripting bits. Scripting everything. But this too conflicted with the ancient set of ideas Phil held about himself. *He never had a teacher*, claim a litany of artist anecdotes, going back to the Greeks. *He was nature's son*. Closely related, both of them, to abrupt social rise, rags to riches. The president's implication undoubtedly hung higher in his mind, a more direct fear of Apprenticeship. And yet it was Phil's very insistence on avoiding any sort of fraud that increasingly began to paint him one. He did not understand that legends and myths are formed in retrospect, that they're built from other, older ones. That Reality *is* scripted, even the bonkers bits. Reality with a little *r*, too. Perhaps above all, he failed to grasp that *being* the magic of showbiz requires, at least to some extent, relinquishing that magic for oneself.

It didn't take long for Phil to develop a reputation for being "hard to work with." He was a "nightmare," a "diva" even, with its disastrously gendered implications, a half step from *hysterical*. Word got around town before they'd even pitched the networks, speculation fornicating with fact. *Distracted by the family, I'd say. A new baby, you know?* And what is Hollywood's quintessential definition of madness but Hitchcock's: of a man pretending to be a mother?

Crewe began to tire of him, false madness begetting a different kind of real one. There was only so much he could do if Phil wouldn't play ball. Crewe didn't drop him, exactly—Phil was still worth something to the agency—but he lost his perch atop Crewe's client list. Phil couldn't always reach him, and longer intervals elapsed between their meetings, calls. By the last week in September, Crewe began passing him off to Charlie, the way wax softens before it properly liquifies.

The pitch for *Medium Rare* floundered, failed to take off. It's hard to say it *fell flat*, because it never really left the ground. The idea was there, not to mention the title, but art, even effective "content," requires execution above all—and execution is something the old myths cannot provide, that they almost explicitly work against, whispering from dusty pages: *Give up, mortal! You do not have wings. You cannot do what I did, what I still do.*

Phil had other problems, too. For someone who'd spent an awful lot of time lobbying against taxes, there were fundamental gaps in Phil's understanding of them, and his financial advisors had probably under-secured his reins. In four months Phil had managed to spend over half his post-tax winnings. And while many of Phil's major purchases were in hard-asset investments, some depreciated frightfully—and basically all generated astonishing maintenance costs. He still had hundreds of millions of dollars, but with every monthly statement he couldn't quite escape the feeling that he had, well? *Less.* Less than Arun Patil, sure, many times over, but worse still: less than former Phil. It was a problem, *less*, less of elevation than directionality. We humans are comparative creatures, and hopelessly future oriented: ever more concerned with slope than coordinates. It is hockey-stick trajectories we want, recoiling when a ball begins to drop, even if it swishes directly through the hoop.

And then there was Sunny, the high reason he'd wanted to spend so much time in LA in the first place. Since Raleigh's apology in Greece, the weighty presence of his wife had clung to his side, throwing off his balance, exposing his underbelly in a way its increasing tautness couldn't counter, the muscles having been developed there entirely for show not strength. Meeting Sunny anywhere else would appear deliberate and risk exposure, the suggestion itself desperate on his part besides. Essential to his ability to attract her was still his flighty air, his unavailability, his perpetual distance. The challenges of competition and secrecy were not barriers to Sunny but fundamental attributes of her desire, what gave their narrative the gravitational pull to keep it revolving. That Raleigh orbited Phil only increased the total mass circling Sunny—and made the latter more attractive by comparison, in that, though Sunny was really much farther away, she managed to take up at least the same amount of space as Raleigh in the sky of Phil's mind, and very often more.

Phil himself recognized it well enough, the essentialness of Raleigh, even in the moments he longed to dispatch her. At times Sunny made her look cheesy, but at others frankly serene. Phil was not desensitized to the appealing wholesomeness his wife and child mobilized, the power Raleigh's body held for Virginia, the power Virginia's held in his arms. As his daughter grew plumper, sat up, stayed awake longer; as she began to look less like a naked mole rat and more like him, alert with his own blue eyes, he softened toward her predictably, humanly, delighting in her growing expressive range—though he was still hopelessly dependent on Raleigh and the nannies at the first sign of quotidian distress.

Phil knew, too, that the tidal pull Raleigh still exerted on him translated to the fans; that she was telegenic in her own way. A brand asset. She was, moreover, tied directly to his harder ones: They didn't have a prenup, and Phil had seen the toll ultra-high-net-worth divorce took even with an iron-clad one in Arun's bad press. It would be an even trickier business for a "prophet." There is something inherently untrustworthy about a divorced medium, an implicit admission of the sort of duplicitous hocus-POTUS Phil was most desperate to prove himself against. For if you don't possess the foresight to choose your own life partner, how much of it can you possibly have?

Phil doubled down at the gym, his trainer at the labyrinth-library nearly every day. And he made an appointment with a high-profile cosmetic dermatologist, one skilled in the sort of *subtle tweaks* Phil had convinced himself Crewe's waning attentions were indicative of his failure to accelerate. It's a common enough self-deception: to project onto one's body deficiencies of the mind; for one's inability to face the truth to manifest in the face. But the chiseling of his abs and jawline went unnoticed at CAA (*well, that's the point of* subtle *tweaks!* Phil's dermatologist said when he complained). It was all so depressing he considered relenting re: the *Housewives*—but then Raleigh wouldn't have fit in with them, and it would be almost worse if she somehow managed to; it would destroy the foiling serenity that constituted her remnant appeal. And how long could he avoid the dissolution or disclosure of his relationship with Sunny on such a show? He saw an even messier, more awful divorce in store than it would be otherwise. And *he'd* be the one kicked off if it happened! It was House*wives* not *husbands*. Embarrassing for him to even consider it, on so many levels, not least of which being the risk of their rejection. Worse still: of Crewe refusing to even try to broker a deal, saving his professional capital for someone else.

But Phil needed some sort of backup plan. The range of products he was hawking on Instagram now were, even as he saw himself getting more conventionally attractive in his photos with them, a marked step down from those he'd been shilling only a couple months earlier. If he wasn't careful they'd be diet tea soon. *No*, he thought, *better to pivot decisively than glide slowly down, losing air incrementally.* The *dramatic pivot* was a life design for which Phil had no shortage of models, not least Arun Patil and the tech set, for whom *failure* was never *really* failure but a *learning opportunity*—provided you were the right "whom." More compelling still were those down the coast, pivoting from drama specifically. Above all his hero, Ronald Reagan, but also Arnold Schwarzenegger and, Phil thought more reluctantly, Donald Trump.

His reluctance with regard to Donald was actually part of Phil's emerging plan's appeal. The latest presidential scandal, not even a fortnight old, of the Ukrainian quid pro quo was looking to have greater sticking power than the previous ones. The Speaker had already launched a formal impeachment inquiry, and the Democrats held a House majority now, even if no one thought the Senate would convict. Shouldn't the moderate Republican electorate be offered a viable alternative? Not just a smattering of overambitious lower-level politicians, but a rival celebrity? Another household name? Phil wasn't so deluded as to think he'd win the nomination, however deranged the incumbent competition—but the very act of running against that level of crazy could have a legitimizing effect of sorts, a priming agent for other endeavors and subsequent campaigns. And wasn't this alone enough to make it a compelling option? If Pete Buttigieg could do it, why not him? The point, after all, was less to reset his coordinates than his trajectory.

Phil *could* win, too, right? Not likely, no, but it was statistically possible. What had Phil's past success proved to him if not the parable of the black swan? *Statistics is never having to say you're certain*, he remembered that math professor saying. Ron Tinaldi's voice also echoed in his mind: *Assuming you were born in America, you have a one-in-ten-million chance of being elected president of the United States. At thirty-five years of age, Phil Fayeton will be eligible to run in the next election*—and his odds would be far better than that: a white, heterosexual man; a six-foot-three celebrity; a multimillionaire (though *not*, technically, an "out-of-touch billionaire"; he could emphasize this point effectively). Phil had already accomplished a far rarer feat.

And Raleigh would help him. More so now, with her subtle little tweaks. She looked every bit the American First Lady, ready to be draped in red and presented to some latter-day Shikler. Phil didn't even need to close his eyes to see her holding Virginia at the inauguration in coordinated Ralph Lauren, his hand encircling her waist as he raised the other high, flying it back and forth in a victorious, patriotic wave to the biggest crowd ever.

# OCTOBER

I think it's the right sport for you, but the worst imaginable matchup, Miles couched, splayed on a green velvet camelback under an Arcadian mural.

We had arrived at Chiswick Farm under the auspices of the Oracle ERP Blue-White Scrimmages Presented by the Virginia Lottery and a first glimpse at Coach Tony Bennett's new team. But politics was the sport most top of mind for Phil that evening, and to which Miles referred, the first real home game still a month away.

It was more encouragement than anyone else had given Phil, *the right sport for you*. Sally Yu, who had left Senator Sheila Campau's employ for a higher-paying job at a top political campaign consultancy over the summer, called him mad. Another consultant—at a slightly *less* prestigious firm—laughed in his face. A third looked at him not with amusement but concern. It wasn't just that Phil would lose, they all insisted. The president would set out to destroy him forever, by any means necessary—and quite possibly succeed. Didn't Phil remember his own meeting in the Oval Office? Being interrupted, disregarded, lied about and to?

That was the president being nice. On his best behavior. Actively trying to support Phil—insofar, at least, as he'd deemed it also beneficial to himself. And anyway, even if the president hadn't been vindictive and conscienceless and able to shoot someone on Fifth Avenue without losing fans, Phil was many months too late: Half the Republican field who'd had the same idea had already dropped out. He'd look like a charlatan declaring now, even with the impeachment inquiry; petty embarrassment the best conceivable endgame. Surely he'd worked in government long enough to know it would be a catastrophic error.

Phil left these meetings in a mix of dejection and dismissal; rattled, but his ego preventing the warnings from achieving full psychic penetration. These were contacts he hadn't spoken to since leaving the AASSS, he reminded himself. *They must not realize the extent of my fame.* Even in the bright light of his own insight, Phil couldn't see the error was his. But then, who can see blindness itself? Remember it is not only the lack of light that blinds, but also too much of it.

—And look, said Miles, not unkindly, having gently reiterated all the points Phil had already heard. Even Reagan ran for governor first.

There was a perceptible shift in Phil's demeanor.

—Newsom's at the beginning of his term, though, he said. Northam, too.

—Senate, then.

—California would never elect a Repub—

Phil stopped, turned to me, our blue eyes meeting.

—You're not working for Maria, are you?

I shook my head. Representative Muñoz had rebuffed my overtures; had again pledged to eschew corporate PAC donations for her senatorial campaign. And why wouldn't she take the moral victory, in a state sure to elect a Democrat, in an election she was so far ahead in it might as well have been uncontested? I saw, now, what Phil was thinking, why he'd asked. He smiled at me conspiratorially.

—Well, you've defied the odds before, said Miles.

—He doesn't have to, I said.

—What do you mean?

Raleigh, too, looked confused, as Phil unbuttoned the cuffs of his crisp blue shirt, rolling the sleeves as if readying for some kind of manual work, smiling wider with every fold.

—I'm going to run as a Democrat, he said.

### 000

Yes, it was a lower office, and he'd fall in his father's estimation with the switch of party, but the California senatorial plan otherwise had much to recommend it. Not just me and Miles but basically all of Phil and Raleigh's newer Hollywood friends and acquaintances were Democrats. Phil's former qualms with the party's "elitism" had utterly ceased when he became a bona fide elite, and now almost enticed him. The appeal of "fiscal conservatism" had similarly diminished alongside his new personal tax rate. He might as well get credit for the hundreds of millions of dollars he'd unavoidably pay on his winnings come April from the party who'd appreciate it. Phil's social positions had always leaned further left, more Democratic than MAGA—and he was not entirely ignorant of the fact, though he never would have admitted it, that the crowning success of Republican public relations had been reanchoring "the center" right of its true point. The campaign itself would be easier, obviously, with less scrutiny and more personal freedom—not just absolutely but in an advantageous ratio, the drop in prestige well worth these gains and more. As a senator? Phil could set up Raleigh and Virginia in DC with a perma-excuse for solo travel to Sunny LA. Raleigh would have her time to shine, too. As far as states went, California was the most glamorous, populous one; they'd still get a Ralph-Lauren wave when he won.

And this was the biggest advantage of all, Phil thought: *When.* His celebrity wasn't at the level he appraised it, but Phil *was* famous, and while I wouldn't say the odds were in his favor, exactly, neither was it a black-swan scenario. Maria had a first-mover advantage, but the late entry that would indeed have read charlatanic in the presidential election could well yield a late splash senatorially. Per California's "jungle" primary law, Phil only need finish in the top two overall to appear on the general-election ballot, meaning he and Maria could both advance to the general over the leading Republican challenger, Cynthia

Duvall. Phil held significant resource advantages over both of them, not that Cynthia stood any real chance. How his white working-class appeal would match up vs. Maria's to California's Latino population was harder to predict, and might be tough to parse from their policy differences. (Not all augury is created equal.) Other parts of the country had seen Latino voters shifting right, though in California the effect hadn't been statistically significant.

Regardless, by splitting the ideological difference between the two leading candidates, Phil did have a realistic shot at winning—and this was what I told him, accepting a drink from the butler and curling into a floral wingback chair. I'd meant this as in *practical enough to be worth a try*, but *realistic* is, in Phil's defense, an awfully artistic word, open to significant interpretation. By the next morning, I could see it inching toward *inevitable* in Phil's mind; by afternoon, careening.

—Maria's kind of a disaster when you think about it, he said for at least the third time en route to the scrimmages. She's basically a socialist. Like, universal health care? That would never work.

—You do realize that basically every other developed country in the world—

—In America, Cassandra. America is different.

—You'll need to embrace Obamacare though, said Miles, at least half backing me.

—I think you mean I'll need to embrace the *Affordable*

*Care Act*—which is now established precedent and failed repeal with bipartisan support. It's a moderate position.

The arena itself was around half full, but the president's box was at capacity, packed with donors and a few especially marketable professors to attract them. No one I knew—no art historians or literary types—but there was a top economist, a charismatic Dardenian, a political scientist widely known for his punditry and "Crystal Ball" election projections. Phil was eager to consult this last one and managed to corner him for the bulk of the women's scrimmage, delighted to reinvigorate the conversations we'd been circling through with a new, more eminent audience. Only when Phil, to his feigned surprise, was publicly recognized as the men's team took the court as a fellow reigning Champion, did he release him, striding to the front of the box with, I thought, a Ralph-Lauren wave-in-training.

There are few events in sports more imbued with hope than a public preseason scrimmage, and I could feel this all around me, how it mixed with the previous season's still-lingering magic into intoxicating dynastic possibilities. Mamadi Diakite was still on the team, as were Kihei Clark and Braxton Key; a few other bench players. And there was some precedent for hope. Possible we were just past the bend of the hockey stick. Holding a whole storybook of fairytales, from which we'd only read the first. John Wooden won ten NCAA championships in twelve years at UCLA in the 1960s and

'70s, seven of them consecutive. Like Tony Bennett, Wooden had been led by a distinctive team-first philosophy, almost a religious creed.

To me? This sort of salivation tasted bittersweet. I didn't see it happening. Wooden's teams had reigned through absolute, almost monarchical domination, winning their championships by an average of over thirteen points, three of them by more than twenty. There were four undefeated seasons; eighty-eight consecutive wins at one point. He had the era's best system, yes, but also untouchable talent. Lew Alcindor—that is, Kareem Abdul-Jabbar—was so much better than everyone else that the NCAA literally changed the rules to reduce his dominance, banning the dunk for nearly a decade. And he still dominated.

Bennett's style, the inherent risk he always ran against far lesser teams, just wasn't conducive to this sort of dominance. Yet wasn't it also what had made their triumph so exciting? That basically every opponent had had a chance against them; that they'd won again and again on a razor's edge; that they *weren't* over-optimized? Randomness—luck—had not only played a role, but an outsized one. Even if they repeated, it wasn't repeatable. Not because they'd won. Because they'd lost. Because no one, not even Virginia, could win another national championship the year after becoming the first to fall to a sixteen-seed.

There was actually a greater magic in this, I thought. In letting go, in unrepeatability, even after reaching the height of the parabola. More basketballic. More black swan. I wouldn't have traded its arc for ten championships. Even if it meant a negative slope now, that we were on our way down.

○○○

Phil had to use Raleigh's phone to get through to Sally Yu on Monday morning; she was clearly screening his calls. But when he blurted out his change of plan, she didn't hang up—and after he walked her through its merits in detail, which he'd now had plenty of practice articulating (and Sally calculated the financial benefit to her firm), she agreed to take him on. Her team filed the requisite paperwork the next day and began scrambling in the backcourt to dial up a last-second splashy announcement: The game wasn't over. And Phil would be ready for overtime.

# NOVEMBER

—H ey Maria, said Will van der Wende into the phone. Do you remember Phil Fayeton?
—The basketball guy?
—Yeah. You're gonna want to turn on CNN.
Though he stood behind a podium, his blue shirt seemed to fill the screen, the crowd behind him a sea of smiling faces holding placards. "Phil for US Senate," they read, with a heavy graphic emphasis on *Phil*. The i dotted with a little star.
—Mother*fucker*, said Maria.
—I know, said Will. I'm getting calls for comment. What do you want me to say?

Maria Muñoz was born in Compton in 1989, the only child of Guatemalan immigrants new to Sunny Cove. Her early years were defined less by realized hardship than the looming, back-seat sort of threat of it, a persistent, low-grade mental anguish that is too often discounted. Her father, a doctor, had a reliable, salaried job as a medical assistant, but her mother's equally essential income from cleaning middle-class houses in Lakewood was subject to greater precarity, and while no ruinous setback ever befell them—illness, rumor, a linoleum slip in well-worn shoes—this was largely a matter of fortune.

As was Maria's own beauty and intellect, of course. But she was diligent, too, excelling in school, and almost more impressively at the sort of complex, fatally boring administrative rigamarole that allowed her to cobble together a patchwork of need-based financial aid and merit scholarships collectively amounting to a full ride to UCLA. Maria graduated in 2011, cum laude with a double major in economics and public affairs, but skipped the commencement exercises. She was already in Chicago, working on Barack Obama's re-election campaign.

It was during this period that Maria's parents traded in their old car, on its last leg, for a more reliable one. The problem was the loan—Buy Now Pay Here financing. No interest, short-term, the dealer had emphasized. What got lost in the fine print? Twenty-four percent thereafter. The skyrocketing car payments started pushing them into credit-card debt—at twenty-*six* percent APR. (Of all the luxuries few can afford, there is none more expensive than being poor.) Maria didn't realize it until she visited after the election, wrote down all the numbers. Her parents owed nearly twenty thousand dollars on a 2007 Honda Civic. A nine-thousand-dollar car.

She stayed in Compton with them, spending her days on hold, filling out paperwork to consolidate the debt, slowly, painstakingly navigating layers of recursive bureaucracy.

Waitressing, then bartending at night because it paid better. She stayed active in liberal and, increasingly, democratic socialist community organizing and campaigning, first meeting Senator Bernie Sanders (no relation to Sunny) in 2015. Enthralled by Maria's charisma, Bernie purportedly hired her on the spot—and later helped jump-start her own congressional run. They had, Maria and Bernie, a charming, Lady Gaga–Tony Bennett (no relation to Coach) type vibe, with far greater collective demographic potential than either could achieve solo. When she unseated her primary opponent in 2018 with less than a tenth of the funding, a star was born.

—What do I want you to say? Maria echoed scornfully. That Republicans are so utterly without an ethos they will literally become Democrats.

### 000

I was picking up the twins from Montessori when Phil called from California, a few days after the kickoff rally, a few days before the House began Donald's impeachment hearings. Right around the start of basketball season.

It was the sort of sunny, late fall day in Washington that reveals the stark differences in individual internal temperature; little kids still running around in T-shirts while their svelte parents swathed themselves in topcoats and fleece performance wear. A couple such mothers glared at me in incredulous horror when I waved off my underdressed children to answer, letting them run amok in the courtyard while we talked on the phone.

—*So.* How's it going?

—Why are you being weird? I said.

—I'm not being weird, said Phil. How's Raleigh?

—It should seriously disturb you that you're asking me that, but as far as I know she's well. I'm about to head over there with the boys.

—Oh, cool.

Percy tackled Tate to the ground, and another mother wearing a puffy, bejeweled headband gasped. (They were fine.)

—I heard Maria called you a mother*fucker*, I said with pointed enunciation, giving Headband a dainty wave.

—Ha. Who told you that?

—Will van der Wende.

—Are they trying to hire you? Phil asked.

—I already told you no, I said.

—Because that's actually why I called.

—Yeah, I thought so.

Phil had spent four million dollars standing up his campaign in the past three weeks, and while, he assured me, he considered it all money well spent, if he *could* recoup it with the corporate donations Maria refused, why shouldn't he? He launched into a paean to my talent, my character, my fit, my résumé. How "every" event of mine he'd been to (I recalled only a couple) had been second to none. I was "brilliant," "innovative," "luminous," and "promising." And he'd make it very well worth my while to help him—monetarily, yes, but also in terms of "advancing my career." A "tremendous opportunity." "Once in a lifetime."

—Seriously Cassandra, please. *I* know you're the best fundraiser out there. It's time everyone else on the Hill did, too.

He wouldn't be the first male Boss I'd had who looked favorably on his own favorable opinion of me and my work as a flattering mark of his own progressivism, as if the existence of my singular mind was his own personal discovery. What *I* knew? That my appraised superiority was invariably contingent on his sense of control over it. My formal subservience. That the second he felt the esteem he'd encouraged in the minds of others reflected more positively on me, myself, than it did on him, he'd find an excuse to "take a step back" or "talk about it next cycle" or outright cut ties on the soft, pliable ground of *style*. It was easy to argue I had too much of it. I "needed to understand how far to press." In pressing for parity, I pressed too far. And so, while I was always "brilliant," "innovative," "luminous," and "promising,"—I never quite *arrived*. It was part of the price I'd paid for the freedom of fundraising, that *Boss* with a capital B was categorically foreclosed, and that was fine. But I would have liked partnership. Respect for my realized abilities as opposed to my "potential." There is an exhaustion to still being seen as an ingenue in your midthirties, especially by a man in his.

—Besides, said Phil. You're a friend. I value your advice.

—Ah, but would you ever take it?

—That would depend on the advice. I'd be retaining you for the advice, Cassandra—and the parties—not to make decisions.

—I'll think about it, I said.

—You wanna to talk to Miles?

—No. I want to talk to Raleigh.

It wasn't that I didn't value Miles's opinion—I almost always talked through the decision to take on a new client with him. I hadn't married him on a whim or something: Miles was thoughtful, intelligent, and socially adept. Plus, in a directly proximate yet tangential professional position, he was able to offer well-informed guidance from another perspective without the slightest risk of competitive envy or ploy. Our material fortunes were directly aligned (the idea that marriage is no longer an economic decision is frankly preposterous), my trust in him bolstered by his sundry incentives to be trustworthy; by our relationship's structural, biological, and legal long-termism; because we *did* have a prenup. I knew my unusual capacity to parse paradox and cognitive dissonance hardly absolved me from the latter (prophesies rarely suffer from a backup plan); that for all my truth-telling, there was a great deal—always more—I didn't know.

No, I simply had no need to consult him with regard to Phil's offer, because I already knew his opinion. Miles was still left of Phil politically, but sat closer to him now than to Maria, whose ambition had emphatically *not* compromised her authenticity, and continued to passionately argue lobbyists should not exist. (Theoretically, I agreed with her. See? Cognitive dissonance.) Phil would immediately become my most profitable client, and the friendship angle—our personal and familial relationships—Miles would deem purely a benefit. Lobbyists are not, in general, particularly concerned with mixing business and pleasure, let alone conflicts of interest.

Considering the narrative proximity the position would provide to Phil, my own instincts likewise lurched toward acceptance. My reservations were two. First, the ideological compromise I'd be making to get it. Not out of some sense of my own purity, but because the sacrifices made for a privileged view can sometimes make it hard to see. I was willing to compromise my ideology, but not my narrative. My politics, but not my art. The facts, but not the truth. I worried that so directly writing myself into the story would imperil my ability to tell it. Who's ever heard of an omniscient first-person narrator?

But this I could quell. I thought of all the blind seers; of Tiresias, of Milton, of Joyce. If my subordination to Phil posed a narrative conflict of interest, a blind spot, it was merely the formalization of a preexisting one. I was already tied.

Conflicts of interest are largely a problem of perception for honest people, anyway—and I would be deemed unreliable regardless. As to the related concern, that I might use my professional capacity to alter the course of events itself—to *shoot the albatross,* so to speak (though the actual risk here would be in propping it up)—well, that was less likely still. It would have meant Phil believing a damn thing I said. And that didn't seem likely, now did it?

My second reservation was trickier. Raleigh. I'd started seeing her more again in the past few weeks, since Phil had started campaigning, but vexingly little over the course of the fall overall. Because they'd been in Los Angeles, Charlottesville, yes, but not only that. Raleigh was still persisting in her contrite deification of Phil, and while I understood the true dishonesty to lie squarely on his shoulders, I also had higher expectations of her. I found her unwarranted atonement almost as infuriating as his unwarranted pedestal. And while I knew our friendship and her marriage were no more zero-sum than mine, her pendulous credence on the matter of Phil's fidelity put us in an increasingly awkward position I feared distance would only exacerbate: The closer I came to confirming my intuition, the farther she flew from consulting me.

So I feared the narrative proximity I'd gain in accepting Phil's offer would come at too steep a price. It would mean significant time in California, and the treacherous,

Sunny clarity I'd inevitably find there would pull me ever further from my ability to impart it. And this was if all went well, assuming Phil didn't ever want to "take a step back" or "talk about it next cycle" or outright cut ties on the soft, pliable ground of *style*. I could lose both the subject and object of my fascination in one fell swoop. Which was why I needed to talk to Raleigh. Art on the order of life is always, to some extent, a sacrifice of the latter, and one I regularly make with pleasure. But my relationship with Raleigh was of such irreplaceable singularity I needed to hedge here in order to consider it. I at least needed her assurances that, if Phil and I ever fell out professionally, our friendship would remain intact.

I found Raleigh in the white Beaux-Arts family room reading a novel I'd recommended to her about spontaneously combusting children.

—How can a book about exploding kids be this accurate? she exclaimed.

—How could it not be? I countered, reclining next to her like a Titian nude. But I need to talk to you about something else. Phil called me today.

—I know! You will do it, won't you Cassandra? I'm positive that with you on his side, he couldn't lose—

—I wouldn't be so sure—

—He's been putting *so* much pressure on himself; I'm

worried about him. Having a real friend on board would terrifically lighten his mood.

—Would Phil call me *his* friend? I think he merely tolerates me as yours.

—How can you say that? Does Miles merely "tolerate" me?

—No, of course not; he adores you.

—Why do you think it's any different with Phil? Raleigh pressed. You rib him as much as he ribs you. That's how you two show affection—it's, like, a brother–sister thing.

—Even supposing you're right, do you think he'd listen to me? You know people don't always like what I have to say.

Raleigh considered this.

—All the more reason you should tell him, she decided. People often don't like hearing the things they need to hear.

—Mm, I said.

—You don't seem convinced, she pouted. At least talk to Phil again before you decide. Tell him all your concerns. I'm sure he'll give you every assurance—

—It's yours I need, Raleigh. I need to know that our friendship isn't contingent. That I wouldn't be risking it.

—Oh my gosh, of course not!

—You say that, but—

She looked injured.

—You don't believe me?

I did though.

—Okay, I said. I believe you.

And I placed the call, Raleigh on speaker. My heart was going like mad.

—Hello? said Phil.

—Yes, I said.

—Seriously? said Phil.

—Yes, I said.

—You'll fly out here tomorrow?

—I will, yes.

# DECEMBER

By the third week of December, the Virginia men's basketball team was 9–1, and Phil was leading in every meaningful poll. *FiveThirtyEight* had him up five percentage points over Maria, though the "Crystal Ball" was more circumspect. Phil was outspending her and Cynthia combined many times over—and his message was resonating. He painted Maria a communist and Cynthia a fascist, drawing significant support away from both of them. *Phil: For Every Californian*, his most-run ad read, though *A Middle Road* tested even better in more conservative areas. Republicans who didn't still support the impeached president, now awaiting Senate trial for abuse of power and obstruction of Congress, seemed willing to vote against party lines for a man who had "put country first" and switched himself, as Phil told it, on account of these high crimes. Democrats, foreseeing how the Senate trial would go in the new year, were wary of asking too much, and likewise inclined to compromise. Phil's absurd wealth, while unearned, at least hadn't been problematically built on the backs of everyday Americans either—quite the opposite. Above all, they wanted someone *safe*. As did corporations. A Republican in the guise of a Democrat? Phil was a wet-dream candidate for them, like the heterosexual anthropomorphosis of Pride Month branding. Invigorated by his success (and the after-hours visits from Sunny), Phil made himself similarly ubiquitous, actively campaigning full-time while Maria balanced her congressional duties. The press circuit following the tournament had been remarkably good preparation for this, and there were points when he demonstrated something close to charisma.

And so, while Phil was spending a lot, we were also raking it in. Everyone left of MAGA was just desperate for stability, for a reality they recognized. For the carefree days of 2015. Phil endorsed Joe Biden—and was feeling so carefree himself in the festive lead-up to the holidays he snuck in a cozy weekend with Sunny in Beverly Hills before meeting Raleigh and Virginia in New Orleans.

—What should I get Raleigh for Christmas? he'd asked me a couple of weeks earlier.

—I'm sure she just wants to spend time with you, Phil.

—What about a house in Charleston?

—I do not think she needs another house, I said emphatically.

—Or Palm Springs? Might go off better with the voters.

—Or they'll think *seven mansions mans-ing* is a bit much, don't you think?

—I want to do something amazing, though, he insisted, oblivious to the grammatical clarity of who this *something amazing* would actually be for.

I had unwittingly given him the idea for just the sort of grand gesture he sought. Phil wasn't about to re-create the entire Twelve Days of Christmas—too many birds, including some rather common ones (French Hens? *Geese?*), and the back-half was overly performative, by the end outright cacophonous. But one of its suggestions was "perfect": imposing, graceful, luxurious, majestic. Quintessentially rare. Or rather, not one, but seven. Those feathered phenomena: *swans*. Black swans, specifically. What could be more appropriate for the Fayetons, for the estate on the lake? On literal Swan Street? They'd provide such exquisite contrast with the white house.

Phil emailed his personal assistant about it. Possible, she told him—the New Orleans climate would suit them.

—But they'll need to be imported from Australia, she said. And it'll cost a small fortune to get them here by Christmas.

—Fortunately, said Phil, smirking, *that* is something I have.

The swans arrived on their eponymous street Christmas morning per Phil's specifications—though much to his ire, one had freed itself from the gleaming red ribbon decking the necks of the others.

—I don't know what to tell you, the deliveryman said

when he complained, gesturing to the red-ribboned Mustang convertible in the driveway—Phil's gift to his father. These are wild animals, not cars.

—But I was told they'd been *pinioned*, said Phil, as if to prove himself a sophisticated avian consumer.

—Just because they can't fly doesn't mean they're domesticated.

Phil visibly wavered as the deliveryman unloaded the crates, as if on the cusp of instructing him to take them back and be gone. But this would have meant admitting defeat, and Phil had no other offering for the mother of his child.

—Merry Christmas, Raleigh! He said brightly, instead.

—Uh—

Virginia's expression uncannily mirrored her mother's, her little brow knit in infinite skepticism.

—Gah! she protested.

—Uh, thank you? Raleigh managed.

—I just thought you might prefer, you know, something symbolic, said Phil, sensing, but not wanting to outright acknowledge her lack of enthusiasm. We've already gotten so much this year; you're hard to buy for nowadays.

—Oh, Phil, said Raleigh. I didn't mean to seem ungrateful. We've been so blessed. And they're beautiful, truly.

And they were—beautiful, that is—if also vicious, loud, territorial, and foul. Actual swans are significantly more Tchaikovsky than Saint-Saëns, and these were especially irritable after their long journey: percussive, hissing and snarling, their thin, shrill wails like demonic violins. Up close, there *was* something a little fiendish about them, with their blood-red beaks and eyes. And while Phil's father had thus far managed to avoid incontinence himself, the swans shat everywhere. One in particular: a pen Phil's father named Odette, she of the shredded ribbon. Swans mate for life, and, while not always faithful, for good reason are generally sold in breeding pairs. Phil's insistence on *seven* had clearly disrupted the group dynamic here, and, in her misery, Odette promptly began wreaking havoc not just among her little swan society, but on the Fayetons' pool. The neighbors began to complain.

—It would be just as good to have *six* swans, don't you think? Raleigh delicately inquired over breakfast a couple of days later.

But Phil's father wouldn't hear of Odette's banishment. Louis Fayeton had taken to the caustic swans in the way Phil thought Raleigh would in their imagined serenity. *For each of us finds lucidity,* as Proust said, *in those ideas which are in the same state of confusion as his own.* Louis was gouty, diabetic, prone to hot flushes, and, aside from the staff, largely alone in his lavish palace. The swans, bred in captivity, provided the sort of needy, vital company with which older adults demonstrably thrive, not to mention a new refuge of trivial considerations—peeved neighbors, pool feces—that gratifyingly, self-righteously invigorated him. Then there was the birds' own reticent coquetry, that alluring affectation of coldness that had always ignited a fire in him with other "birds" too; a brand of fascination that only encouraged him to persevere.

Within a matter of days, Odette and her cohort had become so central to Louis's daily activities that Raleigh grew genuinely delighted with them herself, if only for her father-in-law's sake. Louis looked brighter, healthier, younger even.

It turned out there was a second reason for Louis's rejuvenation, which Phil and Raleigh discovered on their return from a brief romantic jaunt to Chiswick Farm for the Navy game (Raleigh's Christmas gift to Phil). Louis had begun an intense sexual affair with one of the nannies—Frances—and announced, almost the moment they walked through the door, his intention to marry her.

—Very funny, dad, said Phil.

—No, I assure you we're quite serious, said Louis, placing his hand, as if for emphasis, firmly on her not insubstantial bum.

—My god, you're like a walking lawsuit!

—Oh, it's nothing like that Mr. Fayeton—Phil, if I may, ventured Frances.

—You absolutely may n—

—Perhaps you could excuse us for a few minutes, Frances? Raleigh cut in before Phil unloaded on her.

—What's the matter with you, Phil? said Louis as she left the room. You think older people don't have needs? Desires? I assure you I'm plenty virile. And Frances isn't *just* a hot piece of ass. She's charming, companionable—

—*Da-ad!* Phil winced, cringing. The *nanny?* It's so, I don't know. Stereotypical!

—You can find another nanny, son.

—And what about the election? That's my real concern. This could cause a major scandal.

—Would serve you right, running as a goddamned Democrat! But honestly, why should it? It's not like you're sleeping with the nanny. *You're* not having an extramarital affair, I hope.

His words made Phil's rash, the son blushing hard enough for the father to clock it.

—All right, Phil relented, desperate to change the topic. But I need you to promise me one thing.

Louis and Frances agreed to keep their engagement a secret until after the election. In the meantime, Frances would quietly resign and move permanently into the house on Swan Street—where, excluding any future cygnets, her childcare duties would take on a strictly intermittent, grandparental nature.

# JANUARY

Why yes, it *was* exhausting to work for a man in a childish détente with his father; who had, for the moment, only *two* nannies to take care of his single kid. Who for all he'd spent decorating rooms, often still couldn't read them. Who told staffers to "take care" when they so much as went the toilet. Whose policy proposals would provide scant material improvement to Californians. Whose policy proposals were more humane than half the sitting US Senators'. Who was carrying on an increasingly audacious extramarital affair. Who was the husband of my best friend. Who—and I myself cannot believe I'm saying this, but Raleigh was right—had become, separately and distinctly from her, my friend himself.

But I had walked through this door knowingly and of my own volition, between the lions, aware that nearly every house is a temple to Janus; nearly every consequential choice a sacrifice besides. The truth is we all have two faces, and many more. I won't try to cutely parse them. Nothing invites criticism like a subjective taxonomy. But I will say: Nearly all of Phil's moral and intellectual and behavioral shortcomings, his limitations and annoying tics, his cognitive dissonances, possessed some sort of counterweight—if not in perfect balance to his sins. There was an unusual, almost childlike purity to his ambitions, and while the intense beam of his focus shifted mercurially, Phil consistently exhibited the lively, magnetic manner of a man who had not given up on his dreams. Even at the AASSS, I now realized, he had never succumbed to it: that wry, self-aware pessimism that can, for all its intellectual delights, amount to a sort of living death. It was an absence I recognized and appreciated. For I too had avoided its gravest consequences, if by another route entirely. I had avoided its gravest consequences through my art. I had avoided its gravest consequences *through him*. The vicissitudes of his life had given meaning to mine. Whereas my first novel—now on submission—had formed a sort of exorcism, his story eased the usual entrance fees paid for the delights of language and irony: personal suffering. Phil was immensely generous in these subsidies. He was immensely generous in many ways—with his energy, his money—if not in selfless or rational ones. He was an . . . ineffective altruist. And yet, for all his egoic flights of fancy, Phil was almost as charitable to his friends as Raleigh.

This is all tinged with my biases, of course: the effectuation of my narrative fears in going to work for him. The effectuation, I saw now, of my affection. And of a pattern, too. First Raleigh. Virginia basketball. Now Phil. Even Phil. The closer I drew to the people and things I'd defined myself against, the more the lines between us curved toward annularity: an irresistible fiery ring I longed to pass through. My own cognitive dissonance had revealed Phil a paradox: that we were both—well, *both*. The same. I loved him like a novelist loves her flawed protagonist. With the reflective, creative love of artists and gods. Again, a selfish love. Biased. But then, there is no more powerful bias than love.

I had therefore been neither caught off guard nor particularly distressed by Phil's initial reticence to host his marquee primary fundraiser at a private residence in San Francisco's billionaire enclave of Sea Cliff on the grounds it belonged to an antagonistic foil. Arun Patil's team, too, had been hesitant to commit. But I was confident both would walk between the lions soon enough, knowingly and of their own volition; that the great barrier was, in this case, not navigating a labyrinth but simply seeing there was a door.

Being unlikeable is form of luxury, and one Arun was generally content to enjoy, but his bad press the previous March contra Phil had been of a different variety than to which he was accustomed. It had been the product not of envy or half-informed judgment of his conscious choices, but a transparent blunder on Arun's part; a high-profile loss in a head-to-head matchup. Arun could slough off the resentments others bore him as a winner, but not a loser's mockery, especially when it was costing him money. He'd seethed for months, his mind winding, wandering, looping back in its own maze, Daedalus's stock price sinking all the while. He'd scoffed at Phil's campaign announcement—until his advisors analyzed his puffy policies and declared them much the most advantageous to Arun both personally and professionally. Arun's relationship with Donald and his capitulators had long been acrimonious, and Maria, he suspected, would like to see him guillotined. Nothing aligns enemies like mutual enemies—and funds. Arun hardly liked the idea of supporting Phil Fayeton, but by the time our proposal reached him, he was also tiring of exile, homesick for success. Arun remembered MEROPE, the power of a comeback narrative. That the fastest way to kiss failure goodbye was embracing it: giving it wings the surest path to one's own escape. Public sentiment was drifting ever further toward Phil anyway—he was surging in the polls—and passing up the opportunity to reconcile would in no way preclude a future one more rudely forc'd. Better to humbly offer the olive branch now, to willingly hand over the reins. There was, in many ways, no better way to show oneself the superior driver.

As for Phil, his dislike of Arun had largely been predicated on Arun's snub of him, and as soon as this cloud was lifted, he was willing to aid Daedalus and help Arun rehab his public image in exchange for more of his money—plus introductions to his friends and theirs. By the second week of January, Phil had formally accepted Arun's invitation to host him on Sea Cliff Avenue the following month. Not that Sally would have let him turn it down.

Which was how I found myself, a few days later, driving past some of the world's rarest gates, veiling some of its rarest doors, to the grandest in the row. It was a structure of an architectural style they do not teach in art history departments, one I can only describe with any brevity as *American*, or *Californian* maybe. Grey stucco, with teak and slate-blue trim; vaguely traditional, but with an organic asymmetry. The otherwise austere gate featured little panes of ornate decorative glass. It opened before I rang the bell.

—Welcome, said a beautiful woman draped in white linen.

—You must be Helen, I said.

### 000

There was a clean restraint to the interior in spite of its traditional moldings, its almost erratic array of ceilings and floors—coffered and smooth concrete; shiplap and parquet. It had, for all its grandeur, a muted quality, a self-awareness of the structure's almost teleological subservience to the view. Every one of the five floors offered it: an unbroken panorama of the Golden Gate. A view, I thought, more American, more Californian than the house even. A view like Manifest Destiny itself.

Helen was the property manager, a role she embodied with such a relaxed, protean precision as she led me from room to room that she almost seemed a part of each of them. It wasn't exactly that she was a hostess in the hall, a chef in the kitchen, a high priestess on the roof, and in the wine cellar a sommelier. The truth was her cool, professional persona resembled less a hostess than the foyer's magnificent staircase; less a chef (has there ever been a coolly professional *chef*?) than the gleaming, cavernous refrigerator. I speak of only one of her doubtless many faces, but the one I encountered was deeply akin to an expensive human appliance—top-of-the-line and finely calibrated, but a little flat on character. She appeared, in her professional capacity, like the books in the library with their spines turned to the wall, offering a pleasing aesthetic cohesion with their uniform fore edges. They might have been blank inside—or housed the masterpieces of the Western Canon. Most likely they'd been remainders bought in bulk. Regardless, I knew it would have been a grave faux pas to touch them—and I'd need to work closely with Helen for the next two months.

Which was fine by me. The refrigeratorial, fore-edged nature of Helen's affect was not a personality flaw but the mark of her chosen profession's very highest achievement: to be poised and radiant and hollow, an idyllic beauty fading glitteringly into the decor. There were times, as a fundraiser, when I strove for a similar impression. Though I also knew I offered a differentiated, if selective, appeal in my constitutional inability to ever truly achieve it.

The bay-windowed living room opened onto a generous terrace, its swooping outdoor staircase leading down to an even larger one.

—You *could* do the roof deck for cocktail hour, but I'd recommend this, said Helen with a refined gesture. We generally set up the bar on the lower level to avoid a bottleneck.

I chuckled appreciatively at this bit of wordplay, but Helen's face remained stoic. She led me down another level—or, more precisely, two.

—*Wow*, I marveled, almost involuntarily.

—Mm, she said.

An indoor basketball court, past which, through a two-story sheet of glass framing the bridge, arced a vitreous silver infinity pool.

—Is there—any chance we could do the dinner down here? I asked. Instead of in the dining room.

—I did wonder if that would be of interest given your principal's background, said Helen, invoking her profession's preferred lexicon for *Boss*. And I don't see why not, provided we tailor the menu appropriately—

*. . . so the food stays hot enough, given the longer walk from the kitchen,* she implied, and I recognized this as a subtle test.

—Gazpacho it is, I said.

—Precisely.

—*Helen?* A man's voice echoed.

The turn of her swanlike neck was imperceptibly swifter than any other gesture she'd made.

—Arun, my apologies, she said. I wasn't expecting you this early.

But when he saw me, I sensed perhaps he didn't mind.

—This is Cassandra, from the Fayeton campaign.

—Ah yes, he said. Of course. Will the venue do?

His voice rung with false modesty, but I replied with only the slightest edge of rebuke:

—It's stellar.

### ◻◻◻

Dinner on the basketball court was not just on brand, it meant we could sell twice as many tickets, which I relayed to Phil the next day alongside the latest set of names I was considering.

—I only have one addition, said Phil.

—Okay, I said. We can squeeze one more. Who is it?

—Sunny Sanders.

—No.

—But you *just* said we could "squeeze one more"?

—My objection is not on the basis of capacity. Pick someone else. Literally anyone else.

—Why though?

—You can't be serious. You can't invite *Sunny*.

—Sure I can, said Phil.

—Okay, yes, like, technically I can't stop you, but—let me try persuasion. I understand why you want this, but what you want is dangerous. Don't you remember the tabloids during the Final Four?

—Yes, and somehow we all survived.

—You weren't running for Senate then. And Raleigh will be there! You must know how jealous she is. Think about the line you'd have to navigate between them, how thin the margin for error. Best case scenario Sunny's a huge distraction when you most need to be in top form. And that's truly the best case. Look at me! You see my face? I'm not trying to spoil your fun here—you're inviting disaster. Please, Phil. Don't do this. Sunny could singlehandedly crash your campaign.

—You're being hysterical.

—Excuse me?

—Sunny and Raleigh were literally on television together. You think they can't be in the same room?

—I think it's a totally avoidable risk. You're underestimating the power of a rumor. Especially when it's true.

This was, I saw, a step too far. Phil didn't deny, but reddened, less in embarrassment than fury.

—I can handle it, he said quietly. My decision is final.

That night, Tony Bennett's Cavaliers lost their third consecutive game.

# FEBRUARY

I delayed sending an invitation to Sunny, but there was little else I could do until we got through the primary debate. Set for the second Monday in February at Sacramento State University, this event would be cumbersomely official and lack the glamour of Arun Patil's court, but what it eased in the way of Sunny risks it compensated for in darker ones. As impressively as Phil had performed on the campaign trail to date, his public appearances had been largely protected from unscripted moments, let alone dissent. And the moderate positioning that had served him so well to this point would now draw attacks from both sides. Maria in particular was known to be a fierce debater, and there was concern on the team that she'd play some type of "identity card"—of even greater concern: telegenically. The bulk of Phil's prep centered on navigating such an attack with grace.

—The other thing that should be constantly looping through your mind, Sally said to him in a role-play session, is to *never to feel constrained by the question*. Stick to your thematic points whether or not they're directly relevant, and if you're called out for doing so, smile and repeat them again.

Major faux pas aside, what you say isn't as important as how you say it. Regular people don't trust cleverness. Your goal isn't to win the logical argument; it's to prove you can't be riled. Optics are everything. Don't raise your voice, don't roll your eyes—

—*Don't interrupt*, a male assistant of Sally's interrupted, with wry self-awareness, to chuckles.

—Jesus, said Phil, crossing his arms. You don't have to treat me like Biden.

—Oh yes we do, said Sally, cooly, a gesture to his gesture, and Phil released his arms.

We—that is, the campaign team—met Raleigh and Virginia in Sacramento the night before the debate at the sort of local restaurant where politicians dislike to eat but love to be photographed: red vinyl booths, linoleum floors. A fifteen-page menu and the only good order is grilled cheese. Mine tasted even better than it would have normally in view of Phil's goopy chicken parm and Raleigh's salad. She'd lost weight in the few weeks since I'd seen her, a personal success she bore with that specific, self-conscious pride of women for whom it's hard fought. I didn't say anything about it, wary of positive and negative reinforcement alike on her well-being—but Sally did.

—Wow, you look great, Raleigh.

—Oh, thanks! I've just been trying to eat healthy.

—You'll look so good all together on stage tomorrow. A beautiful family, am I right Cassandra?

—Mm, I said.

They were; they did. Raleigh, in a fitted fuchsia cape dress, looking all the slimmer for Virginia's delicious pudge, spilling over frills of the same pale blue as Phil's shirt. I could see Phil saw it, too. A side effect of having convinced Raleigh to largely remain in DC "for Virginia's benefit" was—on the occasions Phil *was* with them and not Sunny—legitimately endearing his family to him more than ever.

—Good luck, babe, she said softly. You got this.

And he kissed them before heading backstage with a sweetness so authentic that it somehow transcended its impetus.

### 000

—Live, from the Hinde Auditorium at Sacramento State University, I'm Chester Price of ABC10, your source for Sacramento's Leading Local News, tonight broadcasting statewide—

—And I'm Elle Gardner with *Politico.com*, where we're also streaming nationally.

—We have, tonight, a history-making debate, folks: the most consequential senatorial race in recent memory. Our three qualifying candidates all boast impressive résumés and serious name recognition, but tonight it's up to you, the citizens of California, to decide which two of them have what it takes to make it past the primary round.

—We'll have ninety minutes for tonight's debate, two forty-minute uninterrupted sessions with a ten-minute break—

—halftime, so to speak, Chester cut in.

Elle smiled falsely before continuing:

—Candidates will have a maximum of one minute to answer each question, with a thirty-second rebuttal for any candidates directly mentioned.

—You can follow and like all the action on social media with the hashtag #*senateshowdown* throughout the debate, said Chester. Here in the auditorium, however, we'll ask you to hold your applause—except for now. Please welcome to the stage: the Democratic congresswoman from Los Angeles, Maria Muñoz; former liaison to the American Association of Stone, Sand, and Shale—and "Medium Rare"—from Los Angeles, Democrat Phil Fayeton; and the Republican Congresswoman from Orange County, Cynthia Duvall!

They entered in a waving row to a standing ovation, Maria resplendent in a red-hot sheath, her matching lips framing a winning smile. The shade suited her brilliantly, and mercilessly outshone Cynthia's burgundy pantsuit. If it had been just the two of them up there, it would have been an optical bloodbath in the tradition of Kennedy–Nixon. But as it stood, Phil stood behind the Lucite lectern between them— and for all Maria's beauty, she couldn't dispose of him so bluntly. He towered over her with a slim, unthreatening boyishness, even as his tonal blues implied gravity, demanding the viewer's attention in that more sophisticated way of appearing not to demand it.

—Let's get started, said Chester. Candidates, you'll have up to one minute for your opening statements. We flipped a coin to determine who would go first, and our lucky winner is: Phil Fayeton.

Maria's brow furrowed attractively.

—Excuse me, she said, but how exactly did that work? There are three of us, and a coin only has two si—

—Whoa, whoa, you'll have your chance, Congresswoman, Chester brayed jovially, as if looking to calm a temperamental horse. Mr. Fayeton, please proceed.

—Thanks, Chester, Elle. Our wonderful audience here tonight, including my family. My fellow Californians. You called me a "lucky winner," Chester, and I want to start by addressing this head on, because it's only half true. Congresswoman Muñoz will say I'm only up here by chance—thanks to a "lucky" bounce of the ball. But I've spent my entire career in politics, if behind the scenes: Of the three of us on this stage, I'm the only one who's served in the Senate already, beginning my career as an aide to the Appropriations Committee. I worked my way up on the campaign trail, and most recently represented hardworking tradespeople at the American Association of Stone, Sand, and Shale. That you probably know me instead thanks to college basketball only goes to show I'm the kind of guy who takes even his hobbies seriously. Behind my perfect bracket were years of observation and analysis—not to mention the sort of teamwork I'd bring to our nation's deeply divided legislature. I know how to reach across the aisle, because I used to sit there. Does a man with the courage to switch parties in order to uphold the democratic values of our country sound like a "lucky" man to you? Or a *principled* one? And when you pick up your pen to vote next month, it's not luck that will guide your hand. No. It'll be *your* principles, too. Luck won't have anything to do with it. I will give you one thing, though, Chester: I *am* a winner. I know how to win. And I can win for you: with A Middle Road for Every Californian.

—Thank you, Mr. Fayeton, said Elle as the audience erupted. Please, hold your applause!

—I'd like a thirty-second response, said Maria.

—We're not doing responses to opening statements, Congresswoman, said Chester.

—But he mentioned me by name—

—It's at our discretion even in the Q and A proper.

—Fortunately for you, Congresswoman Muñoz, said Elle, it *is* time for your opening statement. Please, introduce yourself to our viewers.

Maria smiled, her chin rising incrementally; her straight spine further straightening. This was hardly her first brush with moderator bias, and the muscle memory of her underdog resilience was showing through. A darting, persistent, heel-nipping strategy tended to play to her strengths, anyway. She was gearing up for a bite.

—Mr. Fayeton wants to sell you this bootstraps narrative so you'll forgive his billion-dollar winnings and forget he moved to California less than a year ago. But I know the working people of my home state are smarter than to buy it. I know, because I'm one of you. While Mr. Fayeton's been cozying up to lobbyists and special interests in Beverly Hills, I've been in the House of Representatives fighting for unions and labor. For better, more affordable healthcare and equitable public education. And that's exactly what I'll continue to do as your senator. Mr. Fayeton didn't even bother to mention his milquetoast "policy proposals." Let me be perfectly clear about mine. First: a fairer tax code, raising rates and closing loopholes for corporations and billionaires. Second: a single-payer healthcare system like every other wealthy, developed nation—radically reducing if not eliminating healthcare costs for regular people. Third: aggressive student loan forgiveness and free tuition at public universities. And four: a Green New Deal putting our innovative people to work to save our rapidly warming planet, without which nothing else is possible.

   —Thank you, Congresswoman—

   —You know milk and toast are the bread and butter of our great country, right Congresswoman? said Phil out of turn, his righteous indignation cutting through the claps.

   —*Milk and toast*? Maria echoed in confusion. Oh, no—*milquetoast*? Was that what you thought I said?

   She laughed haughtily at his blunder. And this was hers.

Because at least half the audience had made the same one. What Maria had failed to anticipate was Phil's preternatural capacity for playing the underdog himself. It didn't matter that he wasn't one, any more than it mattered Maria was right. Phil's faux pas was—quite literally—so bland as to be negligible. I could already hear Dana Bash and Gloria Borger breaking it down on *Anderson Cooper* later.

—*Look, was Muñoz technically correct? Yes*, admits Dana, *but she comes off as unrelatable, if not outright elitist.*

—*Exactly*, says Gloria. *And if you consider his delivery, too—bread and butter, milk and toast—it's all very "man of the people," very "everyman."*

—*It's right on brand!*

—*Wait, so* neither *of you think this is embarrassing for him?* Anderson asks.

—*I think it's embarrassing in a way a lot of Americans are used to being embarrassed, Anderson,* Gloria explains. *It's relatable.* He's *relatable.*

—*And he proved he couldn't be rattled!* says Dana.

—*That really was the kicker, wasn't it? Because it was* Phil *who interrupted the debate format initially, but by refusing to engage with Maria's laugh? He made it look like she was the one being disruptive.*

—*Again*, says Anderson.

—*That's right, Anderson.*

—*And then when Cynthia Duvall went after him in her*

*intro, too?* Dana adds, *and less for party disloyalty, by the way, than policy ambivalence—*

—*It felt like they were ganging up on him,* says Gloria.

—*They were ganging up on him!* says Dana.

They were ganging up on him, I thought. And he was playing it brilliantly. Speaking with confidence, but never raising his voice. Never rolling his eyes. Never letting facts get in the way of his narrative. *Regular people don't trust cleverness.* Sally was right. And by her logic, it would have been hard to imagine a candidate more trustworthy. His platitudes bore a superficial profundity and vague unobjectionableness that made it hard for Maria to pierce them effectively, giving her attacks the whiny air of nagging. The same expressive, cutting intellect that had, in conjunction with her beauty, provided such an edge against the dry experience of her wizened House opponent two years earlier faced an unexpectedly tougher matchup against Phil's empty charisma. It is counterintuitive, but personality with substance often succumbs to personality alone.

By the debate's second half, the moderators couldn't ignore this, even if the voters could:

—You've taken a lot of heat from your opponents on the lack of specificity in your policy proposals, Mr. Fayeton, said Elle.

Phil smiled genially, as if she was complimenting his shirt.

—But you'll have another chance with our next topic:

Federal income taxes. Could you please outline, *in detail*, your plan and its expected impact on the citizens of California?

—I'm so glad you asked this question, Elle, because, while I know it sounds boring, tax policy is really important, and the details do matter. The key thing to understand about my plan, though, is that it falls between my opponents.' We can't afford more Republican tax cuts and continue to pay for essential, long-standing services like Social Security and Medicare—services I support, by the way. But Congresswoman Muñoz would pull us too far in the other direction, crushing the economy—

—I think you mean insisting billionaires and multimillionaires like you pay your fair share, Maria interrupted.

—I'll be paying nearly five hundred million dollars in taxes this year, Congresswoman—practically half of what I earned. How much will you?

It was a line he'd practiced a good deal, and Phil delivered it so matter-of-factly, without the slightest trace of malice or even judgment, that even as I disagreed with his lexicon of deserving, his casually presumptive *earned*; even while I wanted to throw tomatoes and get on my soapbox for progressive consumption taxation—I also couldn't help but thrill for Phil. The moment was a mic drop—a slam dunk. The soundbite every outlet would replay ad nauseam with sweeping pronouncements that *Phil Fayeton won the #senateshowdown*.

—I've published my tax returns for anyone who's interested in them, Maria snapped, but even in conveying her openness she sounded evasive. But frankly, I think the people of California care more about how federal tax policy will affect *them*—

—Excuse me, Congresswoman, this is Mr. Fayeton's allotted time, said Chester. You'll get your chance to respond.

Technically, she did—eventually. But it didn't much help her. Maria was visibly hot under the collar; the damage had been done. And as the moderators wrapped, inviting the candidates' families to join them onstage, I couldn't help but notice that next to Raleigh's glowing pink dress, Maria's red looked harsh and almost tawdry.

◘◘◘

Phil was flying high following the debate. Higher after consuming the news the next day, then watching UVa beat UNC. *Too high*, I thought, less out of envy than in my strange, growing desire to protect him. It was as if the publicity of such an official, and by all accounts harmonious appearance with Raleigh had provided a subsequent form of speculative extramarital inoculation. A prospective counterweight. In the ensuing weeks, it almost seemed as if he was going out of his way to be seen in public with Sunny—meals, Lakers games. As if to say: *We have nothing to hide.* He loved his wife "more than ever"; Sunny was just "one of his best friends in LA."

If Raleigh did not particularly enjoy reading about these forays, neither did she express the remotest mistrust of Phil.

Her idealization of him had only increased in the wake of his debate performance; her wholesome stage wave had been no act. Raleigh much admired Phil's "shift back toward public service"—in her eyes, if not his own, a higher calling than reality television. I was less likely than ever to knock him off the pedestal she'd built, even if I could have. I myself was working for him! Remember too my ancient history, all those collegiate accusations of "home wrecking" to no discernible benefit—before there was any real *home* to wreck. *Your discretion* has *improved*, I heard Raleigh say. And what is character growth if not adaptation?

Not that anyone was crowning me in laurels. When I prevailed on Miles and Sally to talk Phil out of inviting Sunny to the fundraiser at Arun's, both thought I was overreacting: Miles on the grounds the flame between them had long since cooled; Sally that it was a baseless rumor to begin with. She even accused *me* of perpetuating it by "making such a big deal" about excluding Sunny. *I* was giving it unearned credence.

—It sounds like you could use a little drama in your own life, Cassandra, Sally said dryly the last time I raised the Sunny question.

—Oh I'm good, thanks, I said.

But I no longer had her attention. Alas, there are some aspects of characterization so deeply ingrained you can never truly escape them. And Sally had the shadow of a point. It was strictly vicarious drama I craved, but my actions were ultimately rendered in the service of maximizing it. On some level, I must have known I was choosing art over life. That Miles and Sally and Phil would rebuff my insights, that my *improved discretion* prefigured not the avoidance of disaster but merely its delay. Like my hand on the lid containing some reactant as it built in pressure, all but certain to unleash a larger, later explosion.

This course was firmly set once Phil invited Sunny to join him on the flight from LA to San Francisco for the event at Arun's. Some fifteen cases of the novel virus that was shutting down parts of China had been confirmed in the United States, and it seemed merely prudent when they'd be in such close contact subsequently—watching the Lakers take on the Warriors together at the Chase Center, the day before the event. (Never mind, I thought, but did not say, the potential exposure of a packed basketball game!) I sent over the invitation. Sunny promptly paid the requisite donation.

I didn't arrive in San Francisco myself until February 28, the morning of the fundraiser, with Raleigh on the Fayetons' other plane from DC. She wanted to keep the trip as short as possible, having left Virginia with a restored triad of nannies, and this well suited me. While not surprised, I had still been miffed by Phil's failure to take my advice on the event, this being at the very heart of my professional expertise, and I must have conceived my physical absence the week beforehand as a form of professional pseudo-punishment. I missed my boys—including Miles—and I missed Raleigh; I had my first call scheduled with an interested editor and I knew Helen had things well in hand onsite anyway. So I largely left them to her, relishing a few days of snuggles and Montessori dropoffs; evenings with Raleigh when Miles worked late; the latest stylings of the Fayetons' personal chef; content to swoop in at the eleventh hour when it came to my own culinary responsibilities. To the extent I foresaw a detonation at Arun's, it wasn't going to spring from the passed hors d'oeuvres.

Still, when we landed I let Raleigh go on to the Ritz alone, heading straight to the house on Sea Cliff Avenue. Things were as I expected: buzzing with a brisk yet controlled energy that mirrored the weather off the breezy bay. Not just Helen and my teams, but the caterers and support staff all oozed easy confidence, the effect of having served in such environments before, the outward imperviousness to the marvelous surroundings as they sliced sashimi and aligned flatware that is a hallmark of first-rate event ministration. It didn't entirely quell my sense of ecstatic dread, but perhaps nothing could have. I was sufficiently satisfied to head to the hotel.

—Cassandra, is that you? Raleigh called from behind the cracked door to their suite, adjacent to my room per mutual request. Ah! How do you make that sort of dress look so beautiful?

It was a tea-length black shift from the Row, loosely darted at front and voluminous in back, that in truth I'd looked forward to wearing, purchased expressly for the occasion if also with the understanding I'd be able to don it many times again. Raleigh sat in a queenly silk robe, her makeup largely done but hair still in rollers. One of several attendants hovered over her, preparing to release the barrel curls. A yellow one-shoulder cocktail dress, draped in flattering asymmetrical pleats, hung outside the wardrobe behind her. I could already tell the tonal effect with her hair would be stunning.

—You're kind, I said. This yellow's going to look wonderful on you.

—Custom Dolce and Gabbana, she squealed.

—It's lovely. I mean it.

—Aww, thank you.

—Is Phil ready now? Or will he come with you later?

—*Phil?* she raised her voice, as he emerged from the bedroom in a yellow tie. Cassandra's here!

He rode with me, hoping to grab a few minutes alone with Arun before things got underway. Up close, I could see little blue quails dotted his tie, their tiny plumes curling into a delicate paisley.

—California state bird, he explained.

—How appropriate. Follow suit, okay?

—What? Phil asked, feigning incomprehension. You're not still chafing about Sunny coming.

—You justify my hesitancy—

—Cassandra—

—*Phil*. We are five days out from the primary. You're leading in every poll. All I'm saying is to avoid an unforced error. Focus on nailing your speech and schmoozing Arun and stay the fuck away from her—oh, and stay away from Helen, too, while you're at it.

—Who's Helen?

—Never mind!

It was an unforced error of my own. How could I have failed to account for the nature of my advice? Failed to adapt, in all my self-awareness, with reverse psychology or sealing my lips? There's no credible explanation; I will not offer one. And yet, perhaps his undoing was not so special, the product less of my singularity than his humanness. For who among us isn't drawn like a moth to the bright, flaming light of a warning? Lured toward demise in pursuit of demise's disproof? It is with the best intentions. Every fatal flaw boils down to integrity in excess.

—Welcome Mr. Fayeton, said Helen, opening the heavy door with a polar lightness.

She wore a black dress similar to mine, and with similar grace, except whereas the absence of color highlighted my eyes, it accentuated her hair: that radiant shade of natural blonde only rarely seen past childhood, which even the greatest colorists on earth can't quite replicate. She wasn't the sort of woman who would have blinded Phil a year earlier, with her minimal makeup, her small chest neatly tucked away—but his tastes had changed, grown subtler, more refined, and I didn't have to turn my head to know he was blinded now.

—Mr. Patil will meet you in the library. If you'd follow me?

—Nothing would delight us more, said Phil. Right, Cassandra?

—Mm, I said.

—This house is something amazing.

—Mm, said Helen.

—There he is, said Arun, rising with calculated ease to shake Phil's hand. Good to see you again. And—it's Cassandra, right?

—Mm, I said.

—Good to see *you*, too.

—Shall I brief you on the preparations while they chat, Cassandra? Helen asked, extracting me elegantly as a pair of drinks materialized for the men.

Reticent as I was to leave Phil without a babysitter, I appreciated her coded kindness, telling myself Sally would be along soon enough. And indeed, as we descended the stairs back to the main floor, I spied her entering the outer gate through the window with a balayage blonde in a yellow dress. My breath caught in my chest, to the point that Helen, piqued by my flash of discomposure, asked if I was quite well.

—Mm? I said, as she opened the door.

What had I half allowed to happen?

—Welcome, said Helen.

The thrill of narrative.

—Sally Yu, Phil's campaign manager, Sally introduced herself curtly.

The thrill of art!

—Pleasure, said Helen.

And the blazing effigy of my best friend.

—Hi! said the blonde, with a full-court smile. I'm Sunny Sanders.

To the powder room! I excused myself to its merciful confines, tucked under the arcing stairs, soundproof, lavender, an oasis of calm. Lock; *breathe*. A retch—dry. Hands on the sink, eyes on my own. The pitfalls of intuition! Impossible to turn off, finicky to override. I'd been so caught up in the job, in the story—so worried about Raleigh abandoning me, I'd failed to realize I was abandoning her. Tears in ducts. Tears, escaping. True:

—I chose Phil, I said to my reflection in disbelief.

And I'd made the wrong decision. How to undo it? What thread to pull? *Think, Cassandra*. Any warning was sure to go unheeded. *Think*. Or—any warning save one?

A knock. *Composure*.

Raleigh herself; my only chance.

Open. Helen:

—Is everything all right, Cassandra?

—No.

—Mm? said Helen.

—I—need to go check the upper terrace—

The preparatory bustle yielded an ironic pseudo-privacy, enough for me to place the call.
—Hey. What's up?
—Raleigh? Have you left the hotel yet?
—Yes—am I late?
—No, no—I am. But I have to ask anyway. Do you maybe have . . . another dress?
—In the car? No—oh, no, did something spill on yours?
—No, I mean for you—
—I thought you liked the Dolce?
—I do! I do, but—
—And no, not really. Custom made?
—Right. It's just—
—I don't want to be conceited, but when you see me in person, I think you'll agree it looks okay.
—Oh, I'm sure you look gorge—
—Cassandra?
The voice was hot on the back of my neck—
—I'll call you back, I said to Raleigh, turning. Yes?
—Sorry to bother you, said Sunny.
Up close, she maintained more of her waxen aura than one might have expected. The labor of her appearance was even more readily evident than it was on television, and yet this did not diminish her hotness but augmented it. She'd had what a lot of women on Instagram would call "good work."

—Have you seen Phil? She asked.

—He's in the library with Arun.

—So not with—what was her name? Helen?

My eyebrows raised, piqued by her jealousy. This was not the direction I had expected it to take. Sunny's insecurity in the face of Helen implied a lack thereof with regard to Raleigh, and I wondered if Phil had made some larger, ill-advised promise to this woman she was worried yet another would usurp.

—No, I said.

—No as in no he's not with her, or as in no he's not *not* with her?

But I didn't have to clarify, because Phil presented himself, if not properly then at least in view, at the indoor/outdoor threshold alongside Sally and Arun.

—*There* you are, said Sunny.

She crossed the terrace, palming his arm—just as Helen opened the front door.

Phil didn't see his wife enter. Nor could Raleigh see his lukewarm face, intent to formalize his interaction with Sunny under Helen's gaze. What Raleigh *did* see: the horror in my otherworldly eyes, seeing *her* see *this* at *that* particular angle; my silent wail at her orbit's cruel arc—which read from Raleigh's perspective as an admission on Phil's behalf. A double Judas betrayal, framed in yellow robes.

—Raleigh! I said, too loudly, so it came across as a warning to Phil rather than the entreaty to her that it was.

She gave me one of those southern-belle nods of irrefutable politeness before ignoring me entirely, stepping between Sunny and Phil with a chaste peck for him, then, stoically, withholding her rage, continuing toward the setting sun, hovering over the Golden Gate—biding her time, I thought with fear, with grief. I was under no illusions as to what Raleigh's friendship meant to me, but the imminent prospect of losing her crystalized it into words. I'm afraid the English phrase, in addition to being clichéd, does not traditionally extend the flexibility I seek, that it would customarily be applied to my partner in wanted sex and wealth creation. I loved Miles. And yet, he was not the "love of my life." Raleigh was. It was Raleigh alone who truly saw me. The only person who had ever believed.

It was the sort of grand epiphany that only the most mundane professional obligations can prevent one from urgently attending. The concreteness of my role, the way its performance had become automatic to me precisely *because* I regarded my job with appropriate perspective, was what barred a scene. Guests were starting to arrive, and my response was all but Pavlovian. The bartenders at ease. The silver trays gleaming between bites of fatty tuna and deep-saffron quail eggs. Sunny had gotten the message from Phil and joined another cluster, anchored by a mid-weight basketball pro. Raleigh had not replaced her at his side. I sensed his fear, too, a mirror of mine, though he hid it well, intently focused on Arun's coveted introductions until an acquaintance of plausible interest to his wife opened the door for him to beckon to her.

—It's lovely to meet you, Raleigh, some heiress cooed. I would have introduced myself sooner, but you and that other woman in the yellow dress look *so* much alike I wasn't sure it was you!

If my professionalism served as an emotional shield, Raleigh's politeness was a veritable fortress. Her composure was terrifying.

—Mistaking me for a television personality? You're too kind!

Every snip of conversation I caught hovered at this tonal altitude of equanimity. Even so, as the pleasantries compounded I couldn't escape the sense of ratcheting tension; of feelings precariously feathered over obscuring ever greater risk. Above all: In Phil's impression he'd successfully escaped already. As the sun slid toward the bridge, I saw him chance a glance at Helen, her luminous hair in the breeze; the chiseled shadow off her fine, seaward face. I saw Sunny intercept it, and Raleigh intercept this interception—or half of it, anyway, decontextualized into a different envy.

The party migrated down to the court for dinner. Generally, this is the inflection point of such events, after which I begin to relax. Formal seating arrangements are less subject to chance than cocktail hours, being thoroughly vetted and planned in advance, thus bearing a certain comfort for a fundraiser assured of her skill. Someone less adept would have sat Phil and Sunny on opposite ends of the room, with their backs to each other—a seemingly rational yet perilous mistake. Nothing is more obvious than a craning neck. I'd been more careful, placing them, rather, at midrange; at an angle of natural if not inevitable eye contact, yet far enough away as to remove any threat of conversation; a defensive row of interlocutors between them, like a social pack line.

Still my palms were cold and my forehead burned, every muscle tense under my tasteful dress. Its precisely tailored billows caught the breeze off the pool as I entered the court. Fewer people were seated than should have been, too many drawn by the architecture's stunning absence to the water's edge, transfixed by the fiery ball hovering over it. Among them: Phil and Raleigh, in quietly intense conversation to the side.

—If you could please take your seats, I pointedly asked a cluster near them, trying to spark a mimetic chain, covering my attempt to listen into the darling conversation I longed to kill.

—... *then why* did Cassandra call to say I should change?

—How should I know, Phil hissed. We can talk about it later. I need to concentrate, okay?

—No, this is more important. Our marriage is more important. You know I trust you, Phil, but I'm not blind—

—Look, let's go sit down.

—*No*, said Raleigh, determined.

—Look, you've misread—Phil tried again.

—I want to underst—

—Look, *I'm sorry*, okay? said Phil. Can we please just go sit down now?

Raleigh's face lost every trace of expression, a blank canvas onto which the setting sun painted a mad grace.

—You're . . . what?

*Apology* is a notoriously tricky word, but no one, let alone Phil, let alone *me*, could have reasonably mistaken its meaning here, that he had wielded apology not as a form of defense, but an admission—*the* admission—of a wrong.

—Raleigh, I said, let's—

—You're *what*? She said again, lion-like, loud enough for the rest of the party to hush.

I saw it all before it happened, in the yellow gleam in her eyes, what they reflected. Her arms outstretched; the imbalance of surprise. His flailing firestorm—and a bath. Falling down, down, down.

—Ra—! Phil screamed.

And he hit the pool with a little splash.

# MARCH

There are some disasters that explode supernovaly, all at once, while others drip, spill over, cascade. For all the drama of the scene at Arun's—the push, the plunge, the ensuing Sunny invectives, the icy *you knew* leveled at me—Phil's infidelity was the latter. Raleigh's exit as he bobbed in the deep end, wetly screaming *fuck* to himself as I called her name, as I ran after her, as I had the exquisite front door slammed in my face: This marked not the end, but the beginning of Phil's downfall. Narratively? It was the climax, of course. I'm ashamed to admit that even in the immediate throes of my anguish, awash in sympathetic ache for Raleigh, my own bereaved failure, my conflicted pity for Phil—still lurked my horrible American intuition that the pain would be artistically profitable. The enduring thrill that I'd willed it all: an early prophesy come to pass, heedless of my subsequent attempts to stop it. Remember desire and suffering are hardly mutually exclusive. Remember we can be smote even by that which we choose.

An alternative scenario exists wherein the damage was confined to the party, mopped up on the court. A small splash in a vast tableau. *An embarrassing event*, they'd have said, *but ultimately, a private one*. Privilege protects itself thus all the time. Self-protection is encoded in its definition—the very telos of privilege, as with so many cruel, organic phenomena, being its own survival and reproduction. But Phil hadn't been a regular in such rooms for long enough to engender the sort of loyalty that can overpower ready iPhones, the zeal of spectators eager to be entertained. By Sunday, March 1, two days before the primary, the video was in every outlet, viral on Twitter; multiple shots from different angles all capturing his fall.

We never found out who leaked it first. Many presumed it was Sunny, trying to raise the hurdle against Phil's marital reconciliation. But this seemed unlikely; her statement to the press was she was "moving on" and "focused on" herself. Others accused Raleigh of pure vengeance—and I knew that was wrong. A few congressional insiders even thought it was me, that I'd always had a whiff of the whistleblower about me, too integrious to be politically trustworthy. I lost two other clients in addition to Phil, not that it mattered. In the videos' background, the soaring heights of my work were on full display for those looking: the exquisite, on-theme private venue, the understated decor, the net worths. My inbox was glutted with inquiries by Monday morning. I didn't open them. Raleigh still wasn't answering my texts, my calls. I strangely thought of Adrienne in my frustration, never more aware of my own failed communications, that motherly conflation of fury and care. I wanted to kiss Raleigh's bruises and stroke her hair and find her a good divorce attorney, drowning all the more in her suffering for her total dismissal of my reciprocal pain.

Phil and Sally continued projecting confidence, working to downplay the scandal as the unfortunate collision of a "personal matter" and an "overserved event"—for which the fundraiser responsible had been summarily fired. *Nothing to see here*, the tone implied, aside from the fact that with this sort of public posture, there nearly always was. In combination with the raw video evidence, the Sunny affair was broadly ingested less as speculation than fact—and in other circumstances, this might have swept the public on to the next one, *certainty* being gossip's mortal foe. Phil continued giving interviews suggesting as much, smiling blithely at Chris Cuomo. Ready to bet the house on the urbane banality of contemporary infidelity, even as he slipped in the polls.

—*So you're not even thinking about going back to your day job?* Chris confirmed, pursing his lips, pantomiming "hard-hitting" journalism in the act of going easy on him. *March Madness is right around the corner....*

—*No, no. Basketball was never my day job. My focus is on the people of California. I'm not even planning on filling out a bracket!*

—What? No way! Didn't Virginia just beat Duke? You have to fill one out, Chris insisted. *At the very least if you lose on Tuesday.*

—*I'm not going to lose,* said Phil.

—*But hypothetically, if you* did *lose the primary, you'd fill out a bracket, right?*

—*If I lose the primary, I'll fill out another perfect one.*

He'd meant it as a little joke, a self-fulfilling display of political assurance playing to a well-established bit; a splashy soundbite to drown out the last press cycle. But I knew, even as he said it, Phil had disastrously miscalculated. *Statistics is never having to say you're certain.* When you say it, you know your luck is running out.

The salient fact that Phil forgot? That to me glared hotly on the screen, in Phil's blue eyes, Chris's white teeth, in Phil's sheepishly unsheepish visit to the polls the next morning, without Raleigh, so conspicuously alone? The jackass! He was running as a Democrat. Only Republicans are forgiven extramarital affairs.

They say the Sun sees all things first, but it had set before Anderson Cooper made the announcement: CNN was calling California's jungle primary for runaway frontrunner Democratic Congresswoman Maria Muñoz and, by a smaller but nonetheless decisive margin, Republican Congresswoman Cynthia Duvall. For the fifth or sixth time in the past few days, I collapsed into Miles's arms, wailing, my nails digging into his flesh frantically, like some feminist inversion of Bernini's *Rape of Proserpina*.

—*Were the polls too high on Phil?* Gloria Borger mused rhetorically. *Sure. But I think the late-breaking affair really hurt him.*

—*Oh, there's no doubt,* Dana Bash agreed. *He totally lost the reins. His wife was incredibly likable.*

Miles stroked my hair.

—She still *is*, I whispered to him, my voice cracking through the tears.

—Hm? Miles soothed.

—I can't stand them, talking about her in the past tense like that, like she's dead or something. Turn it off!

—*I gotta say,* Gloria said in a lighter tone, foreshadowing the segment's inevitable, rosy wrap, *it'll be interesting to see what Phil does now—I mean, that was some pledge he made to Chris Cuomo yesterday.* Another *perfect bracket? We can check in with the data team, Anderson, but—*

Miles shut off the power.

Phil didn't, though. Shut off the power. Long after Anderson gave way to Don Lemon and Gloria hung up her Van Cleef & Arpels; after half-hearted concession calls and showing his team the leonine door, a bottle of Glenfiddich; after midnight, two, four, and day's reprise, Phil continued staring into the gargantuan television, recalling other televisions, televisions of past, present, and future. The wall of black glass in

New York and the cherry cupboards at Chiswick Farm. The painterly Nantucket frames he'd never seen in person. That old fifty-inch flatscreen under a certain synthetically weathered sign—and the opulent Art Nouveau screening room that had replaced it. Raleigh wouldn't be watching. Sunny wouldn't either. But in the lofty columnar palace in New Orleans, where Helios now inched toward mid-sky, his father might be. With pity, even, insofar as pity tends to parentally accompany *I told you so*. Phil had to get out of California. It was the only place to go.

000

—You fucking idiot, Louis Fayeton said. A disgraced *Democrat*, my god. Well, is she gonna divorce you?

—I don't know. She won't pick up.

—Smart woman! Well, bring your stuff inside—*no, Odette, no more treats for you—okay, okay, last one*—

—Phil! Said Frances from the doorway. We weren't expecting you.

Evident from his expression, Phil too was caught by surprise. Frances's very existence, let alone her presence in New Orleans, mistress of the house he'd bought and his own future mother-in-law, had gradually escaped his consciousness over the past few months to the point of total amnesia. Her mental resurrection could not have been less welcome.

—You're still here?

—Phil! Louis roared, with enough force to send Odette

running—and trigger in Phil himself a jolt of posttraumatic childhood fear.

This sensation had the secondary effect of reviving Phil's attentional resources to an observational state unmatched since the night of the primary debate, and he could now see that something about Frances had changed. He would have never conceded to *attractiveness*, per se, but she radiated a new health of sorts; a fullness and a rosy pallor, albeit one more Breughel than Caravaggio. Phil scowled in the assumption he'd been unwittingly footing cosmetic dermatology bills for his former nanny, but passed her without further comment, grabbed a bottle of liquor, and installed himself in front of the television.

But Jake Tapper wasn't talking about him. There were more cases of the novel virus; the Fed was slashing rates. Jimmy Kimmel was hosting the Oscars again. Was it only a week ago Phil had been angling for an invite? After the commercial came politics, but even this segment, discussing Biden's nine-state streak, bore no mention of him—

—Turn that garbage off, said Louis. Since you're here, we want to talk to you about something.

Frances was at his side, blushing.

—Yes, you can get married now, Phil sighed, his eyes still on the screen. What does it matter. I don't care.

—Oh, we plan to, said Louis, smiling. Because . . . well, you're going to be a big brother.

—Surprise! Said Frances.

—Ha ha, said Phil.
—Don't be rude. Frances is ten weeks.
—Ten weeks' what?
—Ten weeks' pregnant! She beamed.
—What? . . . *How*?
Louis chuckled.
—Surely you know how conception works, son—
—Yeah, but—
Phil turned to address Frances:
—At your age?
—I'm thirty-six, said Frances, further reddening. I'm the same age as you.
—Really? Said Phil.
—You're such an asshole, said Louis.
—And *you're* like *sixty*.
—I'm fifty-nine and I've never been fitter. Frances is an excellent cook.
—Yeah, *I know*, said Phil.

There was a pause, Phil's mouth hanging open but emitting no further sound.

—You can stay here, son, said Louis, a bit cautiously, placating yet firm. But you'll be respectful to Frances—

—No, no, I should go, he said, reaching for his phone to call the jet management company. It was a bad idea to come here—Yeah, hi, this is Phil Fayeton. Change of plans; need to get to DC today. . . . Yes today, as in this day, right now. What? When did *that* happen? Shit. Ok—

—You can stay, Phil, Louis reiterated in an emphatic whisper—especially if there's some problem.

Phil covered the receiver:

—Mechanical issue with the wings, but they're working on—Yes, hi, I'm here. . . . Seriously? It was fine this morning. Ugh!

He hung up and collapsed back in the chair.

—Just leave me alone, said Phil. I'll be out of here as soon as it's fixed. They're going to call me.

Frances obliged him. But Louis didn't move. He saw, on some level, Phil's apathy for the deep hurt it was. There was the impulse to draw him out—a flicker of parental intuition urging forthrightness and sincerity. Maybe, with the new baby, Louis would have yielded to it. But the rousing speech that filled his heart could not find form on his tongue. The relational patterns with his large adult son were too firmly trodden to stray from the known path, even when it veered precariously, and Louis exhumed his favorite bootstraps, digging in:

—Poor ignorant boy, he said sardonically.

—Excuse me?

—You win a billion dollars and still find a way to wallow in self-pity!

This was a lower blow than Louis knew. In spite of my efforts at reimbursement, Phil had spent far more on the campaign than he'd originally intended, justifying the expense as an appreciable investment in reputation not unlike his stakes in real estate, sure to yield strong long-term returns in the form of book deals and whatnot. Losing the primary was akin to the Nantucket house sliding into the sea without insurance before he'd ever even set foot in it. The Senate's attraction had been less as a destination than a stepping stone for Phil, its power as much in exit opportunities as within the political sphere; a metaphysical manor providing the infrastructure and foundation for a multi-hyphenate career in celebrity itself.

—You don't understand, said Phil. If it had come out like *three days* later it wouldn't have mattered at all. The timing, it was such bad luck—

—Bad *luck*? Hah! That's what you'll tell Raleigh?

—I never expected you to take my side, but I also didn't expect you to . . . never mind. Just go.

—Humph! said Louis, ignoring another sentimental tug.

He left Phil in the dark screening room, bottle in his lap. Phil took a swig and checked Fox next out of habit before, in a petty act of invisible rebellion, switching over to MSNBC. No word from his private jet people. Nor an hour later, nor the hour after that. No mention of Phil on TV either, not on any of the networks. Even when they recapped the primary results, they only listed the winners this time. The real focus was *Biden, Biden, Biden*, the pundits' partisan glee or terror shining through their painted faces. Phil yawned, flipping back over to CNN.

—*il Fayeton was on this program just last week, you'll recall,* Chris Cuomo was saying.

Phil shot up, as if the plush gold seat had caught fire, watching in horror as Cuomo replayed their conversation, the scare caps of PREVIOUSLY RECORDED fully earning their descriptive title, taunting him redly from the bottom right corner of the screen—

—*I'm not going to lose,* Phil helplessly watched himself say.

—*But hypothetically, if you did lose the primary, you'd fill out a bracket, right?*

—*If I lose the primary, I'll fill out another perfect one.*

—*Another perfect bracket! What are the odds of that?*

—*A hundred percent,* past Phil said glibly.

Present Phil felt an adrenal rush, the putrid kind born not of excitement but mortification, as today's Chris Cuomo straightened his papers superciliously.

—*A hundred percent,* he and Phil echoed together, if in very different tones.

—*You're gonna keep to that, right Phil?* Cuomo continued alone, looking straight into the camera, his finger-gun cartoonishly menacing.

Phil doubled over, emitting a gurgling, primitive sound. He could feel his own faith in himself reflectively collapsing. No one believed he could do it. No one—except—could Raleigh? *Maybe.* It was his only chance for redemption.

He left the screening room in an aftershocked daze. Louis and Frances had gone to bed, a perfunctory note on the kitchen table pointing Phil to leftovers. It was as he chewed his chiles rellenos, bovinely, the way even men like Phil only eat when they're distracted or alone, that his eyes alit on the kitchen hook tray, on the silver horse's gleam. The Mustang—it was as much his as his father's, really; Phil was the one who'd given it to him. And he'd only be borrowing it. Phil checked his phone again: nothing. It was 12:15. He opened Google Maps. Sixteen hours and forty minutes to DC; if he sped—and he planned to speed—he could be there before sunset. Phil popped the last bite of pepper in his mouth and left the dirty plate on the island, grabbing the key.

000

The wee hours were smooth enough, through Mississippi, Alabama. Phil stopped near Birmingham to put up the top, the predawn March chill hitting his now total sobriety like a kick to the face. People at the rest stop acted normal. Warmer and pumped with premium coffee, Phil clipped Georgia's corner. This offered a disproportionate sense of progress, but then the angle at which he hit Tennessee made it seem to last forever, and as the sun climbed his fatigue began to mount. Two, four, eight missed calls, voicemails from his father. Phil ignored them all, finally hid the alerts. He stopped outside Johnson City to put the top back down, get another cup of coffee. The woman in front of him in line for it veered away strangely, abruptly; as if Phil was diseased or something. *The price of fame*, he thought, donning his sunglasses with self-piteous regard. It was going on noon.

    As Phil crossed the border into Virginia, still at least five hours from the District but with the contiguous impression of nearness building, he started to think about calling Raleigh. In the initial throes of Adventure, Phil had harbored the nighttime intention of making his arrival a surprise—first out of genuine romance, then, the more he thought about it, in the shadow of more practical fears. She'd have time to change the locks—worse, simply leave before he got there. This analysis had sat unchallenged in the seat next to him through Tennessee, with the top up, drowsy, but now began to rustle with the highway breeze, in the shifting patterns of free sun on the leather seat. Surely his father would have called her already. It might be better to preempt him—or, at this point, try to unravel the damage. He took a deep breath, looping almost liturgically back through the arguments for his original plan. An hour passed like this, then two, until his decisional framework cracked under the prime horror motivating it. *If I lose the primary, I'll fill out another perfect one.* It was so astronomically unlikely. But it wasn't impossible! Raleigh would know what to do.

    He stopped for gas near the turnoff to Charlottesville, and here everyone was acting weird, paranoid even. Or was it him? Phil briefly considered just taking the exit toward Chiswick Farm, abandoning mission, giving himself a little more time to collect his thoughts—but no, no, he had to see Raleigh as soon as possible, had to know what he was up against. He just had to stick to the plan.

It wasn't until traffic started to slow outside the city that Phil's mind again began to drift off course. *All those people acting weird.* Had one of them sent a photo of him to the tabloids? Phil thought of all its predecessors, the lurid cover shots of him and Sunny. Could she have taken revenge on him? *A hundred percent.* The prickle on the back of his neck bloomed into a twinge, beads of sweat forming between his shoulder blades, dripping down the small of his back.

Phil automatically—almost involuntarily—opened his voicemail, his father's drawling baritone in the Mustang's booming speakers as if Louis and the car were one:

—*Hey, Phil—did you run out to grab breakfast or something? You think you could pick up some—*

—*Answer your phone, son. Are you getting Frances's ice cream or not? She's craving—*

—*Where the fuck did you go, Phil. Where's my ca—*

—*Where—*

—*Answer—*

—*Phil! Goddamn it. I'm calling Raleigh!*

So was Phil, before he realized he was doing it.

A ring—and a pointed little click.

—Fuck! He screamed at the empty seat, slamming his hands on the wheel, veering it dangerously, overcorrecting to stay on VA-120.

—*Hi! You've reached Raleigh Fay*—

Another scream, this one more desperate, avian and guttural. He tried again, but this time it didn't even ring.

—Fuck fuck fuck fuck fuck fuck *fuck!*

And flying into new heights of rage, he dialed another number:

—*Phil?*

—Cassandra? Where is she?

—I don't know, I said. Where are *you*?

—Don't lie to me!

—I never lie, Phil.

—Or "withhold the truth" or whatever. I don't have time for your nuanced shit, Cassandra! I'll fucking fire—I mean, never mind! Just tell me where the fuck she is.

—I wish I did know, believe me. She isn't answering my calls either.

I could hear him breathing hard on the other end of the line, processing, considering it with underslept, suboptimal focus, trying to reconcile his intuition with what I was telling him—and then a beep, a sidewise *fuck you, asshole.*

—Phil, are you driving? Are you in DC?

—None of your fucking business!

—I think you should pull over. We'll come and get you—

—Just tell me where she is, Cassandra! Phil wailed, the pitch of his voice climbing. You *know*! I know *you know.* You *always* fucking *know*!

—Just pull over, Phil, please, I said, the rising desperation in my own voice scaring me. Do you want to talk to Miles?

—No, Cassandra, he said venomously. If I had wanted to talk to Miles, I would have called fucking *Miles*. Ugh, you always act like I'm an idiot! But I'm not stupid, Cassandra. *I'm* the one who filled out a perfect bracket, not you.

—That's true—just—

—I—I can do it again!

—Phil—

I saw it before him: the bridge.

—Remember I *paid* you to roll your useless fucking eyes! To take your precious little notes. Don't think I didn't see you do it, Cassandra. I see—

But the phone cut off, because Phil, knees trembling beneath him, hit the accelerator instead of the brake, his father's wild, plunging animal of a car driving clear off Chain Bridge, freeing Phil from the vehicle midair, rising, falling, *falling*; his white legs disappearing into the Potomac as the sun shone like its own extinguished flame; like a diving, death-divining swan; vicious and elegant and something amazing; beautiful in its suffering, in the radiant light, in the trailing gravity of a perfect arc.

March Madness was cancelled a few days later, due to complications from Covid-19. Brackets would never be released at all.

# SWAN SONG

I didn't see Raleigh Fayeton again until June 2021, a nonevent I can only partially blame on the novel coronavirus. Phil's memorial service was remote, with no opportunity to make amends, and after my virtual and floral attempts at condolence went unanswered I was reticent to press, my grief more bearable than the thought of compounding Raleigh's own.

Through the old sorority network I gleaned a smattering of updates. That she'd considered returning to nursing but couldn't justify the risk to Virginia. That they'd decamped to Nantucket, scaled back to one nanny, one p-jay; donated the proceeds of the other. That she was trying to offload real estate, too. Chiswick Farm went quickly, but it wasn't easy otherwise. Not so much, at Raleigh's level, due to the rising interest rates. Generally, these were cash buyers. But there are only so many people who can afford a twenty-million-dollar property, fewer still in times of economic uncertainty, even if the pandemic was largely benefitting those at the top of the food chain. (Arun Patil recouped Phil's billion many times over.) Ultra-high-net-worth individuals were, like Raleigh herself, fleeing the cities, and the Los Angeles library-labyrinth in particular proved an unmovable beast. She dropped the price twice before it finally sold, shortly after the Manhattan West Egg. I heard she'd considered letting the Musée des Beaux-Arts in DC go as well—but with a vaccine on the horizon, Raleigh decided to keep it. This somehow seemed right to me, in spite of everything. It had always been more her house than Phil's.

For all the lengths to which I went, with delicacy and finesse, to poach this information from our mutual friends, I never dared broach—even with the most sympathetic to me— the question I most urgently sought to know. Raleigh's own actions already matched my presumption: that I was unforgivable—not just for my failure to alert her of Phil's infidelity, but indirectly for his death. That he'd been on the phone with me at the time of the "accident" was common knowledge, though no one else tied any blame to this—the press reporting, accurately, Miles's firsthand testimony I'd been begging Phil to stop the car. But I suspected Raleigh of a more causal interpretation. It would be a natural enough human impulse, I told myself, and if condemning me for picking up quelled her guilt for failing to answer, it was a parting gift I was willing to proffer.

My own efforts to sail calmly on met with variable success. I had legitimate distractions, of course—fear being a particularly effective one (yes, prophets fear pandemics). After the initial wave of toilet-paperless terror, I still had two four-year-old boys confined to a townhouse. No picnic, I assure you, even with charming, hyperlexic ones and Adrienne's begrudging help. Fundraising on Zoom flattened the architectural and ceremonial luster my job once held for me—and I, like everyone else, turned to the schadenfreudic balm of Netflix's docudrama, *Tiger King*.

What was it about a certain breed of men that so violently attracted them to wild animals? Was it about power—or rather, the frustrating lack of it? A kind of coping mechanism for failed efforts to dominate our own kind? Was it about freedom? Akin to the Kerouacian car obsession, but expressed oppositely: not in the promise of an open road, but relief in escaping such visible captivity? Was it about wealth, status? Material profits from the animals' sheer rarity? The personal identification with an exotic mascot? Or the secondhand sale of their own delusions of grandeur to others; some gesture toward an exclusive club? It was obviously—as Miles and I gaped at the television—about fame. But I suspected it was also about love. I thought about Phil and the swans, the fineness of the line between a gift and self-aggrandizement.

Which was I employing now in writing about him?

The question continued to plague me, even as I knew: that I bore no more merit for my gifts than Phil for his. That the same recursive laws of luck spun different fates in a world of asymmetric seeding. *That's just the way the ball bounces* sometimes. I'm not abdicating responsibility, not in art nor in life. Certainly not to Raleigh, to whom I felt—will always feel—utterly, unequivocally culpable. But it is also possible to be responsible without merit, without culpability, and this is how I felt with regard to Phil. Sometimes responsibility only has the appearance of merit or culpability, when the factors and influences driving our outcomes are truly too multivariate and complex—even for generational minds like mine.

It was amidst this growing appreciation for distributed causality that I teared in temporary relief absent (much) gloating following Biden's victory; that I raised my chin at Senator Maria Muñoz's. That I saw my city torn asunder; the deceptive resilience of Trump *l'oeil*. That I embraced Percy and Tate on their fifth birthday, marveling at their distinctness, even from the same egg. That I watched Baylor dethrone the University of Virginia in March—and April. That I relived the prior Madness on paper. That I wrote a lot of sentences beginning with the word *that*.

Raleigh made contact a few weeks after the tournament, surprising me yet again. It was a brief email, a new thread, offering her congratulations on the imminent publication of my first book—not this one, but the exorcism examining an earlier era (alas, such is the nature of publishing timelines!). It wasn't set to be a blockbuster or anything, but had garnered a starred trade review and some pretty heavyweight comps. Just enough institutional prestige, basically, to impress the lobbyists and attorneys, consultants and political types in our orbit who'd previously raised their eyebrows, even if I was nonplussed (rare is the novelist content with her publicity).

I replied immediately. It was *so good* to hear from her. How was she? Virginia? I would love to catch up, if there was any chance at all she'd be willing to meet. I'd be fully vaccinated in a couple of weeks—would she?

She would. And remarkably, she was willing.

### ◻◻◻

We met for dinner, at a restaurant with plenty of outdoor space in Cleveland Park. I'd taken unusual care with my toilette, knowing the value Raleigh attached to smart presentation, but I needn't have bothered. She arrived in a dress even simpler than mine, in less makeup than I'd ever seen her wear; less even than she'd worn in Maine. I wanted to interpret this as a kind of visual peace offering, perhaps something akin to my unusual effort—but it left unmasked a reserved, almost frosty demeanor that didn't reveal my chances so much as further hide them.

Still, my own joy was insuppressible. I was too happy simply to be in Raleigh's presence, so grateful she'd deigned to allow it, even if she was less than thrilled by mine. And I wasn't *certain* this was the case. We'd all sort of forgotten how to be around other people in the last sixteen months. *She's unpredictable*, I told myself as the maître d' showed us to our table, *assume nothing*. Whether or not anyone else did, I was going to take my good advice.

—So, I said, a little awkwardly, offering her the lead.

—I'm still mad at you.

—I know, I said. But, you're here.

—Against my better judgment, said Raleigh.

—I believe I'm on record that sometimes your "better judgment" is not that good.

—Rude! she said, but with sudden animation, a smile lacing her scoff.

—Rude, I agreed. And true?

She considered it, our eyes meeting, locking. Saying more than our lips ever could. Raleigh broke the silence.

—How are Tate and Percy?

—Feral, I said.

—Cassandra!

—But also darling. Tate wants to be a theoretical physicist; he has me reading to him about quarks and shit. Oh, and yesterday Percy told me I was "a hundred percent drama and zero calories."

This garnered a reflexive laugh.

—What does that even mean? she asked lightly.

—I'm not entirely sure—but it sounds true, doesn't it?

—Mm, she said.

—Anyway, tell me about Virginia.

—She's a gift, said Raleigh. So, so sweet. But also serious—and you wouldn't believe how smart—

—Sure I would. Can I see pictures?

She let me scroll through her camera roll, which I did,

captivated. It wasn't just that Virginia was beautiful, or some maternal nostalgia for a child younger than my own. I had no idealized visions of life with a two-year-old. It wasn't even that she was Raleigh's daughter, my love bleeding through— or Phil's for that matter. It was her bearing in the photographs; she had this—this subtle intrigue. It was what she seemed, for all her innocence, to know.

I returned Raleigh's phone with a silent plea to both of them.

—How are Louis and Frances doing? I managed aloud.

—Oh, they're continent enough, said Raleigh.

—Ha!

—Well, except for the baby. I'm not sure if you heard, but it's a boy: Ian. Apparently, Odette's pretty jealous of him. We're gonna try to get down there in the fall.

—Oh, good. And Phil's mother?

(Surely you've wondered about her, too? Realized that even if she didn't have a flashy role in the narrative, Phil must have had one.)

But the server interrupted us before Raleigh could answer.

—*Ladies*, he said. How *are* we this evening?

—Fine, thank you, said Raleigh neutrally.

—Mm, I said.

—Any idea what you'd like?

It was a bit of a funny question at this particular restaurant, with its standard, prix-fixe menu; where everybody came for the same thing. Across the table, Raleigh's eyes met mine, and I thought I saw the corner of her mouth twitch mischievously—but I still couldn't fully read her. Perhaps I'd have to start from the beginning.

—After you, I deferred.

—I'll have the filet, please, said Raleigh.

—Brilliant, said the server. And how would you like your steak?

THE END

# ACKNOWLEDGMENTS

All of the basketball in this book is real. Thank you to Coach Tony Bennett and the 2018-19 Virginia Cavaliers men's basketball team for your truly unbelievable storybook run.

Thanks also to: Sarah Fuentes, Maddy Hernick, Orly Greenberg, and everyone at UTA; Michelle Capone, Mike Lindgren, Katrina Weidknecht, Pia Mulleady, Hanna Lafferty, Jay Pabarue, and the Melville House team; Kyle Matous ("Conservative Kyle") and Kyle O'Connor ("Liberal Kyle"); Jooeun Kim; Jessica Hirschey; Liv Stratman, Isabel Kaplan, Erin Somers, Julia Fine, Martin Riker, and Kelsey McKinney; Anna Gát and Erica Robles Anderson. To my parents. And above all, to my husband, Michael, who made *Medium Rare* possible, and to Dorian, our brilliant, singular son.

**A. NATASHA JOUKOVSKY** is the author of *The Portrait of a Mirror*. Her writing has been published in *Literary Hub, Electric Lit, The Common,* and *Still Alive.* Natasha holds a BA in English from the University of Virginia and an MBA from New York University's Stern School of Business. She lives in Washington, DC.